MARKED

SINS OF OUR ANCESTORS, BOOK ONE

BRIDGET E BAKER

*For Whitney.
I couldn't love you more if you were genetically enhanced.
(Sometimes, like when you ripped that bathroom countertop off
with your bare hands, I think maybe you are.)*

CHAPTER 1

I'm a big fat coward.

I've known this about myself definitively since one month before my sixth birthday. The night I lost my dad.

Case in point: I'm just shy of seventeen. I've been in love with the same guy for almost three years. Even though I see Wesley a few times a week, I haven't said a word. But tonight I have the perfect opportunity to do what I've always feared to try. Tonight, to celebrate our upcoming Path selections, all the teens in Port Gibson play a stupid, risky game.

Spin the Bottle.

I glance around as I walk toward the campfire in front of me. Only thirty-five kids turned seventeen in the past year, so of course I know them all. My best girl friend, Gemette, waves me over. I try to squash my disappointment at not seeing Wesley. When I played this scene in my brain earlier, I was sitting by him.

"You gonna scowl at the fire all night, Ruby?" Gemette pats a gloved hand on the slab of granite underneath her.

"You couldn't have saved us one of those seats?" I point at

the smooth, flat stumps on the other side of the fire. I sit down and shift around, trying to find a flat spot.

"I think what you meant to say was, 'Thanks, Gemette. You're the best.'"

Her straight black hair reflects the campfire flames when she tosses it back over her shoulder. It's against the Council's rules for hair to cover your forehead. Gotta make it easy to see anyone who might be Marked. Except tonight, no one's following the rules. Everyone's wearing their hair down, and Gemette's silky locks frame her face beautifully. I envy her sleek hair almost as much as I covet her curves.

"My bum's already hurting on this," I mutter.

"If you weighed more than eighty-five pounds soaking wet, it wouldn't bother you so much."

Instead of curves, I've got twig arms and a non-existent backside. I shift on the huge slab, trying to find a position that doesn't hurt. I arch one eyebrow, not that she can see it in the dark. "I weigh ninety-two pounds, thank you very much."

Gemette snorts. "That proves my point, you bony butt."

She leans toward the fire and picks up the glass bottle lying on its side. She tosses it a few inches up into the air before catching it again.

"Be careful with that." That bottle's the only reason I'm sitting here, sour-faced, stomach churning.

Slowly the remaining seats around the fire fill up. Wesley shows up last. There aren't any seats left, but before I can convince Gemette to squish over, he grabs a bucket. He turns it upside down and takes a seat a few feet away from everyone else. I guess that's fitting. His dad's the Mayor of Port Gibson and a Counsellor on the CentiCouncil, so Wesley's in charge by default tonight. He'll probably take over for his dad one day, which isn't as glamorous as it sounds since less than two thousand people live here.

He looks around the fire, and his gaze stops on me. He bobs his head in my direction, and I shoot him a smile. I'm glad he can't hear the thundering of my heart.

Although we're all huddled around a campfire, and I've known most of the kids here for years, we maintain carefully measured space between us. Tercera dictates our habits even when we're rebelling. Which we're only doing because it's a tradition.

Maybe Tercera's made cowards of us all.

"Are we starting?" Tom's sitting to my left. His parents are both in Agriculture and he's Pathing there, too. He has broad shoulders and tan skin from working outside most of the day. Gemette likes him, and it's easy to see why. Of course, he's nothing to Wesley.

I glance across the fire in time to see Wesley stand up. He straightens the collar of his coat slowly and methodically, like his dad always does before a town hall meeting. Wesley loves doing impressions, and he's usually convincingly good at them.

"I'd like to take this opportunity to welcome you all to the Last Supper." His voice mimics his father's, and he touches his chin with his right hand in the same way his dad always rubs his beard. Wesley himself is tall and lean with long black hair that he's wearing down, for once. It falls in his eyes in a way I've never seen before, and I feel a little rush. I want to touch it.

Wesley smirks. "I know you may be less than impressed with the culinary offerings for our gathering, but as I always say, Tradition has Value." He cracks a grin then, and everyone laughs. "Seriously though." He drops the impression and returns to his normal voice, which I like way better anyway. "I know the food sucks, but this whole thing started with a bunch of teenagers who were sick of rules and ready to throw caution to the wind for a night."

I look down at the three or four-dozen nondescript metal cans with the tops peeled back, resting on coals. Another few dozen are open but sitting away from the fire. Presumably they contain fruit or something else we won't want to eat hot.

Wesley leans over and snags the first can, his gloves keeping him safe from the heat. "I hope you'll all forgive me, but this was what we could find."

"This is a pretty crummy tradition." Lina reaches down and grabs a can with mittened hands. Her dark brown hair falls in a long, thick braid down her back, like it has every single time I've seen her.

"Traditions matter, even the silly ones. They help pull us together as a community, which is valuable when fear of Tercera yanks communities apart. We're stronger when we aren't alone. Thinking every man should look out for himself hurts all of us." Wesley takes his first bite right before Lina. I grab a can of baked beans.

The food really is as bad as it looks, but at least it's not spoiled.

Wesley talks while we eat.

"As you already know, we come from a variety of backgrounds. Before the Marking, Port Gibson housed approximately the same number of people, but not a single person who lived here before the Marking survived. We cleaned out the homes, burned some to the ground and rebuilt, circled the city with a wall, and made it our own. The Unmarked who live here are Christian, Muslim, atheist, black, white, Hispanic, Russian, German and Japanese. I could keep going, but I don't need to. Before the Marking, these differences divided humanity. Now, we know that what truly matters is what we all share. We embrace the traditions that bring us all together, because we're more alike than we are unalike."

I swallow the last spoonful of baked beans from my can

and set it down on the ground by my feet. I'm almost the last one to finish eating, but several half-full cans are scattered around the campfire. A few people grab a can of fruit. I prefer the stuff my Aunt and I process and can ourselves, so I don't bother.

I rub my hands together briskly. Even in mittens, my fingers feel stiff. It's usually not too cold in Mississippi, even in January, but a late freeze has everyone bundled up. The Last Supper's supposed to be a chance to rebel, but I'm grateful that everyone's as covered as possible. It means I won't look as cowardly for keeping my mittens on. My aunt is Port Gibson's head of the Science Path, so I know all about how Tercera congregates first in the skin cells, even before the Mark has shown up on the forehead in some cases.

The wind moans as it blows through the trees, and we all huddle around the meager fire. Even though the flames have died down to coals in most places, it burns hot. My face roasts while my back freezes. The bottle lies stationary on the weathered flagstones by the fire where Gemette set it, light glinting off of the dingy glass at strange angles.

The quiet conversations die off and the nervous laughter ends. Eyes dart to and fro among the thirty something teenagers gathered.

"So." Evan's voice cracks, and he clears his throat. "Who goes first?"

"Thanks for volunteering," Wesley says.

I suspect no one else asked for just this reason. All eyes turn toward poor, gangly, redheaded Evan.

Evan gawks momentarily. Even though he and I work in Sanitation together, I don't know him well. I haven't been there long enough to guess whether he feels lucky or put upon. He sighs, and then leans forward and tweaks the bottle. It twists sharp and fast and skitters to the right, spinning furiously.

I really hope the bottle doesn't stop on me, and I doubt I'm alone in that thought. Evan's funny in a self-deprecating way, but he isn't smart, and he definitely isn't hot. I bite my lip, worried about what I'll do if it does stop on me.

It slows quickly and finally stops pointing to my left. I sigh in relief, which I belatedly hope no one heard.

Tom gasps, and then in a raspy voice says, "No way. I mean, you're nice and all Evan, but I'm not . . . I don't . . ."

"Yeah, me either. Chill, man." Evan laughs. "So, does it pass to the next person over?" Evan raises his eyebrows and glances at me.

I want to protest, but my throat closes off and I look down at my feet instead.

Evan stands up. "So Ruby . . ."

He may not have saved me a seat, but Wesley jumps in to save me now, thank goodness. "That's not how it works. If you get someone of the same gender, and neither of you . . . well, then your turn passes to him or her. Which means you sit down Evan, and you spin next, Tom."

"Who made these rules?" Evan grumbles as he sits.

Gemette smiles. "They make sense, Evan. I mean, it's not spin the bottle and pick best out of three. Your way, you'd basically pick someone in the circle who's close and kiss whoever you want."

Evan shrugs and glances at me again with a smile. "Sounds pretty okay, actually."

Tom snorts. "I don't hear Ruby complaining about Wesley's rules. I'd say that's your answer, man."

I look back down at my shoes, but not before I see Tom's wink. Jerk. Evan must feel idiotic, and I definitely want to sink into the ground.

I bite my lip again, this time a little harder. Tom's an obviously good-looking guy, but I have no interest in kissing him. I hope his wink was a joke about Evan and not some kind of message.

Cold air blows past me as Tom leans forward to spin the bottle, his body no longer blocking the wind. One thing jumps out at me as he reaches for the glass bottle. In spite of the cold, Tom isn't wearing gloves. He must've taken them off at some point. He's either a daredevil or an idiot. I'm not sure which.

Tom spins the bottle less forcefully than Evan and rocks back and forth as the bottle circles round and round. His eyes focus intently on the spinning glass as if he can somehow control where it stops. I wonder who he's hoping for and look around the circle for clues. Andrea seems particularly bright-eyed. My eyes continue to wander. One gorgeous, deep blue pair of eyes in the circle stares right back at me. Wesley. I've looked at him a lot over the past few years, but this feels different somehow. A spark zooms through me, and I quickly stare at my feet.

No luck for Andrea tonight, or Gemette. The bottle comes to rest on Andrea's best friend, Annelise, instead. She and I were in Science together a long time ago. Her dark brown hair hangs loose, framing high cheekbones and expressive chocolate eyes. She frowns. Tonight doesn't seem to be going right for anyone so far.

"Now what?" Annelise's voice shakes. "We just kiss, right here in front of everyone?"

"No, of course not," Gemette snaps.

"Who made you the boss?" Evan frowns. Judging by his sulky tone, he's still mad about losing his turn earlier.

"Unfortunately, I'm the boss," Wesley says, "and she's right." He points to a dilapidated shed at the top of the hill. "You two go up there."

"Romantic." Tom rolls his eyes as he stands up. He rubs his bare palms on his pants. Gross. At least I know I'm not the only nervous one here. Tom and Annelise trudge a path through clumps of frozen brown grass toward the rundown tool shed.

What a special memory for their first kiss.

Gemette sighs and I pat her gloved hand with my own. I'd feel worse for her, but Gemette likes every decent looking guy in town, including a few boys a year younger than us. She'll recover from missing out on a special moment with Tom.

I glance again toward Andrea, an acquaintance from my time in Agriculture. She and Tom trained together for years. She may have liked him as long as I've liked Wesley. She looks into the fire while her foot digs a messy hole in the soil. I wonder how I'll feel if Wesley spins and gets Andrea. Or worse, Gemette. I'll have to sit here and twiddle my thumbs while I know he's in there kissing a friend. My stomach lurches. Coming tonight was a stupid idea. I clearly didn't think this through.

No one speaks to distract me from my anxiety. The shed isn't far. We could easily eavesdrop on them if the wind would shriek a little less.

"How long does this take?" Evan asks.

"Who the heck knows?" Gemette points at the bottle. "Impatient for another crack at it?"

Kids around us chuckle.

After another few awkward moments, Gemette grabs the bottle and gives it a twist. "No reason we have to wait on them."

"Sure," Wesley says. "Whoever it lands on can go next."

"Wait," Evan asks, "whoever it lands on goes next as in it's their turn to spin? Or goes next as in Gemette's going to kiss them?"

The bottle stops before anyone can respond, pointing directly at Wesley. His perfectly shaped brows draw together under disheveled black hair. Gorgeous hair. His lips form a perfect "o". His bright blue eyes meet mine again.

My heart races and the baked beans sit like a lump in my belly. I shouldn't have come. Of course Wesley will want to kiss her. Gemette's gorgeous, curvy, and smart. Ugh. Am I going to have to sit here while my best friend kisses the guy I like twenty feet away? This is all my fault. If I'd only told Gemette, she'd beg off.

I bite down a little harder on my lip and taste blood this time. I really need to kick this particular habit, especially with kissing in my future. Maybe. Hopefully. I'm such an idiot.

Wesley clears his throat. "I think I'm going to sit this game out. I'm more of a moderator than a participant."

"No," I blurt out. "You can't. You're here, you're seventeen, you have to participate." What am I doing? Why am I shoving him at my friend? But if I don't make him play, I'm flushing my chance to kiss him down the toilet. I want to cry.

"Well, then I guess it's my turn to spin." His deep voice sounds completely different than any of the other kids here tonight. My stomach ties in knots when I hear him speak, which is ridiculous because I've heard his voice a million times.

I glance at Gemette. She looks disappointed and I want to cry with relief, but I don't blame her. He could've kissed her but didn't pursue it. I imagine most any girl here would be disappointed. He glances up and his eyes lock with mine again. Caught. I start to shiver and try to stop it. This look is different somehow from any before, like something shifted. Wesley clears his throat, looks down at the bottle, gracefully reaches over, and snaps it between his fingers.

It spins evenly, not moving to the right or the left. It spins on and on, and I wonder if it'll ever stop. It slows, whirling a little less with each rotation, the butterflies in my stomach swooping and swirling with each pass.

Until it finally stops. On me.

My eyes snap up reflexively, wide with shock. Wesley doesn't even seem surprised. He simply stands and inclines his head toward the shed.

"Isn't it still..." I clear my throat. "Umm, occupied?"

"We can wait over there." He gestures at the hill to the right of the shed. One side of his mouth lifts in a smile and I feel an answering grin form on my lips. Which makes me think about what we're about to do with our lips.

Swarms and swarms of butterflies flutter in my chest.

"Sure," I say.

I stand up and without even thinking, I wipe my palms on my jeans. They aren't even sweaty and what's more, I'm wearing mittens! I really hope no one noticed. Okay, more specifically, I hope Wesley didn't notice. Gemette holds something out to me when I stand. I can't tell what it is from feel alone thanks to my thick mittens, and in the dark I have to squint to make it out at all. A tube of something. "What—"

"Lip gloss," she whispers. "A gift from my mom. I was going to use it, but looks like you need it more, you lucky, lip-biting brat." She winks.

I'm glad Wesley's still across the fire from me and that it's dark. Maybe he somehow miraculously missed both the palm wipe and her wink.

I walk as slowly as I can toward the old shed, partially to avoid tripping, but also so I won't look overeager. I try to hide my face while I apply the fruit-scented lip-gloss so that Wesley won't notice. It's dark, but I don't want him to be put off by dry, scratchy lips, or worse, dried blood. Gemette's a good friend. I feel guilty for overreacting earlier when I thought she might kiss Wesley. Not super guilty, but you know, a little.

Neither of us speaks a word, but I feel the eyes of the other teens follow us toward the shed. We're only a few crunching steps away when the swinging door flies open and Tom and Annelise barrel out. I jump when it bangs shut behind them.

Tom looks as ruffled as I feel, his eyes darting back and forth. He ducks his head and reaches down to take Annelise's hand. They walk out and away from the fire and the rest of Port Gibson's teens. I can't tell where they're headed, but somewhere far away from here.

"Did you know almost a third of the couples in town trace their start to the Last Supper?" Wesley asks.

"No way."

He shrugs. "We've only been an Unmarked town for seven years, so it's even more impressive. Not all of them are matched up from a bottle spin, but I think the game helps people realize how they feel."

A thrill rushes through me. Does Wesley feel the same as me?

My hand reaches for the door handle and collides en route with his. I'm wearing mittens, of course, and he's wearing shiny, brown gloves, but a thrill runs through me when we touch, even through layers. He doesn't move his hand away, but instead draws my hand in his and pushes the door handle back in one fluid movement. My heart skips a beat and time stops. When the door's completely open, he slowly releases my hand. I lower my eyes and step over the threshold into the rundown little building.

Although there's clearly no power, and consequently neither heat nor an overhead light, the walls at least cut the wind. It's at once both warmer and quieter. Two tall candles burn softly on a pile of rusted metal boxes in the corner. Someone prepared this dump, I realize. I wonder whether it was Wesley. The flames provide enough light that I can see his face. His dark brows are an even more startling contrast to his dark blue eyes than usual, accentuated by his hair falling in his face.

"So," I say. "Here we are."

Wesley looks at me from less than a foot away. The shed's small and crammed full of moldering farm implements. The air around us practically hums, but that isn't new. It's always like the moments right before a lightning storm when he's near. Supercharged almost, like the electrons around my body might fly off at his slightest touch. The difference is that here, away from the town's work projects, away from my family and his, it feels like anything really could happen.

Wesley's so close I can smell him, the same citrusy, woodsy smell I've secretly savored for years. It's even stronger tonight, like he put on more of whatever it is he usually wears. I breathe deep, and all the memories of him re-imprint on my brain. Scrubbing, sanding, painting, digging, cleaning, hammering. Projects his dad made him attend, but I suffered through to be near him. When I'm with him, I belong somewhere for the first time in a decade.

When we become adults next week, Wesley's mandatory attendance at work projects ends. Wesley steps into his role as an administrator, and I'll become part of Port Gibson's janitorial crew. It's now or never if I want to make any kind of permanent place with Wesley.

I never thought I'd be close to him like this, and I know I may never be again. I lean toward him and tilt my face upward, eyes closed, ready for what comes next. Maybe I'm even a touch impatient. I have waited for this for years.

Except I keep waiting, and then I wait some more.

Not a single thing happens. The trouble with being ridiculously small is that Wesley, who's on the tall side anyway, towers over me. Even with my face angled up, his lips are pretty far away. I can barely make out his expression, but it looks guarded.

Maybe he doesn't know how to do it?

No way. Wesley must know. I mean, it's not hard, right? You just push your lips onto the other person's mouth. Why isn't he doing anything? This is the moment. THE moment!

Until it passes. And then another moment falls on top of it, and another. All passing. Even the butterflies in my stomach get bored and go look for flowers elsewhere.

I'm not sure exactly how much time has elapsed, but the seconds drag, heavy with my growing frustration. Soon, someone will bang on the door. "You've been in there forever," they'll say. "Make room for the next couple."

I want to smack them in their eager faces.

I know I don't have much time, and I want to say something, anything. I need to tell him how I feel, say the words, take a gamble. But like it always does, my tongue shuts down. My throat closes off. The words stick inside my throat. Why am I such a coward? Our perfect moment withers and dies. Tears well up in my eyes, and I can't breathe.

Wesley isn't similarly affected. He steps back and says, "We don't have to do this, Ruby. It's not safe at all. I don't know why my dad even lets these dinners happen."

"Why'd you spin the bottle in the first place?" I hear the desperation in my voice, but the words pour out in spite of myself. "I know you, and you know me. How's it dangerous for us?"

He takes another step back, his expression registering surprise. "People get Marked, Ruby. It still happens. Every few weeks, in fact. Maybe I'm Marked. You don't know. It happens, even here, even with all our rules. It may take years to die once you're Marked, but it's inevitable."

I roll my eyes. "Well I'm not Marked, if that's what you're worried about." I point at my forehead. "See? Clear."

"We shouldn't be taking these risks." Wesley scowls. "Not now, not right before our real lives begin. This whole thing's supposed to be a time to say goodbye to being a kid, not act like an idiotic five-year-old, breaking rules for no reason."

Our real lives? Maybe he never thought it felt right, the time we spent, the way we are together. Maybe I never belonged with him at all. "Why'd you even come, then? Why follow me in here if you're not going to kiss me?"

Was he hoping for someone else? Was he stuck with me and looking for any excuse to bolt? Am I Evan in this scenario?

I look up, but I'm too close. The hair cascading over his face obscures my view. I want to touch his hair; I want to kiss him; I want to tell him I love him, and that I always have. My fingers and toes and everything connecting them zings in spite of the bitter cold, in spite of the indifference of his words. Energy spins round and round in my body, a closed circuit with nowhere to go.

"Look, Ruby, I don't know what to say . . . but the thing is . . ." He sounds torn, confused.

Suddenly, I don't want to hear "the thing," whatever it is. I've been talking to Wesley for years, talking and talking, and working alongside him, but I don't want to talk to him anymore. I know what I want and I'll never have a better chance to play things off as part of a game, if he feels like I now suspect he does. The notion of an excuse appeals to my cowardly heart. I can't speak the words, but I won't stand here and do nothing, not anymore, because he's the real life I've longed for.

I stop thinking and step toward him instead. He tries to step back and slams up against the back wall. I quickly take one more step and use my gloved hand to pull his head down to mine. I push my lips against his. In my haste, I push too hard and pull a little too fast. Our teeth smack into each other and my tooth knocks against my own lip, splitting it wide open again.

It's the opposite of magical.

I look up at Wesley instinctively. He has blood on his mouth, but whether it's his, or mine, I can't tell. And if it's not awful enough already, Wesley stiffens from head to toe like I mauled him, like I forced him into something torturous.

A tear rolls down my cheek and I inhale deeply. I won't cry over this. I can't, because there's no way I can play it all off as a game if I bawl my eyes out. I turn away from him. If I can't stop the tears, at least he doesn't need to see them. When did this go so wrong? I should be calm, cool, in control. I need to laugh it all off and tell him friends can't be expected to kiss well. Whoops.

Except my heart won't listen to the screaming from my head. I'm not calm. I'm the opposite of cool. I've lost all control.

He grabs my shoulder and tugs me around. I turn, but my eyes stay glued to the ground, too ashamed to meet his gaze.

"Ruby, look at me."

He puts two gloved fingers under my chin and lifts. His head comes down then, but slowly, too slowly. My heart stops pumping and I worry it might never beat again. His lips brush mine gently, then with more pressure. I ignore the discomfort of my torn lip and lean into him, connected to him in a way I can't explain. I need more air, but I want less, because that means more space between us. If this never ends, maybe it'll erase the moments that preceded it.

Suddenly, he lets me go and steps back. Emptiness fills the space where he stood. I reel again, sucking air in and blowing my breath back out to steady myself.

When I raise my eyes, our gazes lock. All my sorrow from before is gone, replaced with a feeling like I'm flying, soaring, floating on top of the world. His sapphire blue eyes reflect candlelight back at me. He's breathing as deeply as I am; he's as affected as me. I can't look away from his strong, almost hawkish nose, his square jaw, his flashing eyes and thick black lashes. I continue to stare as Wesley reaches up and brushes his unkempt hair away from his eyes.

I almost faint.

Such a simple movement. Small in the grand scheme of things, but also vast, earth shattering, all encompassing. My dreams crumble. My world spins out of control. He moves his hair off his forehead, and suddenly things make sense. His reticence to touch me, his skittishness, but also his quick recovery. Once he knew it was too late, he didn't hesitate to kiss me.

Because we'd already touched.

A tiny rash mars his otherwise perfect forehead. Before the world died, it wouldn't have mattered. Before the Marking, no one would have cared about a few bumps. It would be harmless: acne, a bug bite, or a reaction to hair product. It shouldn't matter that his forehead has a blemish. It shouldn't terrify me, but it does. Because that small rash means Wesley is Marked, and in under three years, he's going to die terribly.

And now, so am I.

I can't breathe.

I have so much to say that I don't know how to begin. I spin around to escape the shed and reach somewhere with clean air, but Wesley grabs my mittened hand at the wrist, pulling me back, stopping me from leaving. Touching me, albeit through layers. Again. Except this time, there's no zing.

Only dread.

The floodgates open and I yell. "Don't touch me. Don't you dare touch me." I slap him. Then I slap him again.

His hand snaps up and catches mine by the wrist. "You kissed me! What's wrong with you tonight?"

I shuffle backward until my legs hit something and I fall on my butt onto some kind of metal box. I finally open my mouth. "What's wrong with me? You're what's wrong with me. You Marked me!"

His eyes fly wide and his hand goes to his forehead. "No, I couldn't have." His head shakes back and forth as if he doesn't believe me, but that can't be. He has to know. It explains everything.

I glance around the shed until I see something shiny. I

grab the metal sheeting or whatever it is and rub it with the sleeve of my coat to clean it. I hold it up, angled from a candle so he can see for himself. "The Mark."

He looks at the sheeting, and then he lunges for the candle, bringing it closer. He curses. "I had Perimeter Duty today."

I look at him dumbly. "There wasn't a raid. There hasn't been in weeks." I blink repeatedly, like my eyes are the problem. Maybe if I blink enough, if my eyes clear up, the Mark on his head will disappear. He shakes his head and his hair falls forward again, covering it up. If only it could truly disappear.

But it can't, because there's no cure.

"Not a raid, no, but a single girl."

Jealousy, hot and quick, burns through me. Wesley's Marked, and I'm jealous because it means he touched her. A girl who wasn't me.

Focus, you idiot.

"A girl?" I repeat dumbly.

"She was so young and so very thin, obviously starving." He turns away from me. "She was begging for food, scraps, anything. She stared at my roll with so much . . . longing."

He sits down on a wooden crate behind him. It shudders from his weight and I hope it doesn't collapse, which is a stupid thing to worry about at a time like this. Why do small details pop out when something momentous happens? It's like my brain can't process the problem, so it focuses instead on every other thing that happens.

When he doesn't continue, I ask, "She just showed up out of the blue looking for food?"

He shrugs.

Marked kids' begging is pretty normal, actually. We never have very much food, not anymore, but they have even less. What little extra we have, we leave for them at the designated drop spots. They pick up the food when they come for the hormone suppressants.

My next words shoot out. "Was she pretty?"

"Breathtaking," he says.

My heart breaks a little more.

He looks up at me. "She only looked six or maybe seven, but she might have been older. It's hard to tell when they're half starved. Ruby, she looked so much like my little sister. Before."

Before the Marking. Before the illness spread, killing almost all humans. Before the whole world fell apart. We all had people then, a time we now refer to as Before. I'm not sure how, but I can always hear the capital B.

"She was Marked, of course. The little girl, I mean. I knew she was Marked. I'm not a complete moron. She just looked so much like Adonnia that I had to do something. She wasn't threatening me, or angry."

He closes his eyes. "She sat on the riverbank a few yards from my location north of Mulberry Street, her bony elbows and knobby knees visible through her tattered clothing. I turned and went inside, abandoning my post. I filled a basket with food and took it to her. I set it on the ground and returned to duty. She picked it up with wide eyes, marveling, I assume, that kindness in any form has survived, after all the death and devastation, in spite of walls and barbed wire, guns and bombs."

"Wait. You didn't touch her?" My breaths become short and shallow. If he's Marked without touching her, the virus has mutated. If that's happened, we're all doomed.

He's quiet a moment. "No. I mean, I didn't think so, but I guess I must've." He turns toward the sheeting again, looking at his Mark in disbelief.

"Oh." As I process that, I feel both relief that Tercera hasn't mutated and become airborne and fury that Wesley *touched* a Marked kid, or at least knew he *might* have, and still came tonight, and infected me.

He sighs, long and deep and sad.

"How could you not know she touched you?"

"She grabbed the basket and slung it over her gaunt shoulder." He looks up at me, his eyes haunted. "I should've considered how she'd crossed the river in the first place, but I didn't even think about it." He runs a hand through his now messy hair. "She climbed up an enormous tree, the one clinging to the riverbank before the cutback. She scampered all the way to the top and set out over the branches. She was so young, so small. She couldn't have weighed more than fifty pounds. The branches, even the highest, could hold her weight, but the basket of food was too much. She was too young to consider what would happen when she took it with her."

"Wait," I ask. "How could she be seven years old? That's not a typical kid on the suppressant." She must've come from the Unmarked. Maybe her family lives here in Port Gibson. I rack my brain for someone who lost a young child in the past few years. I can't think of anyone.

Wesley shrugs. "I don't know, but she was very small. Even malnourished, I don't think she could be a normal kid stuck waiting for puberty forever. I doubt she was on the suppressant. She was younger than that, young enough not to consider that the branch would snap. She fell toward the river where the water was flowing fast. I wasn't sure if she could even swim. I ran down the riverbank and finally dove in, desperate to save her, because it was my fault, all of it. I wanted to help her, and I killed her instead. I reached her, and I even grabbed for her hand, but she pulled my glove off and went under."

I remember he's wearing shiny gloves I've never seen, and now I know why. He lost his in the river.

He drops his head in his hands. "Now I'm Marked, and she died anyway."

I understand breaking the rules to give her food. I might have done the same, but to risk being Marked when she fell? That I don't understand.

"Why dive in the river?" I ask. "You didn't know she'd go over the tree branches, so it's not your fault."

"It was stupid, obviously, but I felt desperate not to lose her too." He stands and paces the width of the shed, two steps in either direction. Back and forth, back and forth. "My sister Adonnia was only five years old when my dad left her with his sister. Aunt Valerie was Marked too. We didn't know. We had no idea what would happen, but that was no excuse. He shouldn't have left her."

No one knew at the beginning. That Tercera impacts children differently than adults. Within the first few hours of infection on anyone, a faint but noticeable rash appears, high on the infected person's forehead. After that, nothing happens for more than a year. It's transmittable as soon as the Mark appears, or sometimes shortly thereafter.

It spread like wildfire in the first few weeks after it first surfaced, mostly because no one knew it portended something serious. In year two, infected people began to have sores on their skin. They started out small, but by the end of the year, the sores weeped and burned, or so they say. In year three, organs stop working slowly, and at some point during that third year the Marked die, usually from failure to process food. It's a horrible and slow death.

Unless you're a kid.

Kids get the Mark just the same, and they can transmit it too, but none of the second year symptoms begin until they hit puberty. By the time the world realized pre-pubescents weren't progressing the same, almost every Marked adult was on death's door. Most of the kids in their care died of starvation after the adults passed. It wasn't pretty. A few of the older kids survived, the ones who could forage and fend for themselves. In many cases, starvation delayed the onset of puberty, prolonging their lives before anyone thought to intentionally suppress their development.

Eventually, a team of scientists developed a hormone suppressant for the Marked kids that prevents the onset of puberty, extending their lives indefinitely. Of course, everything has a price. The goal at the time was to find a cure in a few years so all the kids could go off the suppressant. That part never happened, mostly because all the scientists working on it died. Those who are left, like my Aunt, are living in places so afraid of contamination they can't study Tercera properly. The kids on the suppressant formed a Marked society that still exists today. They have a few leaders and a handful of laws. They aren't thriving, but they're alive. No one's quite sure how many there are, but judging by the amount of suppressant they take, quite a few.

"Maybe your sister's still alive," I say. "She could be on the suppressant."

"Yeah," he says, "but she was only five when my aunt died. So probably not."

"You never looked?"

"No," he says. "I wanted to, but Dad refused."

His dad's refusal probably saved his life. I don't know anyone who has returned from a search and rescue trip. I hope it's because no one can come back to rejoin Unmarked society with a Marked kid. I hope they've all found their loved ones and are living with them in the woods, but it seems unlikely we haven't heard from any of them. Especially since we allow scheduled visitation over the wall once a month for loved ones who get Marked. They can't rejoin us, but they can talk from fifty feet away. It's not perfect, but we're too afraid to do anything else.

"I hated my dad for years," Wesley says. "He still hasn't ever tried to find her. I thought he was chicken, but now I wonder. Maybe he did it for us, for my mom and me. He couldn't save Adonnia without abandoning us."

"Like you have to leave now?" I turn away from him and clench my fists. "Like I have to?" I breathe in and out and try to relax my hands, to stop the shaking. "Why'd you come tonight at all, Wesley? You know the rules better than anyone. If you get Marked, you turn yourself in and go to quarantine to say your goodbyes. You certainly don't act like nothing happened. You leave and never return."

Never return. It feels like a knife in my gut. I'm Marked now. I've passed puberty so the hormonal suppressant won't work on me. I have three years left, tops.

Sickness and anger, terror and hatred, misery and fury flood me and I'm drowning. Wesley might not have been thinking when he grabbed the little girl, but that was hours ago, in the heat of the moment.

"You Marked me." I clench my fists until my nails bite into my skin through the knit of my mittens. "How could you?" I stand up and shove him back. It feels good to hurt him. Somehow, causing him pain eases mine. "You've killed me. Intentionally Marking someone's a capital offense, ya know."

He looks like he wants to defend himself, which pisses me off even more.

"What a joke, right?" I snort. "I wouldn't punish someone standing in a freaking downpour with a bucket of water. If you're Marked, you're already dead." I scowl. "Shooting you in the head would speed it up, but why should I? You've doomed me to a miserable and protracted death. Why not leave you to the same? Instead of shooting you, they should shoot everyone you infected and make you watch. That would be more just. That would be mercy."

"I'm sorry." He falls to his knees in front of me. "I'm so sorry I came tonight. Sorrier than you'll ever know, but it all happened so fast. I grabbed for her hand and she pulled my glove off." He pulls a lone black glove, a familiar, worn glove, from his pocket. "I didn't think she'd actually Marked me. I never felt her touch me, not my skin. I ran straight home, terrified I might have been Marked, that I might be doomed, but then three hours passed. I checked before I left and I was still fine. No Mark. I figured I was safe, that I was good to go."

"So you figured, 'hey, why not? I'm supposed to be in quarantine, because I had contact with a Marked girl, but instead I'll go infect Ruby, too?' I hate you."

He flinches. "Look, you know my parents run the First Supper, so they weren't home. They sent Frank by the house to make sure I was ready for the Last Supper."

"No one *has* to come to the Last Supper." I shake my head and step away. "Even you."

"Yeah, right." Wesley stands up and brushes off his pants. "Now who's being an idiot? It wasn't optional, not for me. My parents said I had to come and I swear, Frank was going to grab me and force me when I tried to tell him I wanted to sit it out."

"Why didn't you tell him what happened? Report your incident? Follow protocol? They wouldn't have made you come then."

He shakes his head. "I don't know, okay? Because it didn't feel real. Because I'm a jerk, I guess. I didn't want to admit to myself that I might be Marked." He runs his hands through his hair again. "I swear I didn't think she'd touched me. Not my skin. How would I lose my glove, and her, if she had touched me? It's like some cruel cosmic joke. She dies, and now I will, too."

"And me." He flinches again, but I push on. "You came

here, knowing it was possible, however unlikely, and then you kissed me."

He shakes his head, his boyish grin back. "Actually, I begged off, and I backed away. You kissed me."

I love his grin like a bear loves honey, but not right now. Right now I want to slap it off his face.

"Don't. Just don't."

He throws his hands up as if defending himself from a physical attack. "I should've stayed home, okay? If I could go back and change everything I would, but I can't. It's too late now, and you know I didn't kiss you. I told you we didn't have to do anything."

"You should've told me *why* you didn't want to kiss me. You should've stopped me."

"I had no idea you'd jump on me like that!"

I blush. He's not completely wrong. A jerk, inconsiderate, in denial, yes, but not completely wrong about the jumping bit.

"The thing is," he says, "I've been looking forward to tonight. Everything's about to change. We choose our Paths in a few days." He looks down at his hands and I can barely hear his next words. "I've been wanting to kiss you for a while, so when that bottle stopped on you, well, it seemed too good to be true."

The butterflies are back. Swarming. Swooping. I wave them off. Stupid butterflies. Go away.

He looks at his boots and breathes in and out a few times. "Look, all of this sucks, but make the best of it . . . and come with me."

"What?" I ask, dumbfounded again. This whole conversation feels like a free fall. "Come with you where?"

"To Marked territory. I have to go now, and I'm guessing you do too. I hear they have a whole society out there. Some of them have been taking hormone suppressants for ten years. They have leaders, scientists even. Maybe we can help them figure out the cure. You had years of Science, and I heard you were a natural, like a duck in water my dad said. You'd be invaluable."

I roll my eyes. I'm sure a sixteen-year-old wannabe scientist who washed out will crack the puzzle no one could solve. There've been rumors about a supposed cure as long as I can remember. Heck, my aunt and cousin are in charge of most of that research for the Unmarked, which is how I know we aren't any closer now than we were a decade ago. The suggestion that maybe I'd come up with the magical solution in the next few years is complete delusion.

"There's no cure," I say, "and there won't be any time soon. I also know hormone suppressants won't work for us. We're both past that point."

"We have two good years to figure something else out, then," he says. "Together."

My heart lurches. Together, me and Wesley, like I wanted. Almost what I wanted. "Right. You and me—neither of us actual scientists—are going to figure this out when millions of educated, funded, accomplished, and sophisticated researchers couldn't do it with much better equipment?" I snort. "Thanks for that brilliant plan. I can't wait to give it a go."

"It could happen," he says. "I heard about you, before we ever met. You were a rising star before you quit Science. You had the best aptitude for it they'd ever seen. Some guy from Nashville came to talk to my dad about you, about how soon you'd be ready to move there for advanced training. Everyone always wondered why you quit."

I want to punch him again, as hard as I can. I'm shaking with anger. "Wesley, stop. You're missing the point or changing the subject, and I'm not sure which pisses me off more. You knew you might be Marked, and you stood here and Marked me anyway."

There isn't much light but I see the blood drain from his face.

He reaches for my hand and I let him take it. No point in stopping him now, especially since we're both still wearing gloves. There's a tiny part of me, in spite of it all, that thrills at the prospect of being touched by him. I mash it down.

"I'm sorry. Sorrier than I can ever say. It was never my intention to Mark anyone else, especially not you. I had no idea that coming here would . . ."

He pulls away and presses both hands against his eyes. When he removes them, a single tear rolls down his cheek. "When the bottle spun and stopped right on you, I should've walked away, or begged off. But I thought, what if I'm not Marked, and I swear I thought I wasn't, and what if you thought it meant I didn't like you? This was my chance to finally kiss you, only when we came into the shed, I reached my hand in my pocket and felt my glove. I remembered that I wasn't one hundred percent sure . . . "

He covers his face with his hands again. "I didn't know you liked me. I hoped you liked me, but I had no way of knowing, and no reason to imagine that you'd leap up and kiss me. I stepped back, begged off like I should have to begin with, but then you grabbed me and pressed your lips to mine. It shocked me, but once you did, you were already exposed. It seemed stupid not to really kiss you. Although I'd be lying if I say I was thinking rationally at that point."

I don't know if it's his tone, my feelings, or the earnest look in his eyes and the tear track on his cheek. Maybe it's all of it, but I believe him. I don't entirely forgive him, but I believe he meant me no harm.

"Please come with me," he says urgently. "I'm leaving tonight. I'll write my mom a note and pack some provisions.

You don't have to accept my apology, and you don't even have to like me anymore, but at least we won't be alone out there."

"Any port in a storm?" I ask, a little bitterly.

"No." He stands. "Not at all. I never meant to Mark you, but if I had to Mark someone . . . if I could pick anyone in the whole town to Mark, even in the whole world . . . this is coming out all wrong." He pauses. "Do you remember that first day we met?"

Of course I remember.

"I knew then, three years ago. You were so intense, so smart and quiet. I felt drawn to you, like a moth to a flame."

I arch one brow. "At least I'm not the bug in this analogy."

Wesley rolls his eyes. "I couldn't help but notice you that day because you sparkled, like some energy inside you was clawing its way out. Then you showed up at every single Special Project. At first I thought maybe you loved helping people. I was telling my mom how great you were last year, right after the perimeter fence repair project."

I stayed until long past dark on that one. So did Wesley.

"I told my mom how your aunt and uncle didn't make you go—that you signed up on your own. I told her you were this amazing human being." He laughs. "That was the first time I thought you might like me, because my mom said, 'I'm sure she's great, but don't you think she's getting a little something out of it?' Then she smiled at me."

"Why didn't you say something then?" My heart aches with might-have-beens. If he'd been less unsure, if I'd been less scared, if we'd talked about any of this before now, maybe he wouldn't have been so cavalier during Perimeter Duty. Maybe we wouldn't be Marked.

He clears his throat and I realize might-have-beens aren't helpful. Reality is reality. We're both dead.

"I have to say goodbye to my family. I owe them that." I

think about it for a minute. "In fact, if I don't go explain, they'll probably come after us."

"I like the sound of 'us'." He smiles. "I'll wait however long you need. Go tell them what happened."

"I'll be put in quarantine. I'm following every rule. I'll never, ever Mark someone else, not even by mistake."

Someone bangs on the door.

A voice asks, "You guys alive in there?"

I want to say, "Not entirely," but I don't. I keep quiet.

"One minute." Wesley turns to me. "Please meet me," he whispers. "I'll wait for you in the woods by the willow tree on the other side of the river. If you don't show in three days, I'll assume that means that somehow you didn't contract Tercera."

"Sure." I wipe an errant tear with one gloved hand and open the door with the other. We leave the shed to the sound of jeers and calls. I guess we deserve that. We were inside a long time. I walk with Wesley to the edge of the clearing. Gemette waves at me and I shake my head. I'm not sure what she'll think that means, but I can't go talk to her now. I won't risk it.

Before we part ways a few feet down the wooded path, Wesley squeezes my hand one last time. "I honestly hope I don't see you again," he says.

If I somehow don't have Tercera, he'll leave without me. I'd probably never see him again, just like he said. I think about that second kiss and a life with Wesley, however short.

I almost hope I do see him soon.

CHAPTER 3

I climb up the tree behind our back porch and sneak into my own window so I have time to think about how to tell my family the news. It's a waste of effort since it turns out no one else is even home.

I stare at my forehead in the mirror of the bathroom I share with Rhonda and Job. Now that I'm infected, shouldn't I feel different? A sense of my own impending doom, or tingling, or a sinking feeling in my stomach? I should look different, too, but no matter how long I stare, my forehead remains clear. No rash. It might be a little early to cue the celebration though, since it's been less than an hour and it's been known to take as long as three.

I finally wrench myself away from the mirror and grab a bag. I slide my summer gloves on, and start throwing things in there, things I'll want if I'm leaving to live in the wild. A pocketknife, hair ties, a toothbrush and toothpowder. Every bar of soap we have, which is a lot because we made a new batch last month. I'm not sure how organized the Marked kids are, or what they'll have, but they never look very clean.

Just because I'm dying doesn't mean I need to smell all maggoty.

I'm packed and tiptoeing down the stairs when it occurs to me I should check my Aunt's office. Maybe I should take a few of her science texts with me. Wesley's idea is far fetched, but who knows? With enough motivation, maybe he and I could make progress on a cure before we die. At least, unlike the Unmarked scientists, we'd have access to active viral cells.

I pop my head in her office and start looking around. What should I take? I grab *Clinical Virology*, *Principles of Molecular Virology* and *McKee's Pathology of the Skin*. I'm stuffing them into my shoulder bag when I notice a stack of dark brown leather books in the corner. I pick up the top one and flip it open. It starts with a date. After the date is a handwritten entry. The handwriting looks familiar, and I can't figure out why until a word catches my eye on a line about a third of the way through the book.

My name.

Ruby choked today. I was worried she might die. It's my own fault for letting her play in my lab. She was disassembling one of my molecular models and put one of the components in her mouth.

These must be my dad's journals. My dad, the renowned virologist. My aunt, his sister, is always telling me that if he had only lived, if he hadn't been killed just before Tercera broke out, he'd have succeeded where everyone else failed. No one would've died.

I glance down at the pile. There must be fifteen journals here. I might need them, and technically, they belong to me, don't they? Maybe his research will help point me in the right direction. I can't fit them all in my bags, so I take the four I can stuff inside, and head for the door. Maybe I thought about this wrong. Maybe instead of telling them now, I should go straight to the Defense office and turn myself in. They'll figure it out when whoever's on guard notifies them.

I've almost reached the door when it swings open. I jump backward.

My Uncle Dan walks through first. "Back so early, Ruby? Rhonda and Job were gone half the night their year."

My Uncle walks past me, almost brushing against me. I shuffle away so quickly he looks at me sideways.

Aunt Anne breezes through the door next. "Is everything okay?"

I can't lie and say I'm fine, but I don't know quite what to say. I understand Wesley more with every second that passes, and I pretty much know I'm Marked, whereas he didn't believe he was. It's easy to pretend everything's fine when you don't feel any different.

My cousin Rhonda jogs through the doorway and into the kitchen, and her twin, Job, follows closely after. He pulls the front door shut. Rhonda yanks off her bright red knit cap with the little golden puff ball on top that I made her for Christmas years ago. It's uglier than a hairless cat, but she wears it faithfully. She tosses it onto the kitchen table, and her straight, golden hair cascades down her back and fans around her face. She pulls out a chair and swings it around so she can sit on it backward, her chin resting on the chair back. "I wanna hear the details, all of them. Did you finally kiss the guy, or what?"

"Kiss who?" Aunt Anne asks.

"Yeah, we all want to know." Job plonks down in a chair across from Rhonda and kicks a leg up on the one next to it.

All eyes turn to me.

Rhonda's eyes travel from my coat, to the two bags and then narrow suspiciously. "You extra cold for some reason? What's with the luggage?"

"Well," I say, "about that. There's something I have to tell you."

"Please tell me you aren't eloping," Uncle Dan says.

Aunt Anne rolls her eyes. "That's not a thing anymore. There's not even Vegas anymore."

"Just let her talk," Job says. "What's up?"

"Are you changing Paths again?" Aunt Anne asks.

Rhonda snorts. "Why would she need a bag for that?"

"I don't know," Aunt Anne says, "but she's obviously not a good fit in *Sanitation.*"

I cough. This is not going well.

We're all 'equal' in the Unmarked community, but even so I'm the black sheep of the family because I can't seem to find a place. Rhonda never tried anything other than Defense. She knew what she wanted from the start and advanced rapidly in the ranks of her chosen Path. Similarly, Job never wavered from Science. The presence of two prodigies in the family only highlights my inability to succeed at anything. Or even to fit anywhere at all.

Of course, they don't know my shortcomings have become irrelevant. It won't matter that I never quite fit in once I'm gone.

"Sanitation's not a good fit for me, it's true. I only tried it because I'd done everything else already." I look down and examine my mittens. I need to spit it out already. "Actually, I think one good thing came from tonight." I choke a bit and tears form in my eyes. "You won't have to worry about me finding the right Path anymore." A tear rolls down my right cheek, and I force my eyes up to meet Aunt Anne's sky blue ones. She looks so much like my dad. His absence still stings at the strangest times.

Aunt Anne's brows draw together in concern.

"I'm Marked," I say.

Pandemonium ensues.

Everyone's talking at the same time, so I can't really tell what anyone's saying. Job's ranting about something to do with his research on the hormonal suppressant. My Aunt Anne yells back at him. They obviously disagree on some scientific fact. My uncle jumps out of his seat and checks the door and windows for some reason I can't fathom, yelling about the teenagers and Marked raids.

Rhonda sits perfectly still, so still that she catches me by surprise when she jumps up and reaches for my face. I shove away from her so frantically that I knock my chair over backwards, my feet kicking up and away. My head slams into the floor, but I scrabble backward anyway, desperate to keep her away. My arms windmilling, and my legs kicking furiously. I thwart her efforts to touch my face, barely.

At least our scuffle shuts the other three up.

Job grabs Rhonda, a little belatedly in my opinion, and pulls her back. He glances my way. "You okay, Rubes?"

I sit up slowly, my head reeling, a sharp pain throbbing at the base of my skull.

His question strikes me as funny. I fell on the floor and struck my head, but I feel fine. Other than the fact that I'm doomed to die in the next three or so years, sure, I'm great.

I start laughing and can't quite stop. "Sure," I finally choke out. "I'm awesome."

Job holds Rhonda against him in a bear hug, practically pinning her against the stairwell. They both stare at me in a frightening way, like they're eyeing a rabid dog who could pounce at any moment. Job's trying to protect her from me when Rhonda was the one acting like a nut. What was she thinking?

"I wasn't going to touch you," she whispers. "I just wanted to see your forehead. Has it appeared?"

"No," I say. "I don't think so, not yet. I only got Marked an hour ago, or a little more."

She sags back in Job's arms. "I was hoping it was some kind of prank. Some sick new Last Supper joke." She starts to cry, great heaving sobs wracking her body. The last thing I can make out is, "How?"

They all look at me, clustered almost at the bottom of the stairs, and for the first time it hits me. I'm going to have to tell them I kissed Wesley. It's a stupid thing to be embarrassed about, but I don't want our last conversation at home to be about my first, and possibly last, kiss. I choke up and can't speak, so I shake my head instead. Finally I say, "Does it matter?"

When no one else speaks, I lean over and grab my bag. I know they aren't really my family. Aunts and uncles and cousins aren't the same as moms and dads and siblings. I know that. I've always known that. Even so, I knew losing them would hurt. Nothing prepares me for feeling like I've been gutted when no one stops me from walking out the front door and into the night alone.

CHAPTER 4

My aunt and uncle's house is on the eastern edge of town by the Wintergreen Cemetery on College Street. It's a quick walk to Church Street, and then a few blocks to the old Claiborne County Courthouse. Of course, no one goes to court anymore. The Mayor adjudicates all disputes himself, as part of running the town.

Port Gibson isn't very large, and has only one of everything, except cemeteries. Apparently, each religion needed its own cemetery Before, though I'm not quite sure anyone cares much once they've died. Dirt is dirt, after all. I think cemeteries are more for the living than the dead. One was even dedicated specifically for Jewish people. It's the only original cemetery that still has space left. Pretty much everyone else, Christian or not, is buried outside of town in the New Graves Cemetery. Apparently Unmarked society doesn't put much value on blessed dirt or creative names.

I consider walking off into the night to meet Wesley right now. There's a certain thrill to the idea of bypassing quarantine entirely. Of course, that would leave my friends and family unable to come tell me goodbye. The three-day quarantine rule was developed as more of a safe way for loved ones to mourn than anything else. The thought of watching my friends and family pity me, reliving all the sadness over and over, and suffering through rounds of questions about how it happened makes me feel queasy. It's the first time I've felt sick since seeing Wesley's Mark.

My Aunt Anne catches me before I make a quick turn and walk out to Wesley, instead of heading up the steps to the Courthouse.

"We handled that poorly," she says. "I'm sorry. We all are."

"Thanks for coming to tell me that, but you don't have to come with me to check in." I meet her eyes.

Aunt Anne holds my gaze. "I do." She does love me, after all. I want to hug her, but I don't, obviously.

The Courthouse looms before us, two dozen steps to the front entry. I think the stately red brick building with raised steps leading up to the front door used to be some kind of church, but it was pretty enough that whoever was in charge of Port Gibson at the beginning claimed it.

My aunt walks alongside me, matching me step for step on every stair. I raise my hand to push the door open, but Aunt Anne reaches the handle first and I jump back. I follow her through the entry and into the small office, where Barrett's eyes widen and he leaps to his feet.

He's been over to the house for dinner a few times, so I know him fairly well. He has dark hair and eyes, like both of his parents. Of course, I know all of the guards since my uncle has been Defense Chief in Port Gibson for the past three years.

Barrett shifts uneasily.

"I've been exposed to Tercera," I say. "I need to go into quarantine."

Barrett's mouth turns down. "That's awful. I'm so sorry."

He turns to Aunt Anne. "Unfortunately, you can't stay while she's processed."

"She's a minor," Aunt Anne says.

Barrett crosses his arms, and pins my aunt with a forceful stare. His chocolate brown eyes don't waver. "Talk to your husband. I only enforce his rules."

She stands with her shoulders slumped by the entrance while I follow Barrett's broad shoulders upstairs to my designated cell. There isn't much that needs to be done at the Courthouse anymore, so the upstairs was outfitted as a prison. It hasn't ever held any prisoners that I know of, but the cells double as quarantine rooms. Once I'm in my room and settled, Barrett opens the small window and looks at me through the Plexiglas that's been installed for this purpose.

He asks me a lot of questions about how I got Marked and when.

I choose not to answer any.

What's he going to do? We're pretty sure you have to be touched to be Marked. We don't know of any cases where someone has caught it through breathing the same air or occupying the same room, or even touching someone else's belongings. It seems to require direct skin-to-skin contact.

No one's too keen on taking any chances.

I lay down on the cot and close my eyes. I think about Wesley, shivering in the cold out under a tree. He should've come with me to quarantine. Of course, they might've punished him if he had. It's a capital offense to Mark someone. I'd have argued against it, but I bet my uncle would be angry enough to push. Maybe it's better he didn't come. I try to sleep, but my thoughts return over and over to Wesley and our kiss. Not the first ghastly wreck, but the second one. Wesley's Marked, and after two kisses, there's pretty much no chance I'm not.

I've told my family. I checked in officially. I've done

everything right. Why should Wesley have to wait outside for me in the cold for three days? I've told Aunt Anne and Uncle Dan, Rhonda and Job. They can't hug me, and all they'll do if they come is frown through the glass and maybe cry. I want to say goodbye to my friends, but not if it means Wesley dies three years early of exposure. I'm understanding more and more why he didn't come here.

I hop up and glance through the glass. No one in the hallway, at least, not that I can see. I rummage around in my bag, hoping I have a hairpin inside. I don't find a hairpin, but I do find a ballpoint pen. I twist the cap off and slide out the plastic guts. I poke the long skinny plastic tube into the hole in the doorknob and shove. It takes a moment, but I hear a pop.

Not the best security, but then, this isn't a real prison. It's a quarantine room. I grab my bag and poke my head out the door. No Barrett in sight. I tiptoe down the back hallway. Still not a soul around. I open the rear exit door and slide through. That's when I collide with a brick wall wearing a tight black t-shirt and a black leather jacket.

My uncle's Second in Command, Samuel Roth, reaches out and grabs both of my arms with black-gloved hands.

Well, crap.

"Ruby Behl." Something about his low and raspy voice makes my stomach drop. "Where are *you* going?"

He's the worst person who could possibly have caught me —no chance I'll slip out of town now.

I've known Sam forever. He and his dad lived with us up in Nebraska for most of the time we were there, and we joined the Unmarked together. His dad ran Port Gibson for a while, but then he moved up in the Unmarked leadership and they moved away. Two years ago, when Sam chose Defense as his Path, he came back to town. He's been working with Rhonda and for Uncle Dan ever since.

He's a completely awesome fighter and my uncle keeps promoting him. He's also probably the most gorgeous man I've ever seen, with beefy enough arms to counterbalance his stupidly pretty face. He towers over everyone else in town, with his dark blond hair, and bright greenish gold eyes. I might have even had a killer crush on him when I was a little kid, for like, five minutes. But he never talked to me, and he's quiet and almost dopey, so I moved on. At least him ignoring me wasn't personal. He doesn't say much to anyone.

He releases me. "You can follow me back to your cell."

I wonder whether there's any chance I could outrun him. Even with his bulk, it seems . . .unlikely.

"Your uncle called me in, but your forehead's clear," Sam says. "Why do you think you're Marked?"

I frown. I wish Barrett would come back. He's easier to ignore. "I had contact with someone who was recently Marked."

"What kind of contact?" Sam walks to the back door, which locked behind me, and pulls out a key. He opens the door and gestures for me to follow him through, seemingly unconcerned that I might run. Or maybe he's that confident he can catch me.

"Does it matter?" I walk through the door and start back up the stairs toward my cell, stomping as loudly as possible. "I'm Marked, okay? I'm positive."

Barrett flies around the corner upstairs, his mouth dangling open, his eyes round as saucers. "How did you—"

"She escaped while you were on watch," Sam says. "For now, you're relieved of duty. We'll talk later."

Barrett flinches. "She presented voluntarily, and the door was locked."

Sam's voice barely rises higher than a whisper, "You observe and contain."

Barrett salutes and practically runs downstairs.

When we reach the door to my cell, Sam opens it. He inclines his head as a silent order for me to go inside.

I toss my head. "I'm not a prisoner."

He meets my eyes flatly. "You're to be held in quarantine for three days. You know that."

When I walk through, unlike Barrett, Sam doesn't close and lock the door. He follows me inside.

"Marking someone intentionally is a capital offense," he says. "Your uncle takes that seriously. Defense Path mostly acts as guards against outside threats to our community, but we also police internally as needed. Tell me who Marked you so we can deal with it."

I visualize what will happen if I tell him. Sam tracks Wesley down like he would a deer, his eyes scanning boot prints in the dark, tossing leaves in the air and scenting him or something. Sam's crazy like that. Then Sam catches him at the willow, and shoots him between the eyes.

No thanks.

"No one Marked me intentionally," I say.

"I have to write a report, Ruby. I can't write 'unintentional marking.'"

"Why not? You're concise." That's an understatement. He barely talks at all, and if I tell him, he'll blame Wesley. I may be mad at Wes, but I don't want him dead.

"Give me a name. I'll be concise with it."

"I can't do that."

"Ruby." Sam leans against the doorframe. "Your uncle's not going to let this go, so I can't either. We don't have any reports of anyone else in town who's Marked. Surely you understand why this matters."

"Not at this point," I say. "It was someone from town who got Marked on accident on perimeter duty. He didn't realize it, not until after he kissed me and I saw his Mark. You'll find out soon enough, but I'm not telling you more."

Wesley's parents will be wondering where he is by morning. He'll be waiting by the tree, instead of heading for Marked territory. Even without coming in for quarantine, he may get shot for this.

"If he had contact with Tercera, why didn't he immediately turn himself in?" Sam almost growls when he talks, and I stumble back. I never realized it before, but Sam's kind of a scary guy.

"He didn't realize he had contact."

It feels strange to be defending Wesley, but I kind of understand how the whole thing happened. My Mark hasn't shown up yet, and it feels surprisingly surreal. I don't feel sick at all, which I guess is the point. No symptoms other than the rash until year two. No debilitating symptoms until year three.

"When did all this happen?" Sam asks.

"During the Last Supper."

"Why Fairchild hasn't abolished that absurd practice, I don't know." Sam starts to pace.

I drop my bag on the floor and sit on the edge of the cot.

He stops, suddenly. "I have records of which seventeen year olds had Perimeter Duty, but off the top of my head, I know Tom, Wesley and Robert did. Give me a name, Ruby, and I'll leave you alone. We'll know soon enough anyway."

"I can't do that," I say. "I'm going to meet him outside town when my quarantine ends. If I give you a name and you go kill him, then I'll be all alone until I die. Do you really want that?"

His jaw twitches. "Of course not, but we have to deter this kind of behavior."

"A death sentence without possibility of reprieve isn't enough of a deterrent?" I roll my eyes.

Sam says, "Some little jerk broke the rules and now"—he clenches his fists—"now you're in here. He won't have any symptoms for a year, and then he has a few skin sores. Minor. Two good years, and some decent time his third year, after breaking protocol and killing you? No, it's not enough. But, if you tell me everything, I promise I'll talk to your uncle and we'll decide together when and how he needs to die."

"Good talk, but still no."

I flop backward on my cot and cross my arms. Sam asks more questions and even bangs on the wall once. The room shakes wildly and I worry the light on the ceiling will fall down and break, but it doesn't. I force myself to ignore him until he finally leaves, slamming the door behind him. I don't hear him lock it. I guess he knows that didn't keep me inside last time anyway.

I glance at the clock on the wall. It's been more than three hours, now. The Mark should appear any minute. I touch my forehead. It feels the same. I stand up and walk to the mirror over the sink. I close my eyes, exhale, and finally force them open. I take a good hard look at my forehead.

It's still clear.

This might be the last time I see it, unblemished, unmarked. I finally look away and glance at the rest of my face. We don't have many mirrors in our house—only in the bathrooms. I have curly, blonde hair, but it's almost always pulled back in a ponytail or a braid.

My face is angular, my features all sharp. I'm bony in general, like one of those stick figures people draw with just arms, legs and a big round head. My hair sticks out from my head like I stuck my finger in a light socket as a baby. Tendrils escape from my ponytail, no matter what I do. I take one more look at my forehead and then look away. I can't stare at myself all night waiting for a rash to appear. Maybe I should take a sleeping pill. My aunt makes them to help me deal with the nightmares. Since I was leaving home, I packed all of them before I left. I should take one, but I don't want to sleep until I've seen the Mark.

I pull out one of my dad's journals and start reading. Most of the entries are pretty boring, but a few are about me, and a few are scientifically interesting. My aunt was right when she said my dad knew a lot about viruses. The first journal dates to right after he left his big pharma job to pursue his own research. He had less resources after he quit, but he charted his own course. I don't recall the move we made from the East Coast to Texas because I was so young, but my dad talked about it sometimes.

When Tercera hit, my dad had just died. My aunt took a leave of absence and we stayed at my dad's cabin near Republican City. We hid in a tiny cabin with a big barn, near a lake, for years until our supplies ran out and most everyone was dead. We only left to join the Unmarked, for a chance at a community. I took more than three years of Science before I quit. I advanced quickly and was being taught the same things as the teenagers by the time I turned eleven. It gave me a pretty good understanding of basic scientific terms. Even so, some of these confuse me and I have to look them up in *Clinical Virology*. Good thing I snagged it, too.

When I finish the last entry, I glance at my watch. It took almost three hours to read the entirety of the first journal. It's been six hours since Wesley and I kissed, maybe closer to seven. I take a deep breath and walk over to the mirror.

Still no rash.

I should be elated. I don't know how it's possible, but it seems I might not have been Marked. The rash should've shown up within three hours, four at the most.

Why am I disappointed?

Being Marked meant I was doomed to die, but I finally felt free, like something good could happen, like the worst couldn't fell me. With Wesley, I might have found a place, and someone to build something with. We spend so much time huddled inside Port Gibson behind tall, razor-topped walls, following scads of restrictive rules, that we aren't even able to enjoy anything.

It's almost 2:00 a.m. when I reach down and grab a sleeping pill. I can't wait all night. As I drift off to sleep, I think about Wesley, waiting by the tree alone, maybe forever.

CHAPTER 5

The next morning, Sam's gone and Barrett's back. I wake up to the sound of Barrett sliding a tray through the flap on the bottom of the door. When I glance up, he glares at me. I look down at my breakfast and scowl right back at him. The tray holds a metal box, with lumpy gray blobs on it. Defense rations are disgusting, but this looks even worse. Barrett's punishing me for escaping, which wouldn't have been possible if he'd been doing his job. I eat a few bites until my stomach isn't grumbling, but then I can't force myself to eat any more. I wish I was home so I could pull some things from my greenhouse.

I realize with a start that the disgusting breakfast distracted me. I hop up and run across the room to the mirror. I stare at my reflection, not quite sure I believe my eyes. Still no rash. I'm not sure what it means.

I bang on the Plexiglas. "Barrett, I'm not Marked. Have you ever guarded someone in quarantine who was exposed, but the Mark never showed?"

He coughs. "Nope."

"Very helpful, thanks. Feel like elaborating?"

Barrett's sneering face suddenly fills the small window. "You won't tell me anything, then you run away, and now I'm on probation. What exactly did you expect? I'm the last one who's going to run over to hold your hand and tell you everything's going to be okay. In my experience, things are rarely okay."

"Well, I certainly hope that's not how my husband taught you to talk to people in quarantine, especially individuals afraid their lives may end imminently." Aunt Anne's voice is crisp and clear, even through the window. She's used to being obeyed and it shows. "Not to mention, she's your boss's niece."

Barrett jumps back, his face as white as the walls. I want to feel bad for him, but I can't quite manage it. He brings this stuff on himself.

My aunt's smiling when she reaches the window, her irritation with Barrett already forgotten. "You aren't Marked."

I rub my forehead. "I know."

Aunt Anne breathes in and out slowly. She must've come here from work. She's wearing her typical dark pantsuit and pearls. My aunt's a very put together woman. "As you probably remember, there are no known cases of a Mark appearing more than five hours after contact. It appears quite likely you aren't Marked. Can you tell me why you thought you were?"

I want to protect Wesley, but it's not like she won't be able to put the pieces together herself if I refuse. She knows I was at the Last Supper and every kid there saw us enter the shed together. Once his parents realize he's gone, everyone will know anyway. "I was at the Last Supper. I kissed someone who was Marked."

My aunt gasps. "Why would you do something that imprudent?"

"Obviously I didn't know," I say.

"But *he* knew," she says, "whoever he was. No one just waltzes around Marked without knowing it, and he had to have hidden it or you'd never have kissed him. Your uncle is going to shoot that little miscreant right between the eyes. Who was it?"

I'd never realized how bloodthirsty my aunt could be. Maybe that happens when you're married to the head of Defense and a former Olympic gold medalist in sharp shooting for twenty-five years.

"Who, Ruby?"

I sigh. "It was Wesley Fairchild." I flinch at the fury in her eyes. "But it wasn't like he meant to." My words sound silly even to me. I'm still defending him, and honestly, maybe I should be. Turns out, he didn't even Mark me.

"He didn't know he was Marked, not really, and he wasn't even going to touch me. He told me we weren't going to kiss, but I . . . I grabbed him and I kissed him, okay?" I drop my head in my hands. I'm such an idiot. Living through it was embarrassing enough, but telling everyone? Being Marked might be easier.

"He should've turned himself in the moment he had any interaction with someone who was infected with Tercera," my aunt says softly. Somehow, her soft tone scares me more than her yelling would. "Where did he go?"

"I don't want him harmed," I say.

My aunt ignores me. "Is he lurking around trying to Mark more people? I don't care who his father is, he deserves to be shot."

I bang on the Plexiglas and she jumps.

"Listen up. You aren't me, and this isn't your life. You don't get to decide what to do. I don't want Wesley shot, whether I'm Marked or not. Do you hear me?"

Her eyes flash. "This isn't just about you. He broke the law, and he's still a risk," Aunt Anne says. "He might Mark others. I can't let him wander around. There are consequences."

I speak slowly and emphatically. "He didn't even Mark me."

She steps back and her face blanks. "Are you sure *he's* actually infected?"

I nod my head. "I saw the rash. After."

"After you kissed him?"

I nod.

"Did you touch him, other than the kiss?" she asks.

"Why does that matter?" I think back to last night. I did touch him, but . . . "We both had gloves on."

"We've been studying barriers to infection," my aunt says. "For instance, if you used Vaseline on your lips right before you kissed him—"

"I don't even know what Vaseline is."

"I forget how young you were when the world fell apart." My aunt shakes her head. "I know you bite your lip when you get nervous, and it looks puffy on the bottom where it's split. Any chance you used something to cover that up last night?"

Could my nervous habit have saved me? "Gemette gave me some strawberry flavored lip gloss when the bottle pointed at me, but our kiss was a little bit of a mess. We sort of collided. I'm pretty sure he ingested some of my blood."

"Which wouldn't matter," my aunt says. "Only if you consumed his. And even then, Tercera congregates first in the dermis, so if he was recently Marked, and because the contact took place only at the lips, there may have been a lower concentration. The epithelial cells carry a high load of contagious viral cells, but lips are membranous tissue. They wouldn't have much at all until at least twenty-four hours post infection."

Wesley fails to save a girl from drowning, while wearing gloves, and somehow gets Marked, and I practically jump him and somehow, I don't? I don't know whether to laugh or cry.

My Aunt's lip turns up on the right side. "I think you got lucky."

I take a few steps back and sit down on my cot. When I do, it knocks one of my dad's journals to the ground. I glance up at my aunt. When she sees the book, her eyes fly wide. I grab them and set them back on the cot, but my aunt's gaze stays glued to them. Dates are written on the spine, and she turns her head sideways as if she's trying to make out which journals I brought.

"I grabbed a few of dad's journals," I admit. "I promised I'd meet Wesley today so we could join a Marked camp together. He and I were going to work on finding a cure. I know it was probably dumb, but you said Dad was a genius with viruses. I thought his notes might help."

And I wanted to take something of my dad's with me.

I pause, expecting her to laugh, but she doesn't make a sound. "I wish I could see your face a little better. I'm sure it sounds stupid to you—a kid thinking she could cure Tercera."

I wonder whether I'm about to hear the typical adult refrain from Before. My kindergarten teacher said it all the time. *You can do whatever you put your mind to, kid.* I'm not expecting what happens next.

She opens the door and walks through it. She sits next to me on the cot. "You aren't Marked. They won't let you leave until the three day quarantine period is up, but you and I both know."

Even so, I slide as far away from her as I can.

"You have two days in here. You have to choose your Path the day after you're released. I know you're in Sanitation now, but you had such an aptitude for Science. And now you're talking about continuing your dad's research. I don't think it's ridiculous, I think it's right. It's a family legacy."

When I don't respond, Aunt Anne continues. "There are almost a hundred Unmarked communities in North America, most small like Port Gibson, but some much larger. In almost ten years, no one has shown the aptitude for science that you showed. You advanced through four levels in that first year, and five in the second. Each level was created to take a year for an average student. I still don't understand why you left."

I look down at my hands. I can't bring myself to tell her the real reason, because if I do, she won't love me anymore. I already hate myself.

"You don't have to choose Science if you don't want to, but I need you to know, your dad would be so proud of you. I'm glad you're showing an interest in his work." My aunt clears her throat and I glance up at her face.

It's greenish.

"Are you okay?"

She nods. "There's something I've been meaning to tell you for a long time. The thing is, you were so young when your dad died, that it was easier not to explain everything to you then, and now you're older, well the moment never seemed quite right. You're still so young, but you've handled all of this so well, and you'll be an adult in a few days. I guess it's time I tell you."

My heart rate speeds up. "Tell me what?"

"We told you at the time that your dad was in a car accident."

I nod. They did tell me that.

"It's not true," my aunt says. "He was murdered."

I nod again. "I know."

My aunt stands up and her hands fly to her face. "What do you mean, you know?"

I look down at my feet, because I can't look her in the eye. I just can't. When I finally speak, the words come out as little more than a whisper. "I was there, Aunt Anne. I saw Dad get shot."

My aunt sinks back down on the edge of the cot and she's blinking. A lot. She reaches her hand out and tries to put it over mine. I yank my fingers away and stand up.

"Oh, Ruby, I'm so sorry. We found you at the daycare in the bottom of the building."

"I ran down there. After."

"We had no idea you knew."

I turn to face the wall so she can't see the tear running down my right cheek. She's going to ask; I can feel it. She's going to figure it out.

She walks up behind me and I shake my head. "Don't get too close."

"You're not Marked," she says.

I shake my head again. Tears run down my face freely now, so I continue to face the wall, willing her not to press me about it. "I don't care."

She takes a step back and I relax a bit. Maybe she won't figure it out. Maybe she won't hate me like she should.

"If you knew all this time, why didn't you ever tell me?"

My stomach ties in knots. I shake my head again.

"Ruby? Why didn't you say anything? That must've been a terrible burden."

When she steps close again, I can't help it. I spin toward her with my palms out. "Don't touch me, please. I didn't ever tell you because I didn't want you to know the truth."

My stomach fills with ice. Jackhammers dance inside my skull. She'll figure it out, so I may as well come clean.

"I was there, okay? I watched him get shot, and I had his cell phone in my hands, but I hid in the closet because…I'm a coward. My dad died because I was too afraid to save his life."

My aunt's face falls and my heart breaks.

I expect her expression to grow stony, her eyes sharp like flint. I expect her to back away, to shake her head, to look at me with horror. Instead, a tear forms in her eye, too.

"You were six, Ruby. You didn't do anything wrong. There's nothing a six year old could have done to save him."

She doesn't understand. I'm tempted to let it go, but this is the first chance I've had to stand trial. The judges and juries from Before are gone, but someone should know the truth about me.

"My dad told me to hide in that closet, and he gave me his phone. I watched under the door crack while a man with a freckled nose walked in and they argued. I heard the gunshot and saw my father collapse, bleeding from his leg. I was supposed to stay quiet until the man left, and I did. But after he left, I could've done something. I should've called 911."

"You were six."

"You don't understand. They taught us at school. I knew what to do, and I didn't do it. I ran to the elevator and rode it downstairs to the daycare. They were all on the playground and they didn't even realize I hadn't been there all along."

Tears streak my aunt's cheeks now. "You did exactly what your dad wanted you to do. I only wish you'd told me years ago."

"Do you know why I left Science?" I ask. "We were studying anatomy in Level Ten. That's the day I realized it would have taken him *over an hour* to die from his gunshot wound. If I'd called for help, or if I'd been brave enough to tell anyone, your brother would still be alive."

Now she knows the truth.

I killed my own dad.

CHAPTER 6

My aunt hugs me. She ignores my protests, my complaints, and my attempts to pull away. She doesn't let go until I finally hug her back.

As she pulls away from me, she looks me in the eye. "You didn't kill your father. Your dad's biggest regret, wherever he is now, is probably that you've agonized over this for so long. It was not your fault."

It helps to hear her say it, even if I know she's only trying to make me feel better. It's what adults do for kids. They lie to us so much that it gets easy for them. I don't argue with her because it would just prolong this . . . whatever this is.

"Whoa!" Barrett bangs on the window. "What are you doing? You can't be in her cell!"

My aunt frowns at him before turning back to me. "I know you aren't Marked, but I can't get you out of here until seventy-two hours have passed." My aunt presses her lips together as if she's debating something. She sighs heavily. "I'll bring you the rest of your father's journals so you have something to do." She turns to leave.

"I'm going to have to hold you too now," Barrett says.

My aunt laughs as she walks past him. "I'd like to see you try, kid."

He doesn't bother.

Less than an hour later, a disgruntled Barrett slides my dad's leather bound journals through my meal drawer one at a time. My dad dated all his entries, so I put them in order and start reading. At first, they're a little boring and I almost stop. When I think about Wesley, alone in the cold, and probably headed for the nearest Marked encampment right now, I persevere. I hope he doesn't think I was too angry to go with him. I still can't believe I'm fine. It may be the first stroke of luck I've ever had, other than not dying in the Tercera apocalypse the first time around, obviously.

Rhonda, Job, my uncle, and Gemette all come to visit me in quarantine. Mr. Fairchild comes too, which surprises me. Other than those visits, and eating as little as possible of the regular meals of mush Barrett pushes through my meal drawer, I read. I glance at the clock on the wall. I checked in just after ten the night of the Last Supper. It's almost six p.m. now.

I'll be out in four hours.

I pick up the last journal. It's only half full, and it begins two months before Dad died. I wonder what he'll say in his last journal. Probably nothing great. It's not like you know they're your last words when you're writing them.

The entries are all about a specific virus Dad was working on in order to create his super vaccination. I vaguely remember him talking about it. He combined the worst viruses on earth in order to create a virus for which he could make a vaccine with the intention of protecting mankind from everything with one shot. It's nine-thirty when I reach the second to last entry. It's dated only ten days before he died.

I can barely breathe, because I remember that day. Dad

promised we were going to play on the beach. The beach and ocean were visible from the window of our condo, and I pestered him to walk in the sand and splash in the water every day. He put me off a lot, but that Sunday we were going. Until he changed his mind at the last minute. He said there were too many jelly fish, but I saw the flag. It wasn't blue, it was green. No jellies.

I squash the memories down and force myself to read what he wrote; I want to find out what he worked on instead of spending time with me. I hardly believe what I read. He bailed on the beach because he had a breakthrough in a new viral treatment method.

One of the things I learned at some point, but had forgotten, was how viral vaccinations work. All viral vaccinations take one of three forms: first, a live but weakened virus, second, inactivated or dead viral cells, or third, a partial virus. In each case, the idea is that after vaccination, the human body will prepare a defense to a less devastating version of the virus that keeps the person from getting sick if they're exposed to the full strength virus. Of course, the most effective vaccinations use a live virus, but there's a significant risk to the very young, the very old, and the sick members of the population, since even a weak virus can still do some damage. It creates better immunity, but it results in more substantial illnesses too, or in rare cases, even death.

None of the three normal vaccination methods work with Tercera because it reproduces too quickly. The human body doesn't even recognize it as a threat when it's first introduced. It spreads like wildfire, and then sits inert for a long time. By the time Tercera starts attacking vital functions, it's too late. The virus is already everywhere, shutting everything down. When it was introduced ten years ago, it spread so fast that most people couldn't have been vaccinated, even if they'd had a working vaccine.

His entries explain that my dad's breakthrough isn't a vaccine at all. In the process of splicing viruses to create a consolidated one, he spawned another virus—a more aggressive one. Instead of taking over human cells, or repopulating in the human body itself, the virus takes over other viruses, including malignant ones. It lays dormant until it encounters other viral cells in the host body, and then it gobbles them up, creating more of itself as it goes. It was more aggressive than Tercera, but if his notes are right, it's less damaging to humans. The only side effect my dad identified in primates was a stimulation of brain function that reduced the need for sleep.

He was preparing forms for government approval to move forward with human testing. It tested one hundred percent effective with no negative side effects in lab rats, sheep and monkeys. Why didn't someone find his notes and do something with this after Tercera broke out?

The next passage in his journal answers my question.

I miss the resources of my big lab so badly that I almost called my old boss to bring them in as partner, but I already have one partner who adds nothing and creates problems. I don't want another, even if Philip would pay the fees for this application in a heartbeat. If I hand it over to Pfizer, I'll lose all control. I wish Jack had the money for the application right now. He thinks we should create a demand first, and then our requests would be expedited. I refused of course. Jack never worries about the human lives at risk.

Create a demand first? As in release a disease that could kill people? Something that would need to be cured? My blood runs cold. Who was this partner Jack? Thank goodness my dad refused. What a monster.

Jack's a much bigger idiot than I realized. Even with him creating issues every step of the way, I'm going to get approval and release this. It will cure every virus that presently plagues the human race.

Holy crap. If he hadn't died, my dad would've saved the world. I force air through my nose and exhale through my mouth. I need to finish this entry.

Despite the difficulties, I really strive to keep my work life separate from my home life. My father never let up and I resented him for it. I want to be there for Ruby. I didn't want to bring work home at all, but my partner and I are at odds right now so I needed a place to work that he couldn't reach. He wants to sell the Triptych virus. I used components of Variola, HIV and Influenza to make it, and modified them all. I even coded it to only impact human cells so it won't be as likely to mutate, but you still need a loaded gun to invent a successful bullet proof vest.

I only created it to formulate a durable vaccination, one that will prepare human cells for most anything. I created Triptych first, but now the hacker virus should render Triptych unnecessary. I built in a three-year waiting period so if it ever does get out, there'll be plenty of time to treat for it before anyone dies.

Unfortunately, that very thing makes Jack think we should release it. He says it'll improve the market for the hacker virus. He even has a buyer lined up, a political activist who—it doesn't matter. I refused him. I locked Triptych up so he can't reach it. I'm only keeping it in case my hacker virus fails human trials. Then I may need to reopen Triptych to try again with my multi-faceted vaccine.

I know we need money—I'm in debt up to my eyeballs—but Jack's not thinking straight. He hasn't been sleeping well, and I understand marital problems well enough to empathize. He says the vultures are circling. Since he does the books, I guess he'd know.

He thinks we'll have plenty of time to deal with the fallout if we sell. Since I work alone, no one will ever track it back to us. The scariest thing about selling Triptych is actually the quirk I engineered into it. Since it lays dormant for so long, any humans infected wouldn't even know anything was wrong. It could spread to most of the world's population before anyone realized what was happening. I set it up to pass from person to person through the epithelial cells like leprae, because I wanted the vaccination to do the same. I'm tired of big pharma making a killing on everything. I want to make the world better, not worse. But if it ever got out, it would proliferate unchecked.

I engineered an early warning system so if it ever did get out, even by accident, I'd be sure to notice. At first I planned to use hair loss, but it was too hard to code so I ended up adding a facial rash. It's innocuous enough that I don't think he'll notice it, but I'll know if it's ever released. Thousands of people with the same facial rash should hit the news.

My dad created Tercera.

He would've stopped it before anyone died, if he'd survived his partner shooting him. Ironically, if my dad had let Jack sell it, he wouldn't have stolen it, and maybe my dad would have survived to disburse the cure. If my dad had been more of a villain, civilization might have survived.

The final entry is short and dated the day of Dad's death.

Jack and I had another fight. He threatened to call Ruby's mother if I don't agree to sell Triptych.

I almost drop the book. My mother died giving birth to me.

The sky is blue. Tercera kills. We all need sleep to function. My mother died the day I was born. These are all things I know for a fact.

My dad, my aunt, and my uncle have always told me my mom's dead. I have one photo of her and my dad from years before I came along, and nothing else.

If Jack's threatening to call her, that was a lie.

I still refused, and he knocked me out and removed the virus right out of my safe. I paid a fortune last week to put in a hidden safe that can only be opened by me and mine. He won't steal from me again. No one will.

I'm so close to the solution that would render this entire discus-

sion moot. I've isolated the special mechanism by which Triptych passes. It builds up first in the epithelial cells so it transfers via simple touch. I only need to incorporate that transmission method for the hacker virus and it'll be complete. Jack doesn't want me to add it, because if I do it's not marketable. Why would anyone pay for something that will be transmitted by touch almost immediately after it's released?

He's missing the point. My goal was never to make buckets of money. It was always to create a new world—a better world. He accuses me of wanting fame. He may be right. I miss the renown of working at a big lab, the respect, but that's not my only reason.

If I'm being honest with myself, more than anything else, I want to come out of hiding.

Come out of hiding? Why were we in hiding? I was so young when we moved to Galveston that it's mostly a blur. I thought he gave up his fancy job to have more time to spend with me.

I gave up a lot when Ruby and I ran, but more importantly, I want Ruby and her generation to lead a very different life than I led as a kid. She won't get sick. Her body won't betray her.

He gave up a lot when we ran from what?

I don't know if the hacker virus will work against Triptych once I change its transmission mode, or what other side effects might manifest in humans. I can't risk using it before it's been tested, but I have the data, and the samples to develop antibodies for Triptych. It's tricky because the human body won't develop these on its own. The miserable virus I made knocks out the antibody response almost immediately.

To combat that, I developed an extra zealous antibody here by reverse engineering the strands. The bad news is that it would be tremendously hard to administer, not to mention cost prohibitive. With the rate at which Triptych would spread, there would be no way to immunize everyone in time. I made the antibodies I reverse engineered self-replicating with contact from any virus so they'll last indefinitely once injected. I have no idea how they'd react with the attack virus I'm working on. I'd be nervous to give the same person both.

I'm putting the rest of my research somewhere safe. Somewhere only my blood can reach. If anything happens to me, Ruby will be safe. At least I know Ruby will have what she needs.

A huge chunk of pages following the last entry are torn out. Nothing but blank pages follow. The clock says it's ten minutes til ten.

My mind spins furiously. My dad invented Tercera. He must have. His partner Jack stole it and infected people. Before Dad could cure it, someone murdered him. But how did all of that happen? What happened to the hacker virus? Did he put it in the safe and lock it up, and if he did, is there even a remote chance it might still exist?

Highly, highly unlikely, but maybe his research shows how he engineered it.

Except the rest of the pages he wrote are missing. These journals discuss the hacker virus, but don't contain hard data. I glance at the clock. Five minutes.

My aunt—the person who brought me these journals— including this last one, has had them in a stack in her office. They were just sitting on the floor in a pile, so it's a safe bet she's read them all. Which means she already knows about my dad's research, and she knows my mom's alive. She never said a word about either to me. I had no idea we were on the run, or why. It slowly occurs to me that my aunt never told me my dad had been murdered, either. She actively lied to me for more than a decade.

What's more, she knew about a cure to Tercera ten years ago, and did nothing. Maybe the reason she didn't hate me for letting my dad die is that she allowed billions to die.

My aunt's a bigger monster than me.

At ten o'clock, I barely make eye contact with Barrett as I

walk out the door to head home. Aunt Anne owes me some answers. I may have failed my dad, and my aunt may have failed the human race, but I won't let Wesley or anyone else die when there may be a cure.

I'm going to fix the mess my Dad made if it kills me.

CHAPTER 7

I prepare what I'll say to my aunt the entire walk home. Three main things upset me. First, why did my aunt conceal that my mother was alive? After my dad died, shouldn't she have contacted my mom? Second, why didn't my aunt ever tell me my dad created Tercera? I get that it might be depressing or stigmatize us, but she should have at least told *me*. And finally, if she knew my dad cured Tercera, why didn't she go to Galveston to recover the cure herself?

I pause in front of the door, take a deep breath, and shove it open.

"Welcome home, Ruby!" a large banner proclaims.

"Welcome home!" my family yells.

Rhonda, Job, Uncle Dan and Aunt Anne crowd around me. They don't take turns hugging me, so it becomes a giant jumble of arms and legs. The smell of rabbit stew makes me smile, until I catch sight of what's resting in the center of the kitchen table.

An enormous cake with chocolate frosting! Cocoa beans only grow in Latin America and Hawaii, and we no longer communicate with or travel to either location. Cocoa is basically impossible to find, and I haven't had chocolate in years.

"How is that possible? Or am I hallucinating?" I glance at the cake and back at Rhonda.

She smiles greedily. "The Fairchilds had some cocoa powder, and Wesley's mom brought over an entire tin of it to apologize for the horrible ordeal Wesley put you through."

Wesley's poor mother. Her only son is Marked, and she's sending me an apology gift. A valuable one at that.

I intended to immediately pin my aunt down, and not let up until she'd answered my questions, but now that I'm here, it's hard. When Job stands up to start on dishes, I realize I can't wait any longer.

"Aunt Anne," I say.

She turns to face me across the table, and squares her shoulders. She gestures at Uncle Dan to sit at her side. "Job, please sit. The dishes can wait. We need to talk."

She brought me the journals. She knew exactly what I'd find, so she's had two days to prepare.

Uncle Dan reaches over and takes his wife's hand. He clears his throat. "Kids, we need to tell you something that Ruby recently learned, but we've kept from you until now."

"What's going on?" Job sits down and glances from his parents to me, and back again. "You're freaking me out."

"It should," Uncle Dan says. "This is big news. We've been waiting until you were old enough. We planned to tell you when Ruby turned seventeen."

I don't know whether to believe them. It seems awfully coincidental that I found out days before they 'planned' to tell me.

"Ruby's dad, my brother," my aunt says, "created Tercera."

Rhonda's jaw drops. Job's mouth quirks up in a smile, and I shake my head. Not a joke.

"How long have you known?" It's the most crucial of all

my questions. If they knew all along, they really did let the world burn. Please have an excuse, some reason why you didn't know until recently. Please.

"We know about your dad's development of Tercera from reading his journals," Aunt Anne says. "We didn't read those journals until it was too late to do anything about it."

I want to believe that. Badly. "Why didn't you read them right away?"

Aunt Anne and Uncle Dan share a glance, then Aunt Anne says, "All we ask is that you listen. Listen to our explanation of what happened first, and then make judgments later. Because Ruby already knows that's not even the most shocking revelation."

Uncle Dan frowns. "It's not. The worst part is that Ruby's father also engineered what he believed was a cure."

"A cure?" Rhonda gasps. "That's not bad, that's good!" She glances at me. I can see when the realization hits her. She turns back to her mom and dad. "How could you sit on information like this? All those people died."

"Yes, millions died. Billions. You know that academically, but you don't remember what it was actually like." My aunt leans back into her chair. "None of you do. You don't even understand why so few humans survived. We're not sure exactly how Tercera got out, though everyone suspects World Peace Now released it."

World Peace Now, or WPN, pronounced like weapon by its detractors, is a religious cult that proclaimed early on that Tercera was more than a simple rash. They claimed it would end humanity. They secluded themselves right away and are currently the largest group of survivors in North America. The Unmarked have nearly one hundred small communities, most with only a few thousand survivors. No one's quite sure how many Marked kids are alive out there, but we donate enough hormone suppressants for a hundred thousand a year. WPN has at least seven heavily fortified ports, with more than half a million citizens. They outnumber the Marked by hundreds of thousands, and they outnumber the Unmarked by a wide margin as well.

"My dad's business partner sold it," I say.

My aunt says, "Your father's partner stole the virus and released it, yes, but we aren't sure who Jack is, and we don't know who he sold it to. It could have been WPN or one of its founding members."

"How do you know my dad wasn't involved?" I need to know. He did something that sent him on the run, and later he did something that got him murdered.

"From what we can tell, when Tercera emerged," my aunt says, "your father had been dead for at least a week. He couldn't have had anything to do with its release. The blood of millions is on his partner, or if they aren't the same, possibly the man who murdered him." My aunt's eyes widen and she stares at me. "Who you saw. I hadn't thought about it before now. Can you describe him?"

He still stars in my nightmares several times a week. He stood taller than my dad, and thinner, too. His light brown hair was cut short, and angry blue eyes stood out above a strong jaw. Freckles sprinkled his long, straight nose, but his cheeks were smooth. His mouth never stopped moving, and his perfect, huge teeth flashed as he spoke. He talked smoothly and clearly, as though he could talk his way out of anything. Even in my dreams, his voice makes my skin crawl.

"Wait," Rhonda says. "Your dad was *murdered* and you saw it?"

I nod. It's strangely satisfying to know Aunt Anne concealed the truth from more than just me. "He had light brown hair and blue eyes. He was taller than Dad, and thin. He wore nice clothes, like a blazer and a blue button down shirt, with shiny shoes. He had freckles on his nose."

My uncle asks, "Was his name Jack?"

I stand up and pace from one end of the kitchen to the other. "I've been trying to remember. Dad yelled on the phone a lot, and I remember him yelling the name Jack, but I don't recall what Jack looked like. Dad met his partner at their main lab several times, but it was always while I was at school."

"So the freckle faced man *could* be Jack?" my aunt asks.

I close my eyes and go over that night again. "I guess, maybe, but the more I think about it, the less sense it makes. Dad seemed surprised when he saw the freckle nosed man through that little hole in the door. He bundled me off to the closet and told me not to come out, no matter what. I doubt he'd have been shocked to see his partner, or made me hide in the closet. He would've been angry possibly, but not surprised."

My aunt exchanges a glance with Uncle Dan I can't interpret.

"Regardless," she says, "it was bad timing that the one man who could've stopped Tercera died shortly before it spread."

"Bad timing?" My laughter's about two octaves too high, but I can't seem to stop myself. I force my mouth shut. "Dad created the virus that decimated the world. Weeks before it was released, someone killed him. You don't think he had any culpability?"

My aunt draws herself up in her chair and squares her shoulders. "Your father was a good man. He did his utmost to keep the dangerous parts of his research safe. In fact, I'm positive his attempts to stymie this Jack caused his death, though I can't prove it."

I sit down hard on one of the wooden kitchen chairs, too numb to process any more. My dad was a giant among men, a genius, gifted, the perfect father, a devoted single parent.

I've known all these things were true my whole life, but now I'm not so sure.

And apparently he wasn't a single parent at all—not really. "What about my mom? You haven't mentioned her yet."

My aunt sighs. For the first time ever, my aunt looks old. She puts her head in her hands for a moment, and then she straightens up and meets my eye.

"I should've told you this part years ago. My only excuse is that the days blur and somehow, in a way I can't explain, I woke up one day and you weren't a baby anymore. Or maybe if I told you your mom was alive, and confessed that I lied about it, you might hate me for it. It's always felt like you were my daughter, ever since we lost Don. Admitting you have another mother, well. It hurt me. I guess it doesn't matter. I should've told you years ago and I didn't."

"Is my mom still alive?"

My aunt reaches across the table and puts her hand on mine, but I shake it off.

"She's almost certainly dead now," she says. "By our best estimates, Tercera wiped out more than 98 percent of the world in the first three years, closer to 99.9% in North America where it originated. But she wasn't dead before that, no."

"Why were Dad and I on the run? Why did Dad lie to me at all?"

My uncle clears his throat. "Your mother left your father. It happened a lot Before, people falling out of love. She didn't want you when you were born, and your dad took you home from the hospital with her blessing, but your Mom and her new husband showed up a few months later and tried to take you away. Instead of fighting them in the courts, your dad decided to run from it. He couldn't face the possibility of losing you."

"That's insane," I say. "Why not just share me? I had a kid in my kindergarten class Before who lived with her mom most of the time, but then went to visit her dad sometimes too. I could've done that."

My aunt reaches for my hand again, but catches herself and balls her hands into fists. "Your mom's new husband wasn't stable. Your dad didn't think he was safe. The scariest part to Don was that the new husband had a lot of money and influence, and your dad worried that he'd lose you entirely."

The room goes utterly silent for one moment. Then another.

Finally Rhonda asks, "Why didn't you go after the cure, after you found out it existed?"

My uncle says, "We read the journals too late. Years ago Don had a huge job with a very prestigious company, Pfizer. They made all the best vaccinations. To protect Ruby from her mother and abhorrent stepfather, he gave it up. He bought a tiny cabin in the woods with most of his cash, and planned to do odd jobs for cash around the area. Harvesting, woodcutting, handyman type work."

"Don was a terrible handyman." Aunt Anne snorts. "He was bored, and it showed. It wasn't a good enough life for him, or for you. You needed friends and social interaction. He found an investor to fund his work on an idea."

"Jack."

Aunt Anne nods. "He'd been talking for years about combining viruses to create one vaccination. Limit the exposure to these kids of all the toxins. Limit the incessant visits. One shot to stop it all. He kept the project quiet, but as it progressed he needed access to more sophisticated equipment. He gambled when he moved out to Galveston to be near UTMB, the University of Texas' Galveston campus."

"It seemed to pay off," my uncle says. "He told us everything was progressing perfectly. We didn't know anything about his investor, not even his name. He said the identity of his investor was confidential, and we didn't press. When Don was murdered, we knew the identification documents your dad was using for you wouldn't hold up. The authorities would discover who your mother was and contact her."

My aunt stands up and starts to pace the same track I walked moments ago. "We flew to Galveston immediately. I left my hospital in the lurch, but I didn't care. Your dad had given up everything to protect you. I wasn't sure what to do, but I knew my brother didn't want you to go to your mother. Besides, for all I knew, she was involved in his death. She'd been searching for you. I wanted to see what the police investigation turned up before I made any decisions I couldn't unmake."

"So you took me back into hiding?" I ask.

"I was grief stricken." A tear rolls down my aunt's cheek and she doesn't bother to brush it away. "My only sibling, who was also my best friend, died. I needed time. We all did. I needed to identify the best course of action for all of us."

My aunt, the doctor, took me and ran, just like my dad. I actually felt sorry for my mom.

My uncle's voice is softer than I've ever heard it, almost gentle compared to his usual barked commands. "It might have been an imprudent decision. It might even have been rash. But running to your dad's cabin in the woods in Nebraska saved our lives. All of us. It's the only reason we didn't contract Tercera. So while you're tallying up your father's crimes, remember that his running away with you, and his murder, and the weeks we spent grieving in Nebraska while we tried to decide what to do, are the only things that kept you alive, kept this family alive."

"How did we not come in contact with anyone?" Job asks.

"I thought basically everyone had Tercera within a few weeks."

My aunt nods. "They did. When we ran, we ordered enough food for a few weeks. The cabin was already well stocked with long term supplies from when you lived there before, Ruby."

My uncle says, "Anne hated shopping, because the only decent store was over an hour drive. We'd been there about two weeks when we decided to replenish our supplies. That was about the time we started hearing reports of a strange rash. WPN started broadcasts before the news even picked up the story, but not many people gave credence to its claims that the strange rash on everyone's forehead was a Mark of impending doom. Still, we worried. Life went on, but we thought, like others, that prudence was appropriate. After all, we were free of this Mark, whatever it might portend, and very few people were."

"We emptied out our retirement funds and used them to order more food. Large quantities." My aunt reaches for Rhonda.

Rhonda pulls away, too. I'm not the only one who's upset.

I'm tired of them delaying the answer. "When did you read my dad's journals?"

My aunt shakes her head. "Not for a long time. We didn't even know we had your dad's journals right after he died. The day we ran, we contacted his assistant. She hadn't been paid in a month. We offered to pay her, if she'd send us all his things. We couldn't risk being seen if the police showed up."

I close my eyes and think of Aunt Anne and Uncle Dan acting like criminals, sneaking around and having other people sneak for them.

Aunt Anne continues. "Within a few weeks of the news picking up the story, Pfizer scientists determined that the Mark was the first symptom of a viral illness that would worsen with time, sort of like HIV progresses into AIDS. By that point, almost everyone alive was already Marked, and there were plenty of people willing to cater to the paranoid, as long as enough money was involved. Very few people credited WPN's ranting about a plague, but Pfizer's analysis had everyone nervous. John Roth joined us immediately. He and his son had been on a hiking trip, and when they returned, everyone was talking about it. He called me right away."

"And you just took them in?" I ask.

Uncle Dan nods. "He's my oldest friend. He brought his son Sam up to Nebraska the first week after the Mark appeared. He was more nervous than most, since his dad died from some bizarre illness after traveling to Africa twenty years before."

I remember Sam coming to stay with us. We hadn't been in Nebraska very long, a few weeks, maybe a month. He seemed so much older than me then. I was six, and he was nine. "I remember, but what about—"

"We had a little money, but John Roth had a lot. Without him joining us, we might have starved," my uncle says. "But we made it that first year without being exposed. Once the sores started showing up in year two, the whole world went crazy. We kept people away any way we could. You were all so young, I don't know what you remember, but we tried to make sure you stayed inside as much as possible, and even outside, the cabin was fairly isolated. Ruby, you were only seven then. Rhonda, you and Job were nine."

Aunt Anne stops pacing and reaches for Uncle Dan's hand. She squeezes it tightly, like thinking about all this hurts. Maybe it does. "WPN predicted the sores would worsen and death would follow. People were listening by then, since they'd been right about the virus progressing. They insisted it would carry a one hundred percent mortality rate. People were terrified. Mobs formed, riots spread. By that point, almost every human on Earth was Marked and most of them were dealing with weeping sores. WPN's followers weren't. They had holed up in their compounds from the beginning, casting out anyone who got infected, but everyone else who wasn't Marked was like us. Some combination of paranoid and lucky. Lucky enough to have a bug-out spot. Paranoid enough to have been cautious once the Mark appeared."

"WPN told the government they had a cure," Job says. "I remember this part. They said it had to be taken within a month of the first sores appearing. It was all over the radio programs. There were debates over whether to believe WPN, whether to take their deal and get the cure, or keep trying to find one ourselves."

"WPN had terms," my aunt says. "They argued with the government for over two weeks, but in the end there were only three days left for most government officials, including the President, to take it before they were outside of the window of efficacy. WPN demanded control of communications. They demanded weapons, food, and access to energy plants, tools, and resources. Their list went on and on. They claimed they needed it all to administer the cure effectively."

"It wasn't a cure," Job says. "I remember that, too."

"Right." My uncle stares at the wall, his eyes glassy. "WPN somehow discovered a way to accelerate the progression of the virus. They fooled everyone so they could wipe out the only group that could've broken into their compound. As far as we knew at the time, there wasn't a cure."

I look sharply his way.

My aunt notices. "Even with your dad's work there's no guarantee, sweetheart. It seems very likely your dad created the Tercera virus that was released, but we don't know for sure whether he completed his solution, or how the virus might have changed since its release. Even if a cure worked then, it might not work anymore."

I raise one eyebrow. "When did you find out? I keep asking, and you keep talking about timelines."

My uncle says, "The police conducted an investigation after your dad died that turned up no answers. It did, however, turn up the fact that he was on the run, and he wasn't who he said he was. We only have the journals because his office manager snuck them out before the police cordoned the lab off. She shipped everything she could sneak out to the cabin, and it all got stacked in the garage, and then later, they got buried under the tons of supplies we bought."

"When did you read them?" I ask.

My aunt looks at me for a moment, searching my eyes for something before she speaks. "We moved here, to Mississippi, a little more than three years after the Marking began, roughly two years after the acceleration of the government, and a year after the bulk of humanity died. Most people who had survived were starving at that point, and there was no one left to produce and prepare food, or to care for the sick except for pre-pubescent children. Everyone over the age of twelve or thirteen was sick. A lot of people committed suicide. All that was left were roaming bands of Marked kids, more desperate than ever, and slowly starving. There weren't as many as before so it seemed safer to travel."

She closes her eyes, massages her temples and reopens them. "We'd heard rumors that a society was forming. A society of unmarked people like us were banding together. Instead of raiding decimated towns and braving trips out to empty houses looking for undiscovered food caches, these people supposedly grew their own food, defended themselves and most of all, had a sustainable plan, which we needed. We were running out of everything fast."

"We calculated we had less than a month of supplies left when we left," Uncle Dan says.

"Which meant the garage wasn't so full?" Job asks.

Aunt Anne nods. "Bingo. We sifted through our belongings to decide what was important enough to bring and what we would leave behind. We found the box of things from your dad's office manager from three years before. The journals were in there, along with a briefcase and some files. When I realized what they were, I read them all. It had occurred to me before that if anyone might have leads on how to deal with a super virus, it would be your dad, but he was dead. I didn't realize I had his research in my possession. By the time I read through to the end, it was already too late."

Rhonda hasn't moved or spoken a word, but she looks up then. "Too late for what, Mom? What about all the children?"

The children died by the billions, most of them starving when their parents died. Some of them starved slowly over a period of years.

"Most of them had already starved, Rhonda. We were thinking about *our* children. You, Job and Ruby." My aunt puts her hand on my head and I don't shy away this time. "We couldn't risk pursuing it. The journals don't have any specifics about the virus or your dad's solution. They contain no coding or information on where he started in his research. There's not enough for me to work from. The mentions in it of the viral delay being linked to GnRH allowed me to develop the first hormone suppressant. I led the Unmarked initiative to make and distribute it."

"It's not enough," I say. "You could've done more. You should've done more."

Uncle Dan slams his hand on the table. "Stop. Your aunt's not telling you the biggest reason we didn't take action. You know where your dad's lab was, Ruby. That's why we couldn't pursue it."

"Galveston, Texas," I say. "WPN's home base. Their main compound."

"The most heavily armed area in North America." My uncle leans back. "Even if your dad's lab hadn't been controlled by WPN, there are hundreds of miles of countryside between here and there, most of it teeming with Marked kids, who we very much pitied, but we couldn't risk traversing it with you three."

"We did ask you about it." My aunt turns toward me. "You may not remember it, but we asked if you knew anything about your dad's work, or where he would've stored important things. You said you didn't know where he'd put secret stuff. Anything you knew at the time, back when your dad wrote this, you'd forgotten by the time we asked. We don't know what he meant, but it was such a long stretch to think that we could've reached the lab, much less found anything once we arrived."

I remember lying to them about it, because I lied about anything to do with Dad's death.

Rhonda stands. "Why didn't you tell the Unmarked when you arrived? Surely they'd have sent a team. WPN may be full of lunatics and zealots, but even WPN must want a cure for Tercera."

"We didn't tell the leadership with the Unmarked because of a line in the journal," my aunt says. "It implies that only Ruby can reach the cure. We didn't want the Unmarked to take our child. We kept the secret to protect her."

I remember the line. "He says something like, 'I'm putting the research somewhere only my blood can reach.' That's what you're talking about?"

My aunt nods. "But, I've been giving it some thought, and I think that statement may include me, too. We went yesterday to talk to Mr. Fairchild, who's about as motivated as anyone can be. He's passing word of this along to the

Unmarked leadership in Nashville, including John Roth, and once we get approval, we'll leave to pursue it. We're only waiting to find out whether John might have ideas on how to initiate contact with WPN. Maybe they'd grant us permission to search. If John thinks it's a bad idea, we'll sneak in."

I square my shoulders. No more secrets. "My dad had a safe. I didn't tell you about it because I was scared you'd make me go back. What if you get there and you can't get it open?"

"How can we be sure *you* even can ten years later?" my aunt asks. "It's a risk either way, but we want you here. We've waited to act until you were safe. It's time for us to take that risk. Not you."

"I remember my dad putting it in, and I can reach it. I'm the safest bet."

"Ruby, you can't know for sure that you can open it," my uncle says.

"I'm his blood. I have the knowledge of where it is, and I need to do this." I pause. "For Wesley."

My aunt and uncle both frown. "We've decided you're staying. We leave tomorrow, or the next day at the latest."

"That's not fair," I say. "If—"

A loud moaning sound fills the air, and I cover my ears. The Unmarked warning alarms sound across the entire city in one circumstance. The Mayor sounds the alarm when the perimeter's been breached by hostiles.

Port Gibson's under attack.

CHAPTER 8

Uncle Dan and Rhonda shoot out the door without comment, both presumably armed already. Aunt Anne and Job stand up and walk to their rooms to grab their guns. We all use guns on perimeter duty starting at age twelve, but a personal gun's issued on each citizen's seventeenth birthday. With my past experience, I haven't minded the lack of one. Being left home in a crisis chafes, though.

I put on my coat, and when they return to the kitchen I ask, "Maybe I can borrow one of Uncle Dan's tranq guns? I'm old enough, and I've used them on perimeter duty a lot. I can help."

Aunt Anne stops. "You've been under supervision when guarding the perimeter at all times. You haven't passed your certification for a real gun, so no. You can't bring a tranq. The grim reaper spared you once this week. You'll go to the Courthouse like protocol dictates, while Job and I report to our designated zone."

I open my mouth to protest, but cut off when she clenches her teeth. She never budges after that, and we don't have time to argue.

I follow her and Job outside, but when Job goes south toward the Medical Center, and my aunt heads for the middle school, I turn north. Back to the Courthouse, yuck. At least this time I won't have to sit in a tiny room on the second floor and stare at the wall. I sit down on the front steps when I arrive, and put my head in my hands. Gemette won't be here, because she turned seventeen a month ago. She already has her gun and a security assignment.

Parents drop their kids off in waves and head for their assigned areas. Claire Hartford wipes her son Adam's nose and tells him to be brave. Robert Emler can't get his clinging toddler Colby to release his leg without yelling. Annie Bettin deposits several children, one of which only has one sneaker. When Tina notices the missing shoe, she starts to cry. She's not the only kid sobbing, but I can relate to her distress. The tears began over missing footwear, but they've morphed into a reflection of her feelings of helplessness.

Something's wrong with the world, and we can't do anything about it.

I walk inside and squat down so we're eye level. "Hey, Tina." I grab the puffy sleeve of her coat with my gloved hand. "You remember me, right? I'm Ruby."

She nods.

"Your dad loves to go fishing, right?" I pull her a little closer.

She nods again and wipes at her tear-streaked cheeks.

"Your mom and dad are doing some important stuff out there, keeping us all safe, but we get to do something really neat here. We get to play some games with all the kids in Port Gibson. And you don't need a shoe for that. Look."

I take my shoes off and toss them toward the wall in the entry hall.

When she sees my gray wool socks, she cries harder. Her nose starts to run. Great job, Ruby. "Oh, no, I—"

"Did you say games?" A little girl with red pigtails peeking out from under her cap interrupts me.

"Yes." I turn toward the redhead. Distraction is the goal, so maybe she can help. "You were all in bed at home, right? Thanks to the alarm, we get to be up and out of bed. It's basically a celebration. You don't need shoes for a pajama party."

Two other kids take a few steps toward me and Tina's bawling deescalates to hiccups.

"Have you ever played duck-duck-goose?" I ask.

Heads shake back and forth all around me. Pretty much every kid in the room inches closer. Tina's still sniffling, but the rest listen quietly.

"It's a great game," I say. "But you need gloves. Can you all show me your gloves?" I hold up my hands to show my gloves, and all the kids around me do the same. I sit down on the floor in the middle of the Courthouse foyer. "We all sit in a circle on the floor with your shoes off and your gloves on. Who wants to give it a try?"

Within a few minutes, all of them are sitting in a circle, except the youngest who's probably no more than two. She sits on my lap with her gloved thumb in her mouth. I play with them for a while, but eventually Maris, a twelve-year-old girl with long dark hair who's training for Agriculture takes over. I slip gratefully off to a quiet corner. When the baby on my lap falls asleep, I lay her down on a cot and drape a blanket over her.

I spent all day reading in quarantine, and then went home and argued with my aunt and uncle. Now it's past 1:00 a.m. and I'm tired. I want to sleep, but I can't with an attack underway. I hope my family's safe. I wonder whether the Marked attacked. It seems more likely them than WPN, since their cities run along the coast, and Port Gibson's a river port —nowhere near the ocean.

I wonder whether Wesley's found a place with the

Marked. I hope he found the encampment that's closest to us. I can't imagine he'd join any kind of attack on his hometown. I listen for gunfire, my breath puffing out in front of me as I wait, almost like time has frozen around me. I sit outside for a while counting shots. Twelve so far. Ice crystals have formed on the weeds at the base of the steps since I came out. I ought to go back inside before I freeze, too.

"You shouldn't be out here," a deep voice says.

I turn toward Sam. He's leaning against the doorjamb, arms crossed over his chest. How long has he been standing there?

"You pulled babysitting duty?" I ask. "How sad for you."

I turn back and rest my chin on my arms. I hate that I'm sitting here like a kid, listening and vainly trying to figure out what's going on instead of seeing it for myself. Less than a week stands between me and a security assignment. I've dreaded being issued a firearm for years, but with Sam watching me sit with the children, I dunno. I may finally be ready.

"Why are you here anyway?" I ask. "Aren't you my uncle's top guy?"

"Your uncle sent me. Ask him."

My stomach clenches suddenly. What if my uncle dies? Then who would go after the cure? I hear another gunshot. A lot of bullets are flying around tonight.

"I hope he's okay," I say.

"He was fine half an hour ago when he sent me here," Sam says.

That answers my question of how long he's been standing there. I wonder how long he sat and watched me staring off into nothing before saying something. "What's going on out there? Who's attacking?"

"The Marked," he says. "Who else?"

"But why? What do they want? They haven't attacked in

over a year, and that was during a drought. They were starving, which made sense. It was less of an attack and more of an emphatic petition."

He shrugs, then walks down the steps and sits next to me. He sits so close, I can feel the heat radiating off of him. Everyone seems big to me, with my slight frame, but he's massive. He even makes Rhonda, at almost six feet tall, look delicate. I'm like a kitten next to a Rottweiler.

We sit in silence for several minutes, both immersed in our own thoughts. I smell him, but not like I always smelled Wesley. Sam certainly isn't wearing cologne. He smells like leather, gunmetal, sweat, and the woods, but for some reason, it isn't gross. I almost like it.

He obviously doesn't feel the need to fill the space around us with words. I'd always thought of Sam as being kind of dumb, but after all the arguing that went on at home this evening, I have a newfound appreciation for silence.

When he stands suddenly and without apparent reason, I feel bereft, cold, and alone. Several moments later, a patrol comes into view. How had he seen it that far out? When I stand for a better view, he moves in front of me so fast he's a blur. The wall of his body blocks my view completely.

"Who's there?" Sam asks.

"Trevor Stayley and Jonas Hill," a high tenor says.

"And how's it going?"

"They've pushed them back out beyond the wall. We still have to secure the perimeter and do sweeps." When I lean around Sam, I can barely make out the short stocky man who's talking in the dark. It's Trevor. "It was definitely an attack, not a raid. They weren't after supplies."

"I know. I was in Zone Six earlier." Sam's shoulders are tense, like he's ready for a fight.

"Is something wrong?" I whisper.

He shakes his head slightly in response, then says, "Any orders?"

Trevor says, "No, I think it's almost over. They don't have the resources to really push. Stay in place. Once the alarm sounds again, you can release the kids to their parents."

Sam's shoulders relax, and he sits down. I circle around and sit next to him.

He raises one eyebrow. "Minors stay inside. They could've been a threat."

I toss my head. "Oh, please. It's not like they could even see me around your ginormous chest."

He cocks his head to one side and raises one eyebrow, but his eyes scan the street. That's Sam's problem. He's always too focused on work. I should go inside. If nothing else, it's warmer in there, but for some reason, I want to stay and see more. I've never seen him like this, and I scoot a little closer. Heat rolls off him in waves, like a furnace.

"The Marked attacking without provocation is weird," I say.

Sam grunts.

I wonder. "Who would be in charge of Defense for Port Gibson if my uncle were to leave? Temporarily, I mean."

Sam turns toward me. "Did it get approved?"

My jaw drops. "You know about my aunt and uncle's plans?"

"Your uncle tells me most everything. He had to in this case, because I'll be in charge while he's gone."

"I should go with them," I say. "If they insist on going, that's fine, but it's my dad's research, and I know more about that condo and the safe he installed than anyone else."

Sam sighs. "Your uncle got a gold medal in sharp shooting at two Olympic Games. He's the perfect person to run the ops on a trip down to WPN, and he has the best odds of getting through in a tactical op."

"I'm fine with letting him come. He can even run point, but they should bring me."

"Why?" Sam asks. "So you can feel useful?"

Blood rushes into my cheeks. "They may need me, my blood, or my DNA or my fingerprint, to get into the safe."

"Your aunt is the Unmarked's foremost medical researcher. If anyone can figure out how to crack a safe that's biologically linked, it's her. We receive training on breaking safes in Defense, too."

"Why?" I ask.

"When the CentiCouncil wants something hidden, who do you think pursues that?"

"Defense?"

He nods. "Besides. Even if your aunt couldn't go or went and couldn't extricate the information from the safe, your uncle can bring it back to Port Gibson. You can open it here, in safety."

"He'll bring it how exactly? Rip it out of the wall?" I wonder about Sam sometimes. I really do. "You're right. Tearing hidden safes out of concrete sounds simpler than letting me tag along."

He quirks one eyebrow at me.

"You think I should sit here and wait for them to come back with the cure?"

Sam glances back at the kids behind us. "You're young and untrained. You should stay inside the walls of Port Gibson where we can keep you safe."

"Who's we? You and Rhonda?"

"She's almost as good a shot as her dad."

I wonder whether anything's going on between Rhonda and Sam. They're in Defense together, and now that I think about it, Rhonda talks about him a lot. They're both prodigies in every form of fighting, and they're both so gorgeous it's like a slap in the face to look at them. Besides, Sam may be the only guy in Port Gibson tall enough to date her.

Why hadn't I considered this before? And now that it's occurred to me, why does it bother me? I need to know.

It's better to be completely clear with Sam. He doesn't pick up on my subtle questions, or if he does, he ignores them. "How long have you been seeing Rhonda?"

He glances my way, face scrunched up. "What?"

"I'm pretty good at reading people, you know."

He laughs, full-throated and deep. Sam doesn't laugh too often.

"What's so funny?"

"You talk a lot."

"You never say anything."

He rolls his eyes upward.

"I can do this all day," I say. "I'm like a squirrel with a nut."

Still nothing but a lopsided smile.

I need to shake him up. "At least tell me if she's a good kisser."

Sam looks gob smacked. "I would never kiss Rhonda."

My heart stutters. Why am I relieved? Wesley's face flashes through my mind. I feel guilty for even talking to Sam when I should be inside instead. Which is stupid. Even if I did like Sam, which I don't, I'd have no reason to feel bad about it. Wesley's gone. He and I aren't anything.

"You wouldn't?" I ask.

"She's like my sister."

"Oh." Which makes me the annoying younger sister. We did all grow up together, so that makes sense.

The alarm bells sound.

"Wait until the kids are gone, and I'll walk you home," he says.

Great. Sam thinks of me like his sister, and now he wants to walk me home to make sure I'm okay. "Are you crazy? I'm not a dog. I don't need to be walked. They wouldn't sound the alarm unless everything was clear."

He stares at me for too long. "Fine."

I run home as fast as I can. I want to talk to my uncle and convince them to take me along, but when I get home, no one else is there. I brush my teeth and change into pajamas. Still alone, I lay down on my bed and close my eyes.

Memories of Wesley crowd my mind, jumbling my thoughts. He's Marked, and my dad created Tercera. Dad's partner released it, and I can find the cure, I just know it.

Ten years ago, I hid in a closet while my dad got shot. I didn't step out to defend him against the freckled man. I didn't call the police or the paramedics. I was too cowardly to act, and the world fell apart. My aunt compounded the problem by thinking our safety mattered more than the lives of hundreds of thousands.

No more catastrophically bad calls. My aunt and uncle want to go without me? Too bad. I'm leaving tomorrow headed for Galveston, with or without their permission.

CHAPTER 9

The rumbling of my belly wakes me up. When I finally pry my eyes open, I glance out my window and realize I slept in pretty badly. I want to stay here, tucked inside warm blankets. Except I need energy to confront my aunt and uncle and demand they take me along. My whole body shivers with cold, and my stomach growls while I check on the chickens. I pump some water for them, fill their grain bin and take the eggs back inside. I fry the eggs and stick some crusty two-day old bread in the toaster oven. I wolf down several pieces of toast and three eggs before my stomach stops threatening to revolt.

Now that I'm not starving, I wander around the house. Everyone else should've slept in too, but no one's here. I look on the kitchen counter and breakfast table for notes. No luck. I walk by the front door, and notice two pieces of paper jammed in the crack between the door and the doorframe.

I pull them both out. The first is wrinkled and worn. I smooth it out enough to read it.

Kids,

In light of last night's aggression, the CentiCouncil's moving up our timetable. From what we gathered, they worry the hormone suppressants are failing. They're not working at all for some and the side effects are worsening for others. We're leaving this morning, bound for Galveston and the cure. Stay here, be safe, and trust in us to fix this.

Love, Dad

They left before I could even try to convince them? I crumple the note without thinking and realize Rhonda must've done the same.

I open the next note.

Ruby,

Mom and Dad left early this morning. Rhonda and I thought you needed sleep. Besides, you don't have to work today because your Path is due. Mom said you're thinking of Pathing Science? I think that's great. Just make sure your selection's handed in by noon today. See you tonight.

Love, Job

Rhonda was probably as upset as me at being left behind. It looks like Job convinced her to wait it out. I'm not so willing to sit on my hands. If the Marked are attacking and things are desperate, now's not the time to hope for the best. They need me to have the best chance of reaching Dad's research.

A razor wire fence surrounds Port Gibson, and guards are stationed around the fields of crops too. They keep people from coming in, but they also make it hard to leave without permission. I could stay here and Path Science like my family wants.

Science among the Unmarked has two main tasks. Scientists create the hormonal suppressant for the kids who are Marked so they don't undergo puberty. It keeps the Mark from progressing, but it doesn't allow them to really live. They're adults trapped in the bodies of pre-teens. It was a Band-Aid meant to be ripped off, only we never cured the underlying problem. The only other task for science is treatment of the population of the Unmarked. Pharmacists manufacture small batches of medicine, and physicians administer it. I don't want to slap Band-Aids on the Unmarked, or the people of Port Gibson either.

I want to fix the real problem. I need to go after my aunt and uncle, but how can I catch them? My uncle would've taken one of the Defense trucks. I don't know exactly what time they left, but I'll never catch them without comparable transportation myself. Luckily I learned the basics about automobiles during my time in Defense: driving, maintenance and basic repairs. Now all I need to do is locate one to steal.

Uncle Dan should have the location of each Defense vehicle in Port Gibson written down somewhere. Defense protocol dictates they check and move them after every Marked attack since occasionally the Marked kids would find and hotwire one. Better to know it's missing right away than need one and be without. In fact, if I find a truck and escape, Sam and his people will likely assume it was stolen by the attackers.

Of course, for my plan to work, I need to find the truck before the locations change. I run to my uncle's desk in the shared office and rummage around. I don't find anything in his drawers or file folders. The coordinates must be in the safe under the desk that's bolted into the floor. I groan.

I try my uncle's birthday. It doesn't work. I try his anniversary. No go. I try my aunt's birthday. Still no luck. I try Job and Rhonda's birthday and the light still blinks red. I slam my hand against the top of the safe. My birthday, the year Job, Rhonda and me were all born in order, Dad's birthday, Dad's death date, the date of the acceleration of the government. None of them work. I should've woken up earlier. I should've paid more attention to my uncle.

I try the day we joined the Unmarked here in Port Gibson. When that works, I breathe a heavy sigh of relief. I pull out a stack of papers and shuffle through them until I find it. The list of cars. I scan it for an automatic truck. I learned to drive standard transmissions, but it's been months since I've done it, and I sucked at shifting. I mark a map with the location of the closest automatic truck, and rummage around my uncle's desk again until I find a map that shows all of Mississippi and Texas. I glance over the possible routes to Galveston from Port Gibson. There aren't many, especially since the smaller roads have almost certainly become so overgrown they'll take forever. I need to make up time to catch them, not lose it.

I dress for travel and start packing, tossing in anything that comes to mind. I head back downstairs to look for food. I empty out the last of the granola bars I made last week, wrap them in cheesecloth, and stuff them into my backpack. The rest of the pantry looks surprisingly bare, probably because Uncle Dan and Aunt Anne already raided it for food. I grab the end of the bread, a hunk of goat cheese, and a few packages of dried fruit.

I duck out back and grab my rabbit snares from the shed. I usually only use them in the spring and summer to keep the garden pest free, but they might come in handy if I can't reach Aunt Anne and Uncle Dan quickly. I snag a handful of small herb sacks too, in case I get stuck eating rabbits on the way. I pull up some potatoes and carrots from the green-house and zip up my mostly empty bag. I'm rummaging around in the fridge when I hear it.

A knock at the front door.

I jump and hit my head on the shelf above me. I run through a list of possible visitors before deciding not to answer. None of them would know what was going on, except maybe Mr. Fairchild, and no adult in town will ever allow me to leave, including him. Luckily, no one could see me from the door where I'm crouched. We have a big window in the kitchen over the sink and another in the breakfast room, but as long as I stay down low, they can't see me from them.

I turn back to the fridge and fish out a pack of batteries. Why keep batteries in the fridge? As far as I know, there's no sensible science behind it. I bend back around to check the drawers at the bottom. A small early season tomato we picked before the freeze, and a single, shriveled bell pepper that survived the previously mild winter in the greenhouse. Rabbit stew's looking more and more likely.

Another knock, harder this time. Who would be this persistent? Gemette wondering what I'm Pathing? Job or Rhonda would walk through the door, not knock.

"Ruby!"

A voice I know. It's Sam, of course it is. Uncle Dan probably asked him to look in on me since he sees me as a sister. Kids need checking on, after all. Ugh. Maybe if I stay the course, he'll think I'm sleeping and go away.

"You may as well answer, Ruby. I hear you moving around."

He's lying. He can't possibly hear me rummaging in the fridge from across the room, through a solid wooden door. Nice try, but no way. I check the last drawer. A handful of mushy strawberries and a squishy onion. I grab the berries and leave the onion, push the drawer closed, and shut the fridge.

"Ruby, you're digging around in your icebox. Answer the door."

I drop the berries. How could he possibly know that?

He knocks again, harder this time. "Ruby. Door. Now."

Or what? No way I'm listening to some lecture. I suspect most of the adults in town would try to stop me from leaving, but I *know* Sam will. He's trained to notice small details. If he comes in, he'll notice my backpack, probably try to preempt my trip, and dump me in some kind of daycare prison. 'For my own good.'

I think about it. He may have guessed right, but he can't have heard me, not really. I'm not afraid of him—he's not going to stop me. I duck behind the island in the kitchen, prepared to wait him out.

CRASH.

What was that? When I peek around the corner of the island, Sam's glowering at me from our entryway, the oak door hanging askew behind him.

I hop up without thinking. "You broke our door down? What's wrong with you? Why didn't you just go away like a normal person?"

"I'm abnormal?" Sam asks. "You're hiding behind the island, holding . . . what is that?"

"A honey pot, not that it's any of your business." I brandish it at him, which isn't the best idea. Honey spills over and drips down my arm.

"What would you do right now," he asks, "if I meant you harm? Pray I had a honey allergy?"

He steps toward me and he doesn't look happy.

"Do you mean me harm?" I put the honey pot down and put my hands on my hips, forgetting my right hand's sticky. Drat. "Oh, stop glaring at me. I'm not the one who just broke into someone's home, destroying his boss's property in the process." I look more closely at our front door. "You splintered the hinges right out of the wall!"

"Sorry," he says.

"You're sorry? What about offering to fix it? Apologizing profusely might help."

"I said sorry."

"You should be." I narrow my eyes at him. "You will be, actually. I fully intend to tattle on you."

Sam rolls his eyes. "It'll take like two minutes to fix. I'll replace the hinges."

I look at the door again. Chunks were torn from the wall. Think again, Sam. This is a major repair, you big ox.

"You never answered me." I huff for emphasis, and lift my chin in the air defiantly. "Why are you even here? What do you want?"

"Your uncle sent me."

"When?" I ask. "My uncle's gone, so he couldn't have sent anyone."

"He asked me to look in on you today. Before he left last night."

"Wait." I put my hands on my hips. "You saw him after the attack? You knew he was leaving?"

"Yes."

"Enough with the vague responses. What's going on?"

"Last night, after they released us and you ran away, your uncle came by. He made me promise to take care of you while they're gone."

I stomp my foot. "I'm an adult."

"Not for a few more days you aren't. And you aren't going anywhere."

"Why would you think I'm going somewhere?" I kick my backpack around the edge of the island, covering the sound with a snort.

"Why, indeed." He strides past me into the kitchen and leans over, muscles in his back rippling visibly under his t-shirt. He picks up my backpack and dangles it from his index finger. "You usually pack a bag with," he pokes around in the bag with his big ham hands, "garden snares, potatoes, and dried herbs for no reason? Maybe you meant to carry them up to your room. Are you planting a window garden or dealing with a rodent problem up there?"

"I was going on a hike." I huff. "I thought I'd set some snares while I was out to supplement my meals here for a while. I happen to love rabbit stew. The granola bars are in case I get hungry while I'm outside laying snares." I reach toward him to take the backpack, noting he isn't wearing gloves. He has enormous hands, which makes sense. Every part of Sam's oversized. He doesn't resist when I yank it back. I pull it open and shake the contents around as though he hadn't just rifled through them. "Six granola bars, some water bottles, carrots and potatoes to lure the rabbits, and a snare. Hardly provisions for a long trip."

"Rabbits eat a lot of potatoes these days?" He cocks his head sideways and narrows his eyes at me. Intelligent eyes, eyes I can't quite pin down as green or gold.

"They do. They'll eat most anything."

Sam rolls his eyes. "Or maybe your aunt and uncle cleared out your pantry when they left and that's all you could find."

I sit down and throw my hands up in the air. "Fine, you caught me. I was about to make the most pathetic attempt ever to follow them. How could you possibly have known that? I didn't decide myself until this morning."

"I've known you for more than ten years."

"Wait, you talked to my uncle. Did he say which direction they're heading?"

He raises one eyebrow. "Why would I tell you?"

"You're saying you knew me so well that you knew I'd try to follow them?"

He shrugs. "I came to remind you that your Path choice is due today."

"Excuse me?" I stand up and put my hands on my hips. "I don't need reminders. I'm not ten years old."

"You only have an hour and a half left."

I scowl. "I'm not a child."

"You are for three more days," Sam says.

I scowl at him mightily, but he doesn't budge. I walk across the room and snatch my Path form off the entry table. I scrawl "Science" in the box and hand it to him. "Here. If you care so much, you can go drop it off."

Sam glances down at the form and both his eyebrows rise.

"What? You expected me to stay in Sanitation?"

He shrugs. "None of my business." He folds up the paper and tucks it into his pocket.

"No," I say, "it isn't."

He walks out the door and down the road. He glances back once, and I hurriedly duck, but not before he sees me looking and smiles. Once I'm sure he's out of sight, I can leave. Rhonda or Job could come check on me next, and they won't be as easy to redirect.

I pull a knit cap down over my head and wrap a scarf around my neck and over the bottom half of my face. I don't think anyone else will be looking for me, but covering up my most recognizable feature, my curly blonde mop, seems like a good plan just in case.

I sneak out of the house, watching for Sam. He's smarter than I thought, and if he only pretended to leave . . . but when I don't see any sign of him, I take off at a jog. My uncle always had the emergency trucks moved from the closest in to town outward as a simple matter of expediency. The least likely truck to have been moved would be the one farthest away, which happens to be an automatic. I'd normally walk right through town to get to the northwest side, but today all the seventeen-year-olds have the day off and most of them are hanging out or celebrating. I'm surprised Gemette hasn't come over, actually. It'll be hard to explain my large back-pack if I run into one of them, so I need to avoid that.

An enormous wall surrounds Port Gibson, from McComb Avenue on the south side up to Bayou Pierre on the north. The Bayou isn't walled off as consistently, because it's used to water the crops, but guards are posted along every section with a gap, and the water itself forms a natural barrier. The wall runs along the outside of Bridewell Lane down from Bayou Pierre; on the west it runs down behind the middle school.

The wall itself consists of a ten foot wooden fence, topped with razor wire. Behind that, on the Port Gibson side, there's a second fence of chain link. I think that went up first, but then Mayor Fairchild didn't want the Marked kids to be able to see what was going on, or where crops and buildings were located. We worked on the fencing by sections for years, and now we maintain it the same way.

The easiest way to get down to Galveston would be to take a truck south out of Port Gibson and hop on Highway Sixty-one, but since I'm not approved to go and I'm basically stealing a truck, I need to avoid the Unmarked *and* the Marked. I also need the truck to still be where Uncle Dan last logged its location, which means I'm hiking way past the fence.

That leaves me heading northwest, which incidentally means I didn't lie to Sam. I *am* going for a hike. At least it's all on the Unmarked side of things. Most Marked kids don't seem hostile, the attack last night notwithstanding. They usually keep West of the Mississippi, at least down until Baton Rouge when they sprawl all over. They'd already staked the claim on Baton Rouge when the Unmarked asked for the east of the Mississippi.

The roads around Port Gibson stay clear to allow travel to the other Unmarked cities. I think Oil Mill to Grand Gulf, followed by Sixty-one to Natchez Trace will work. Then I can circle around Port Gibson so I'm not stopped. It'll eat up a lot of gasoline, and I'm not sure how much each truck has. I bite my lip, because there's nothing I can do about that.

I hike along the edge of town until I reach the first gap, where Bayou Pierre meets the wall. I pull my boots off and roll my pants up, then I wait in the bushes until shift change. As soon as Mark leaves, I sneak around the edge of the wall, sinking into the Bayou up to my knees. So much for rolling my pants up.

Gah, the water's freezing. I only pass undetected because they train us to watch for ingress, not departure. Once I'm through, I run to the closest thicket, wincing when I step on sharp twigs and rocks. I hide long enough to wipe my feet as clean as possible, and put my socks and boots back on. I can't help my pants being soaked, or the fact that they're now dripping annoyingly into my boots. I move up Oil Mill Road until I pass the abandoned Addison Elementary school. Weeds fill the grounds, and vines climb the walls. A deer bounds across the playground, startled by my presence.

I spot the section of forest past the school where the truck's supposed to be hidden, and I'm moving toward it when I hear a crackle somewhere behind me. Probably the snapping of a twig, but from what? I jump and spin around.

"Who's there?" I ask.

Sam steps out behind me and grins. "You look just like that deer. The question is, can you run as fast?"

"How long have you been following me?" I'm beginning to wonder whether he snapped that twig on purpose, so I'd know he was here.

He shakes his head. "If I were following you, I'd have wet pants too." He looks pointedly at my dripping jeans. "I came over the wall, not through the Bayou. I'm here on official business."

He's moving the truck I'm headed for. Dangit.

"My aunt and uncle left alone, but they're gonna need me," I say. "I need to go to Galveston."

Sam shakes his head. "Not in one of my trucks, and certainly not alone. It's not safe right now, Ruby. The Marked are acting almost as crazy as you."

I clench my fists and refrain from biting down on my lip so I won't scream at him. This is already a long shot, and yelling won't help my case. "You don't need to watch me. This isn't your problem. Just let me go. You can report that the truck was already gone. You said yourself you've known me for ten years. Do me one favor. Please."

Sam shakes his head. "I'm done talking about this. We're going back. If I have to tie you up to keep you there, I will."

I square my shoulders and plant my boots shoulder width apart. "I know what I need to do and I'm going to do it."

Sam laughs, steps closer to me, and lowers his voice. "Look Ruby, I get that you want to help, but you need to let the adults handle it. People are getting Marked out there. Stay here."

I want to scream. "I *am* an adult, Sam. I won't just sit here in Port Gibson while my aunt and uncle go alone. They need me."

Sam rolls his eyes. "Before your uncle left he made me swear an oath to keep you safe."

"Then come with me," I say.

Muscles work in Sam's jaw. He seems to be weighing something and I wonder what. "What is it? Tell me."

"Your uncle left abruptly for a reason."

My stomach drops. "Don't you mean my aunt and uncle left abruptly?"

"Your aunt was Marked last night. She's in quarantine."

No. "Why didn't they tell us?"

Sam shakes his head, but I already know. Because without

my aunt, my uncle needs me to get into the safe. He knew I'd insist on going.

"Where did my uncle go, Sam?"

Sam sighs. "Your aunt needs the cure, but she made him promise not to tell you. She wants to keep you safe. Your uncle went to ask my dad for help. He thinks WPN will listen to my dad in a way they won't if we just show up at the bridge."

"Uncle Dan's asking your dad to petition WPN as leader of the Unmarked?"

Sam nods.

We're finally about to leave to look for the cure, and my aunt gets Marked. We should have better communication channels set up with the Marked. Dropping messages with the hormonal suppressants is completely insufficient. Everyone's too afraid to risk anything. What if they're trying to get our attention, or tell us something that we need to know?

I ask, "Why did the Marked attack?"

"Your uncle didn't give me details, and he made me promise not to tell you any of this. They'll try diplomatic channels, and if that fails, they'll send a tactical team."

I want to cry. "But there's no way they can get into my dad's safe, not without my blood or my aunt's. I have to go, don't you see?"

Sam crosses his arms and sighs. "Diplomatic requests won't get us anywhere. I requested to be on that team, Ruby. I'll get the cure, if there is one. I promise."

A tear escapes to roll down my cheek, and I wipe it away. "Why can't we go now? Before WPN knows anyone's coming? We could get in and get out. When the diplomacy fails, if we go in with a strike team, it could spark a war."

"Our strike team would be disavowed. My dad might suck, but he's a decent leader."

"He wouldn't ever send his only son on a secret mission. Be reasonable, Sam."

He shakes his head. "You really don't know my dad. Come with me to get the truck moved. We can keep talking, but I have orders to follow, Ruby. I don't run the world."

It's the best offer I'll get. Sam sets out across the clearing and I follow.

"So you're in charge, but they still have you moving trucks?"

"Port Gibson doesn't have that many defense personnel. As you know, all citizens are required to help, but with your uncle gone and Roger injured, there aren't many people with clearance to know vehicle locations. Emergency transportation's important. Plus, I have an aptitude for hiding things." Sam shoves a tree branch aside and I belatedly notice the truck. I might never have found it without him.

He tosses me the keys and starts shifting branches to clear the way for us to move it.

"We could take this truck and head out right now," I say. "If you're brave enough to risk doing the right thing, instead of following orders."

Sam sighs. "Sit inside with the doors locked until I finish clearing the way. Also, don't beg. It's sad."

"I'm not begging! I'm cajoling, sure, and maybe insulting a little, but not begging."

Sam slams me to the ground in the same instant I hear a gunshot. Does he have some sixth sense I don't possess?

He curses by my ear.

"Get in the truck," he growls.

Another gunshot, closer this time.

"Scratch that," he whispers. "Follow me."

Sam crawls along the ground quickly, reaching the truck and sliding under it to the passenger side.

"Stay on the ground behind the wheel." He leaps up lightning quick and pulls a big black bag out of the truck bed.

"What's that?" I ask.

"More ammo. I have a feeling we're going to need it."

"How many are there?" I ask. "And who is it? Do you know?"

"I don't know." He swears again. "It's probably Marked kids. They've all lost their minds."

"You can't kill kids."

"They're on the suppressant, Ruby. They're probably older than either of us."

"They're still people."

"People who want our truck and are shooting at us."

Sam pops up, gun in hand, and squeezes off half a dozen shots. He drops back down and spits in the dirt.

"How many?" I ask again.

"Way too many."

"Five?" I ask. "Ten?"

"More. Forty, maybe fifty."

"Did you see anyone you know?"

"Are you asking me if your aunt is out there?"

I shake my head. I know she's got to be back home in quarantine.

"You're asking about your boyfriend."

I want to know if he's shooting at Wesley. I nod. "Is he out there? We can't shoot forty people. Maybe we should surrender." If Wesley's out there, he'll keep us safe. I know it.

Sam shakes his head. "I didn't see him."

I sigh with relief.

"You're wrong, though," Sam says. "I can shoot them all."

"You can shoot forty people without being hit?"

Sam doesn't answer.

"If you might be hit, that's unacceptable to me." I put my hand on his arm. "There's got to be an option B. One that keeps us safe, and doesn't kill forty of them. What about a tranq gun?"

Sam grits his teeth. "I'm a great shot and I have perfect vision, but they're out of range for a tranq."

"We could run."

Sam shakes his head. "We have a car that runs, and we have supplies, but they have guns themselves, and without some kind of distraction, we'll never get in the car alive unless you let me start thinning the herd. Once I've killed ten or twenty, the others will run."

Another gunshot cracks behind us, and dirt sprays to my left. It startles me, and that gives me an idea. "Do you have any gunpowder?"

Sam pops up again and shoots off a few more rounds over the hood. He slides the bag over to me. "Maybe. Why?"

I sit up to rummage in the bag, but Sam yanks me down to the ground again. "Don't give them a target."

"Sorry." I look in the bag again, but this time I stay flat on my stomach. It's harder, but I find it. A little keg of gunpowder for reloading. Perfect.

"We need to get into the car and drive away, right?"

"Right." Sam fires off three more shots. I cringe. By my count, he's pulled the trigger twelve times now. If I know Sam, that means a dozen hits.

"You aren't killing people, right?"

He sighs. "I'm accurate, Ruby. To my knowledge, I haven't killed any of our very precious attackers. Yet."

"Speaking of, you won the sharpshooter award, like, six times, right?"

"What's your point?" he asks.

"My aim sucks, but my uncle did something on our trip down to Mississippi. Remember when he scared off that bear?"

His eyes widen. "He filled a metal box with gunpowder

and had my dad throw the box as far and as high as he could. Your dad shot it. The metal sparked from the shot and ignited the gunpowder. The explosion scared the bear and it ran off." Sam eyed the metal keg of powder. "It might work, but there's no way you can throw it far enough."

He's right.

"You can't," Sam mutters, "but maybe I can."

I shake my head. "Won't work. No way I could hit it. I barely know how to shoot at all."

"I'll throw it into a tree. If it lodges in the branches, I can shoot it. I need some armor piercing rounds though, or it'll glance off." He looks at me for a long moment. "How many kegs are there?"

"Two." I pull out the other one.

"I can miss once," Sam says.

He holds out his hand and lobs the small keg into the air. It flies far and high and branches crash above the heads of the group of kids. Then I hear it thunk onto the ground. This time, it's me that curses.

He doesn't speak. He just holds out his hand. My hand shakes when I place the last one in it, but his holds steady. He breathes in and out a few times and then throws it. It sails up far, too far, and high, too high. Leaves rustle as it passes, but then I can't see anything else.

"Crap, Sam, I can't even see it. No way to hit what you can't see. I'm sorry. It was a dumb idea."

Sam ducks down and grabs a rifle. He places some rounds in a clip and snaps it into place. "I see it."

"No way. You threw it way too far."

Sam stands up and fires off two rounds. An explosion, followed by lots of shouting. Sam grabs my arm and hauls me into the truck. He slides over to the driver seat while I pull the door shut. The Marked kids are running the wrong way. They're heading for Port Gibson, forming a loose group in the road blocking our path back home.

Sam turns the key in the ignition and the truck roars to life. "Get down. We're leaving." He floors it and the truck lurches forward, slamming through underbrush and onto the main road. Gun shots fire behind us, but none hit the truck.

We drive for a long time in silence, only stopping to clear the road when tree limbs or other debris block our path. He takes Grand Gulf Road like I planned to, but instead of taking Sixty-one South to Port Gibson, he takes Eighteen East toward Natchez Trace Parkway.

"What're you doing?" I ask.

"The Marked are blocking Sixty-one, but we need to get south, right?" He glances my way, and raises one eyebrow. "I know some back roads that'll take us down from Hermanville."

"Why would we drive to Hermanville?"

He shrugs. "It's on the way to Galveston."

I gasp. "You changed your mind?"

"Your uncle made me promise to keep you safe. With the Marked kids acting insane, it's not safe for you in Port Gibson."

But is Port Gibson safe without Sam?

CHAPTER 10

We drive in silence so Sam can pay attention to the road. Potholes, rusted out cars that ran out of gas and coasted to the edge of the road, and debris clutter it up this far from town. Animals unfamiliar with the perils of cars periodically shoot across the road too. Sam guides the old, four-wheel-drive truck around branches, over crumbling sections, and through water over the road.

Just before we reach the abandoned town of Fayette, about twenty miles away from Port Gibson, we encounter a trunk that's too large to drive around. Sam shuts the truck off and climbs out. His eyes dart back and forth, scanning the woods around us, as though he's expecting an ambush. Maybe he is. Sam squats near the largest part of the fallen tree and reaches around the trunk.

"Wait," I say. "I can help."

Sam doesn't roll his eyes or scoff, which I appreciate. I jog around to the other end of the trunk. I throw my arms around it, but I can't seem to grip anything very well. The trunk's so large that my hands keep slipping. I'm still scrabbling at it when it lifts off the ground. Sam grunts and the enormous trunk slides back four feet. An exhalation of breath and it moves another three. I finally abandon any pretense of helping to watch as his muscles bulge, and the enormous blockade disappears from the road.

Once the tree has been relocated, Sam circles around to the truck. Instead of getting in, he starts rummaging around in the bed.

I walk up behind him. "What are you doing?"

He doesn't pause in his search. "Checking our supplies."

"What do we have?"

"The basics stored in every emergency truck. Fuel, tools, weapons, ammo. A mix of tranqs and bullets. Blankets and a tent, a hatchet. Water purification tablets and a little food."

"Good thing you have food, because all I've got is what you saw earlier. Granola bars, carrots, potatoes, and a handful of sad strawberries."

Sam climbs back into the truck. I follow his lead and circle around to hop in and slide up onto the bench seat.

He says, "You won't be impressed with Defense rations."

I remember. My stomach rumbles. "I think I'll have a granola bar now. You want one too?"

He holds out his black-gloved hand in response. I set a crumbly granola bar in it, careful not to brush my glove against his. "So you didn't see anyone you knew back there with the Marked kids?"

"Still worried about your boyfriend."

"He isn't my boyfriend," I say, "but no. You already said Wesley wasn't with them, but I know you shot quite a few. I'm wondering if you knew any of them. Today or last night."

"I didn't shoot anyone I've met either time."

"How can you be sure?" I ask. "They were pretty far away."

"I have excellent eyesight, and even better aim."

"You don't know everyone I've met."

He eyes me sideways. "Don't I?"

I roll my eyes, but Sam isn't looking, so it's pointless. I glance at the road. It's clear, but we aren't moving yet. Maybe Sam needs some help navigating. I rustle around in my bag until I locate my map. I glance down at the road. "You just missed the turn off for thirty-three, but if we go back a half mile and take it south, I think we may get to Galveston faster."

Since I'm puzzling out the roads on the map, I don't see him until he's right in front of me. He's leaning across the seat, his face hovering inches from mine, breathing my air. I smell him again, stronger than last night. Leather, metal, and something else. I breathe it in greedily. I should shove him away. I have no idea why he's invaded my space, but I like it.

The butterflies in my stomach swoop and swirl. I wonder whether he's going to kiss me. I close my eyes.

Then I hear a click. He buckled my seatbelt. The seat shifts when he slides back over to his side. I force my eyes open, when what I really want to do is sink into the seat and disappear.

"Safety first." He doesn't even glance my way. "If we take thirty-three down, we'll hit Baton Rouge before we hit I-10."

How humiliating. I closed my eyes. Is there any possible reason I would've done that while someone buckled me in? Maybe I had something in my eyes? I rub at them both.

Why would I want him to kiss me, anyway? What's wrong with me? The last time I kissed someone—scratch that—the only time I've kissed anyone, I almost got Marked.

Plus I love Wesley, and when I get this cure, or figure one out from my dad's research if we can't find an actual cure, Wes can come back to join the Unmarked. So why would I want Sam to kiss me? Sam, who's like a brother, like a big, quiet, maybe-not-as-dumb-as-I-thought brother.

Maybe it's because I'm mad at Wesley. I should be pissed,

really. He was far too cavalier with my life. But I feel excited, giddy almost, every time I'm around Wesley and I've never felt anything like that around Sam.

Not until today, at least.

I shove my dumb thoughts away, tossing them right out the window. Why should I care if Sam thinks I'm an idiot who closes her eyes for no reason? I refuse to fret.

Sam pulls back onto sixty-one headed south, but doesn't speak at all. I wish he'd say something, if only to pass the time. It's not a very smooth ride, and we slow down frequently to drive around stuff, and stop periodically to clear the road. I help with little branches, but Sam moves all the big stuff.

After our third stop to clear the road Sam says, "You might want to try and sleep. I'll drive as long as the light's good, but when we stop for the night, if you've taken a nap, you can take first watch."

"We won't drive after dark?"

He shakes his head. "The roads are too bad to risk the tires."

I look down at the big bench seat. I'm huddled on the far-right side. Even though Sam's massive, there's a lot of space between us. His coat's draped over the worn, cloth seat next to him.

He sees me eyeing it. "Spread out. Use my coat as a pillow if that helps, but keep your seat belt on."

Maybe his suggestion triggers it, but a wave of exhaustion rolls over me. I pull on my seatbelt to loosen it and lean over, balling his coat up under my head. I shift my feet and I'm almost asleep when a big bump jolts me awake. "I'm not sure this will work."

"You've slept five or six hours in two days," he says. "I know, because I've slept even less. Try harder."

I punch his stiff leather coat with my fist. It's not a great pillow. It feels more like a rock.

I slide out of my jacket and into Sam's, and wad my jacket up under my head. "If I do fall asleep, promise you'll wake me up when you get tired."

He quirks an eyebrow. "Do you even know how to drive?"

I snort. "I took Defense, remember?"

"I do remember, that's why I'm asking."

He taught a class on self defense and I didn't do very well. I slug his shoulder. "Rude. I might have bombed hand-to-hand combat, but I aced the section on automobile use, maintenance and repair. It was one of the only things I did passably. Maybe because cars are like the human body, if the human body always followed the rules."

Sam quirks one eyebrow. "The one area of Defense you liked was the one area that reminded you of Science?"

"I guess so." I close my eyes and this time, I actually fall asleep.

CHAPTER 11

A sequence of large bumps jars me awake. I sit up and rub my eyes.

"Sorry," Sam says.

The sun sits low on the horizon. I slept longer than I expected.

"Where are we?" I ask.

"We made good time."

"What road are we on now?" I squint at the road sign. "Does that say 165?"

"I had to get creative in Alexandria. The exit ramp was in bad shape."

I sit up. "Creative? What does that mean?"

Sam grunts.

Whatever it was, it didn't wake me up, so I don't press him about it. We're headed for Galveston like I wanted, even if Sam's taking an odd route. We drive in silence until the sun sets. Vines, trees, and weeds have overgrown the abandoned houses and buildings we pass, checked only by abundant animal life. Sam slams on the brakes and swerves several times for deer, and once for a raccoon.

He pulls off onto a small road just past a big sign for something called a Cracker Barrel. Did people really eat crackers from a barrel? Or maybe they sell barrels? The truck lurches over weeds, branches and twigs. The highways traversing from one settlement to the next aren't entirely overgrown thanks to Unmarked efforts, but the smaller roads that haven't been maintained are almost impassible.

We drive a few dozen yards down the road before he jerks the wheel hard and we fly into the underbrush. He obviously isn't worried about keeping the truck's paint job pristine. Sam slams on the brakes and the truck halts abruptly. He hops out, grabs some branches and disappears down the path we drove to get here. He reappears a few minutes later, using the branches to smooth over the tire treads and his own tracks in the dirt, leaving the road behind him far less noticeable. My door is so tightly wedged against the underbrush, I'm not sure it will open at all. I squeeze out of the door he left askew instead, dragging my bags out behind me.

"What can I do to help?" I ask.

"Start hunting for branches and bring them to me. I'm going to refill the truck and then hide the gas tanks before I cover it over."

"Why?"

"So no one steals them."

"People steal gas?"

"All the time. Cars are easy to find. Clean gas, not so much."

"I was in Energy for a while. I know a little about gas production, but I didn't realize people steal it."

Sam shrugs.

Before I start gathering fallen limbs, I quickly lay my snares. Dusk's a great time for rabbits.

After that, I jog back with the branches in an attempt to

make up for lost time. We work quietly. I forage, and Sam arranges branches. He has a real knack for it. I know the truck's there, but I almost don't see it until I run right into it with a new armful of sticks.

I return from my final trip to find Sam stretching his bare hands over a small fire, now that it's dark enough the smoke isn't visible. Someone close might see it, but they'd have to be awfully close. Traveling at night's a difficult prospect these days, so I'm guessing we're fine. Humans may not have fared well the past few years, but wildlife's prospering. Wolves howl in the distance and I shiver.

A little pot rests on the coals.

"You cook?" It sounds idiotic when I say it out loud. He lives alone. Of course he cooks.

I can barely make out his grin with his face cast in shadows from the moonlight. "You eat? Dang it. Then I've probably miscalculated how much we need."

"Funny."

"I didn't cook anyway. It's stew from a can," Sam says. "Only marginally better warm than cold. Still gelatinous, but the fatty chunks melt a little."

"Great."

"Are you mocking me with these short answers?"

"No." I suppress a smile.

"Brat."

I sit next to him on the log and reach my hands out toward the fire, hoping to thaw my stiff fingers. Gloves have nothing on mittens for warmth, but mittens aren't practical. I peel my gloves off so the heat can reach my skin.

I lean in close to the fire and look into the pot. Sam's right. It looks disgusting. I reach over and snag my bag. I pull out a few handfuls of herbs and roll them back and forth between my fingers, mashing the dried leaves. I crumble them into the stew. It smells a little better but still looks unappetizing.

I stand up and click on my flashlight.

"Where are you going?" Sam asks.

"I thought I'd check my snares."

"Pretty unlikely you caught something in an hour."

I shrug. "We're in the middle of nowhere and animals aren't used to humans. It wouldn't surprise me."

A little brown rabbit struggles in my second snare. "Sam!"

He reaches me in three seconds flat. He moves wicked fast. "What's wrong?"

I shine the light on the wriggly little guy, then swing it back so I can see Sam's face.

"Nice work." He shoots me a baffled look. "Why'd you call me?"

"I'd rather not kill it. Would you mind?"

He lifts one eyebrow. "Don't you kill them at home?"

"Never. If Rhonda isn't around to do it, I go for a walk and let them go in the woods. I mostly set snares to keep my garden safe."

"What were you going to do alone?"

"I figured if I got really hungry. . ."

I can practically hear his eyes roll. "I'll do it."

When he pulls a knife from his boot, I walk away as fast as I can without looking like I'm running. Unsurprisingly, Sam's pretty handy with his knife. I watch him skin the little critter and then roast it on a stick before passing it to me. I pick off the meat and drop it into our pot.

Finally, Sam pulls out two big metal mugs and pours half the stew into a mug for me. It tastes surprisingly good. The meat's a little gamey, but not terrible. Our little rabbit must've been doing pretty well on the grass and bushes around here.

"I get half?"

"Seems fair. I probably eat more, but you need the reserve."

I speak without thinking. "You do, too. I bet your body fat percentage is lower than mine."

Sam raises his eyebrows. I should not have gone there.

I can't help it. The firelight makes all the muscles flexing in his shoulders, back, and arms even more obvious. I remind myself that Wesley's attractive in a completely different, and less physical way. More impressive in presentation, and less. . . bulky. I definitely like Wesley, not Sam. I figure I should repeat it a few times in case the moonlight and fire are confusing me.

Wesley Fairchild makes my heart beat faster. Wesley Fairchild makes me laugh. Wesley Fairchild always says the right thing.

Wesley's gone, though, and Sam's right here.

Thank goodness Sam can't read my mind. How he would laugh.

I shovel my stew to distract me from errant thoughts. I usually eat slowly, but I haven't eaten much in the past few days and as Sam mentioned, my body needs fuel. Plus, eating fast helps me pretend I'm not eating the cute little bunny Sam killed and roasted. I'm halfway done when Sam hands me a hunk of bread and a chunk of cheese.

"Where'd you get these?" I ask.

"They were supposed to be my lunch today."

I shake my head and hand them back. "That reminds me." I set my mug down and reach into my bag for my hunk of bread and goat cheese. My hand brushes against something hard, and I remember the water bottles. I pull them out and pass one to Sam. My hand brushes his warm one when I hand it to him and he gasps softly.

He sets the bottle on the ground, reaches over and takes my hand in his, chafing my icicle fingers between his beefy paws until they regain sensation. He does the same with my other hand, neither of us talking. The warmth spreads beyond my hands, but guilt comes with it. I wonder whether Wesley's warm, and if he has enough to eat. Has he made new friends? Is he moving on with life, whatever that looks like? I doubt he's sitting around thinking about me.

Or maybe he is.

I turn back toward the fire and use my bread to wipe out the dregs of my stew, gobbling the chunks of bread like a stray dog until it's all gone. "How can I help clean up?"

"No need."

"Seriously, I want to." I stand up and brush at my pants.

"I have a system." Sam cleans up our meal quickly, and methodically.

I stand around, shifting from foot to foot, wringing my recently warmed hands. Finally, it occurs to me to bank the fire. I've done that for years in our fireplace in Port Gibson.

"Thanks for dinner," I say.

He doesn't respond.

"This is where you say, 'you're welcome.'"

"Right," he says. "You mentioned that earlier."

"What would your mother think?" The words fly out before I remember and wince. His mom's dead, like I thought mine was. Like she probably is by now.

He's quiet for a moment and I want to curl up into the ashes of the fire and hide.

"She'd probably be appalled," he says. "She was classy, like you."

I never knew his mom, but I think about Sam for a moment. I might give him a hard time, but he's a good guy. "I'm not sure classy fits me, but if she's like me, I think she'd be proud. You saved my life. You made us dinner, and now you're cleaning up. You may lack polish, but the essentials are there."

"Thanks."

He kicks dirt over my carefully banked fire.

"Hey what're you doing? Don't we need that? You know, so we don't freeze?"

"We can't risk someone taking the truck while we sleep. We'll sleep in the cab."

"I thought we were taking shifts? One sleeps, and the other keeps watch?"

"You're a good guard, huh?"

I scowl. "I have eyes, and I thought that's why I took a nap."

"You needed the sleep. You don't seem to listen to me unless there's a purpose. I haven't slept in more than twenty-four hours, and you actually didn't sleep much in the car. I set some warning wires, and no one knows we're out here." He taps a black box on his belt. "They run around the perimeter about a hundred yards out. If they're tripped, I know we have company. The truck's the safest spot, though probably not the most comfortable. It's camouflaged now, and we'll lock the doors."

"Oh."

"We should move our supplies inside to be safe. I wouldn't put it past any scavengers to pick our pockets while we sleep. It's what I'd do."

"Alright." I reach into the truck bed to pull out a bag. I tug on the handles, and then I tug a little harder. It doesn't even shift. I alter my hold and pull one more time. Nothing. I move my hands to grab the bag to the right of it, hoping Sam hasn't noticed my epic fail. I can't lift that one either, though. I try the third bag and fail again.

"Geez Sam. What's in these bags? Rocks?"

Sam leans over and snags one with each hand, lifting them from the bed and setting them on the floor of the truck cab carefully.

A stupid show off, that's what he is.

He grabs the third one and tosses it in, too. They cover almost the entire floor of the cab. I climb up into the truck and slide over on the seat. My knees are hiked up to my nose because of the bags. There isn't much room with all the supplies crammed inside. When Sam slides in, his feet barely fit under the steering wheel.

"How's this going to work?" I ask.

"Well, that depends on you."

"What does that mean?" I lift one eyebrow.

"Take off your coat," he says. "Apparently mine makes a terrible pillow, so we're using yours."

We're using? I shiver.

"Cold? Don't worry. We'll use mine as a blanket."

I pull off my coat and rub my hands up and down my sweater-covered arms. The sweater doesn't block the wind very well, but it's not so bad when Sam closes the door. He turns and pulls me against him, my back to his chest.

"Think you can sleep like this?" His breath rasps against my ear and I shiver. He pulls me tighter.

Ummm, heck yes, I can sleep like this.

He takes my silence as consent and shifts, stretching his legs out and pulling my down coat under his head, a big puffy ball. His chest becomes my pillow, and it isn't nearly as soft as my jacket.

Of course, I'm not complaining.

He pulls his heavy, brown leather coat over us both. His breath shifts my hair slightly, warm and constant. His arms tighten around my waist and he stretches again, settling in.

Keep quiet, I think. Even if you can't sleep, don't keep Sam awake. I lie back and try to relax. I'm warm and safe. But, also guilty. This should be Wesley. If I'd left with Wesley like he wanted, we'd have three years, tops. It wasn't my fault he got Marked and had to leave. But if I get the cure, Wesley might come home. Thoughts roll around in my head like tumbleweed in a barren field.

Sam shifts.

"Am I hurting your arm?"

His only response is a low laugh I both hear and feel against my back.

"Seriously, am I cutting off your circulation?" I try to turn around.

He tightens his grip. "You can't hurt me, sunshine. Shhhh."

Sunshine? I try to sleep. I really do, but I have trouble sleeping in normal circumstances and this isn't even odd. It's almost otherworldly. This time I shift. Then I shift again. I move my head.

Sam sighs. "What's wrong?"

"I'm sorry. I have trouble sleeping. Maybe I should've mentioned that."

He snorts.

"I could take a sleeping pill."

"No, bad idea."

"Okay, well. Maybe you could tell me a story."

"Are you serious?" Sam asks.

"No."

"You are. Okay, about what?" His breath blows pleasantly on the back of my neck when he speaks.

"I don't know." I think for a minute. "Something from Before. Do you remember much?"

He's so quiet, I wonder if I asked the wrong thing. When he speaks, the words are so quiet that I almost can't hear them. "I'll tell you about the last time I saw my mom."

I tense, guilty about asking for a story now.

"You mentioned her earlier."

"Never mind." I sit up and reach for my bag at our feet. "I

have sleeping pills right here." Sam pulls me back against his chest.

"You don't want to be groggy if something happens."

"Oh."

"It's the last thing I remember before Tercera hit. My uncle, my mom's little brother, was named Chaz. I don't know what his real name was but that's what we called him. Uncle Chaz. He wasn't always the best guy, I guess. Anyway, he was in prison."

I shift a little to see Sam's face while he talks.

"My mom visited him every month, sometimes twice. When my dad was away on business, she'd take me and my little brother Raphael with her, even though my dad got mad if he found out. We lived in California, near San Francisco. My dad left that morning on a business trip and we were all supposed to go on vacation to Disneyland the very next day. He said he'd be back in time for us to leave. Since we were going for ten days, my mom wanted to see Uncle Chaz before we left. We got all dressed up that morning and I drew Uncle Chaz a picture. It was our family in front of Disneyland, and Uncle Chaz was standing with us."

"Mom drove us to the prison. I remember it was on the beach and it was pretty, you know, for a prison. The men all wore grey jumpsuits. They led us to a little cubicle and Uncle Chaz came inside like always. My mom was so happy to see him. I couldn't really remember a time before he got locked up, but that morning, seeing how much my mom loved him, and how much she missed him, I asked him why he had to be in prison. He said he did something bad, and since I was only eight, I asked what. When he wouldn't explain, I pushed. Mom got mad and I went to pout in the corner. That's why I didn't touch him."

A chill runs through me. Why should that detail matter?

"That day he looked different. Raphael noticed it right

away. He asked Uncle Chaz what was wrong with him." Sam's arm tightens around me, pulling me back against him. His entire body tenses.

"What was it?"

"He had a mark. Little red bumps that almost looked like a backwards number six."

I choke.

"On his forehead."

I push up on one arm and turn to face him. "He was Marked?"

"Yes, before that meant anything. No one had even heard of it then. He unwittingly Marked my mom and Raphael, too."

"How were you spared?" I ask. "And what about your dad?"

"Like I said, I got mad at my mom for scolding me and went to the corner. When we left, she fussed at me even more for acting like a baby. I was so mad, I ran straight up to my room. That happened to be the very day some guy served my dad with divorce papers. She thought he wouldn't get them until after our trip, but Dad flew home early and got served at his office."

"That's a sad memory." Sam's dad, John Roth, is an imposing guy. Large, sure of himself, and decisive. I doubt he took the news well.

"Dad charged in the door, eyes flashing, fists clenched, jaw muscles popping. He accused Mom of fighting dirty, but she shook her head. He took one look at her face and realized she was serious, I guess. He told Raphael and me to grab our bags and come with him. We both loved Mom way more, but I was mad at her, and I didn't understand what any of it meant. When my dad promised me ice cream and said we could still go to Disneyland if we followed him, Raphael stayed with Mom."

Sam breathes in and out slowly. "I should've stayed, and with any other set of circumstances, I would've stayed. But that day, I went. After that Dad wouldn't give me up. Even knowing I'd have been Marked, I've regretted leaving with him ever since."

Sam would rather be dead than be with his dad? I don't know his dad that well, but that seems harsh.

I lean my cheek against his chest and breathe in deeply. "I'm sorry I asked, and sorry you went through that. It sucks your dad's a jerk too, but I'm glad you're not Marked."

"I'm not sorry you asked. I've never told anyone else." He pulls me tighter.

I don't think I'll ever go to sleep—not now. I keep thinking of Sam as a child—the boy I knew. He seemed so big and brave, even then. After a few minutes, Sam's breathing evens out and the rhythmic rise and fall of his breath lulls me to sleep too.

CHAPTER 12

We get lucky that night.

Not like that.

No one trips Sam's wires, and we pass the night undetected. We sleep until the light wakes us the next morning. Sam is the perfect gentleman.

I wake warm, comfortable and finally rested. I blink my eyes several times to clear the sleep from them before I remember where I am. Sam's arms still encircle me. My hand flies up to my mouth and I breathe a sigh of relief that it's dry. No drool, thank goodness.

The hand motion wakes Sam. His body tenses, and then a second later, he relaxes again.

"Morning, sunshine," he whispers against my ear.

His arms rub up and down mine. Somehow his coat slid off during the night. "Cold?"

"No, I'm okay. You?"

"I'm great." He stretches and with his arms around me, I see his forearms ripple as he moves. I shift up on one arm to take the weight of my head off his right bicep.

"Sorry about squishing you all night."

"Stop already," he says. "Don't bring it up again."

"All right."

I wonder whether I upset him and turn to see. He smiles brightly at me in the early morning light. I duck my head.

He reaches up and tousles my hair. "I like your hair better down like this than in a braid. It's fun."

"Fun isn't something I associate as a priority for you." I smile at him.

"I guess you don't know me as well as you thought."

"I really don't."

I sit up and he pulls back, swinging his legs out and over the supply bags. I yank my legs up next to my body. When he sits up, it strikes me again how much bigger he is than me. He gazes out the window peacefully.

The moment's so quiet that it startles me when he says, "I'm going to take down the perimeter wires. Can you start pulling down branches?"

"Uh, sure."

Sam's wires were so well laid, I can't see them when I look. I force myself to stop watching him so I can take down the branches covering the truck. I pile the biggest ones into the truck bed.

Sam raises one eyebrow at the pile when he returns.

"I thought if we put your bags down over them in the back of the truck, maybe we'd save ourselves some time tonight."

He shakes his head. "It's a good idea, but I don't have twine and I can't risk the bags flipping out the back. They're heavy, but it could still happen with wind gusts. Plus, I'm not sure what kind of trees we'll stop near, and the cover for the truck has to match or it won't be very effective."

"Duh." I'm an idiot. I hop up on the truck bed and start pulling the large branches out. He reaches over easily and grabs all but one remaining branch in a single, smooth movement.

I pick up the last one just before he swings the bags from the cab back into the truck bed. I pull three granola bars from my bag and hand him two.

"Breakfast. That I can handle."

"Thanks."

"Oh!"

"What?" Sam asks.

"My snares." I hop up and run out to check them.

Nothing else. I'm not too disappointed. I don't relish the idea of a dead critter in the truck with us, or even worse, a live one stuffed in a bag waiting to die.

I stuff the empty snares back into my bag and open the door to climb back into the truck cab. "We're off now, right?"

"Not yet. We left hot yesterday so I didn't have time to stop for this. We're still in a hurry, but it's important."

"More important than surprising WPN to sneak in and then back out with a cure for the disease that almost elimi-nated humanity?" I ask.

He reaches into the back of the truck and pulls a black box from one of the bags. He opens the box, pulls out a gun, slides a clip into it and holds it out to me. I've avoided guns pretty uniformly since I watched my dad bleed out from a gunshot wound. Even on guard duty, they always let me choose a tranq gun.

I take a step backward. "I'm good. I passed basic training."

"Not with me, you didn't. I need to know what you know." He holsters the gun, grabs a bag, and walks away from the truck and down a path toward a clearing.

I jog after him reluctantly. "Assume I'm useless and maybe I'll surprise you in a pinch."

He ignores me. "Because you're so tiny, we'll start with a twenty-two." Once I reach him, Sam places it in my hands and wraps my fingers around it. "Normally you'd get a firearm of your own after you Pathed and someone from Defense would teach you a refresher and give you marks. Those marks ensure your basic aptitude and let us assign you an emergency security post. Since you haven't had your evaluation, I need to see what you can do. I can't have you running around without a gun anymore. Not if we're going in tactically."

The black handgun's heavier than I remember from basic. I try to recall what to do with it, but it's been too long. I try to hand it back to Sam. "I hate guns, okay?"

He looks at me flatly, ignoring my attempt. "You need to know how to use it."

"Show me with a tranq gun. I remember those details way better."

He shakes his head. "We have one tranq, which I will carry and use whenever I can. We don't have two, so you won't even have one. Plus, its range sucks and it's harder to use, which is why I'll hold on to it. If it's safe to use a tranq, I will. Otherwise we use regular, old, bullet-filled guns. I'm not saying you have to fire this live. I hope you never do, but if it comes to it, it won't be my fault you aren't trained."

I try again to pass it back, spinning the gun around by the circular area near the trigger.

Sam holds up his hands. "Whoa tiger, let's go over a few rules first. Number One, always assume a gun is loaded. Number Two, never point this at someone when it's loaded unless you plan to shoot them. They should've taught you that in basic."

"It's been a while." Plus, I tuned out most of what they told me. I turn the firearm toward the ground. "Is this loaded?"

"Do I look stupid to you?" he asks.

"You really want me to answer that?"

Sam scowls. "You saw me put in a clip, but you didn't notice the clip was empty. In any case, if you don't know, you behave as though it is."

"I assume that means I need to load it first?"

When it becomes clear I don't know how, Sam shows me how to pull the clip out, put bullets in it, and put it back in. He makes me show him the safety and the trigger and pretty much all the other gun essentials. I remember some of them, but I stop him before he starts in on cleaning techniques. "Is this really critical?"

"Not interested in cleaning, huh? Typical girl. Only the showy parts."

"Umm, I think you mean typical guy. I'm focusing on what matters."

"I think you're ready to fire." He reaches over and plucks the gun from my hands, keeping it pointed away from both of us. I follow him to the edge of the clearing. He circles behind me and reaches his arms around to place the gun back in my hands. Somehow, in those few seconds, he screwed something onto the end of it.

"What's that?"

"It's called a silencer or sometimes a suppressor. Typically, you wouldn't use one. It'll mess with your aim, but I don't want the report from the gun to attract anyone's attention. We're still annoyingly near Marked territory and they're bizarrely aggressive right now."

"Okay."

He presses my hands back over the gun and moves his hands down to my hips. It's hard to focus with him wrapped around me, but I'm grateful for the distraction. I do not want to be touching this thing.

He shifts my hips gently. "Stand like this. Now, go ahead and shoot at that big tree whenever you're ready."

He steps back, and I almost drop the gun. I need to learn,

though. I'm tired of being a drain. I think about the kids shooting at us. I should be able to help defend us if we're cornered again. And what if Sam's in danger and he needs me?

Ha. Yeah right. Focus, Ruby.

I close my eyes and open them again before any nightmares can spring to life behind my lids. I breathe in and out deeply and pull the trigger.

"I missed," I say, disappointed.

"No, you didn't. Look right there." He points, and I squint.

"I missed."

"No, you hit right below that branch that juts off to the right. See how it's dangling?"

I bite my lip. "I wasn't aiming at that tree."

He laughs. "All right. Let's keep practicing."

I improve slightly. Sometimes I even hit what I aim at. "At least it should be easier to hit a person than a tree."

"Harder, actually. People move, plus you feel guilty about it your first few times."

"You don't feel guilty?"

He shrugs. "Not anymore."

My eyes widen. "Well, that sucks."

"Part of the job. Keeping Port Gibson safe means guarding resources, and food's scarce. Energy, too."

"It's a good thing I don't want to path Defense, because even if I got over the guilt, I can't hit the broad side of a barn."

He chucks me under the chin, which makes me feel about five years old. "You did great. Better than most."

Most? My head fills with images of Sam shifting lots of women's hips and wrapping his amazing arms around them to do it. I'm surprised when my nostrils flare, my fists clench, and bitter words erupt from my mouth. "Train a lot of young women, huh?"

"Young women, young men. They make the newbies do them all. I trained pretty much everyone for a year before Rhonda came along. New trainees have a tendency to follow the person who certifies them around like a puppy. It's irritating."

I suppress a snort. "I think they might have imprinted on you for more than your adept skills at handling a gun. I'd think you might like the adoration, actually. Most guys would."

Sam's brow furrows. "Why would I like it? Rhonda's always trying to foist the training off on me. Says I'm better at it. Truth is, we all hate it, and she'd make up any excuse to get out of it."

He says it so nonchalantly, like it's nothing. I guess it's a routine part of his job. I've watched girls flock to him for years, and it never bothered me before. Why do I care now? I probably feel sorry for him, getting hounded like that. He obviously doesn't appreciate the attention.

"What part of the job do you like?"

He takes my gun and unscrews the suppressor. "I like most of it, and I don't mind the rest."

"You like shooting, right? Didn't you get first in marksmanship in the Unmarked Games last year, and the year before?"

Sam shrugs.

"I didn't realize you were so modest. You've taken it every year since you Pathed. That justifies a little pride."

I remember Sam winning medals year after year. He never even smiles when they award him. I want to know why he's so stoic about it all, so I keep after him. "Your dad must be proud. You medaled in like, seven things that first year, right?"

"Dad wasn't proud. He said it doesn't mean much to win against a few hundred thousand people. He medaled in the real Olympics. Before. The Olympics that mattered, competing against the entire world. Millions. Billions. I'm the biggest fish in a pet store tank, and he swam in the ocean."

"That's a pretty crappy thing to tell your kid."

Sam shrugs again, but it doesn't bug me. Not anymore. I used to think he thought he was better than everyone. Now I know he's as modest as they come.

"Is that why you transferred to Port Gibson? To get away from him? Nashville must be way more exciting. Since your dad's the leader of the Unmarked, you could pretty much go anywhere. You could've stayed there, in the largest Unmarked city, the capitol."

"I wanted to get as far from him as I could," he says. "And I know people in Port Gibson."

People, not just my family, or he'd have said he knows *us*. Which reminds me—Rhonda mentioned a week or two ago that he liked someone. Maybe he came to Port Gibson for a girl? Even though he denied liking her earlier, I wonder whether he came for her.

"You wonder if what was for who?" he asks.

I must've said that last part out loud. Ugh. "Nothing."

He looks at me funny. "What're you talking about?"

"Rhonda said. . .Nevermind. It's just, I heard you liked someone. I was wondering who."

He looks away when I mention Rhonda's name. I rack my brain trying to think of who I've seen with Sam, but I can't think of anyone. He's a serious loner. He comes to our house to hang out with Job sometimes, and he stays for dinner occasionally. Other than visiting our house and going to work, I never see him with anyone. Not that there's much to do or many people to be seen by or with in crummy little Port Gibson. Plus, with as often as I get out, he could have girls at his place every night and I'd never know.

Finally, he speaks. "Rhonda told you that?"

Now that he's talking, I realize I don't want to know. I don't want to hear about the girl he likes.

"No, she told me . . . never mind. I was teasing you, that's all. It's none of my business."

"You don't want to know?" He opens his mouth and closes it again.

"Definitely not. It's none of my business, and I'm sorry I asked."

"Right." He shakes his head. "Port Gibson's pretty small. Hard to keep anything a secret."

"What do you mean?"

"I've known all about your boyfriend for a while, for example."

"Then you don't know anything," I say. "I mean, Wesley's—"

"Your boyfriend."

"It's not that simple."

Why do I even care what he thinks? Maybe because Sam seems to be changing so much. Although, if I'm being honest with myself, Sam might not be the one who changed. I clearly made some snap judgments about him years ago and never took the time to check them out. I spent all my free time signing up for Special Projects, trying to get to know Wesley. How would I know what Sam's really like?

Maybe I'm the one changing.

"He's Marked now, so I guess that complicates things." Sam walks back toward the truck.

"Wait," I say. "What about your turn?"

"My turn for what?"

"I want to see you shoot." I put quite a few holes in the tree during my lesson. I wonder how much better he is.

"We need to go."

"We have sixty seconds to spare," I say. "You'll be fast, and I bet I can learn something from watching you."

"I don't use this caliber."

"I thought you were the best shooter the Unmarked has." I put one hand on my hip. "Is the great Samuel Roth nervous?"

Sam whips the gun out so fast that I step back reflexively. "I could fire off a few, I guess." He loads the magazine and clicks it in place.

"Wait," I say. "You need the silencer." I walk toward the box, but he waves me off.

"I'm not using it. It ruins your aim, remember?"

"Male pride."

He smirks. "We're leaving, so we can risk a little sound. I'm not sure I'd ever live it down if you told people my aim sucked."

I roll my eyes. "Who would I tell?"

He reaches into his bag and grabs two pair of ear covers. He hands me one. "Put these on. You'll need them without the suppressor."

He slides his on while I do the same, then he holds the gun out, takes aim, and fires off several shots in quick succession. Before I can ask what he's doing, he shoots several more times. They hit the trunk of the beech tree he told me to target earlier.

"Go check it out for me," he says. "See if any of them hit."

I raise one eyebrow, but walk across the clearing like he asked. When I'm close enough to see the tree, I gasp and run my fingers over the beech bark. It's still hot around the new holes. His twelve shots fill in the blanks around the seven of mine from before. They transform my messy, erratic holes into the outline of a perfect heart. Unbelievable. I knew he was good, but not that good. I couldn't even see the target clearly from so far away.

"Holy crap, Sam. How'd you do that?" He didn't just have

perfect aim, he put it into a shape. When I turn back, he's looking at me intently. I'd always thought of Sam as a cartoon cut out. A big, dumb, brawny kid who never spoke. I mistakenly assumed it was because he had nothing to say. Maybe I never let him get a word in.

I turn back toward the trunk and touch it one more time. When he clears his throat right behind me, I jump. I'm beginning to hate how quietly he moves. I punch him on the arm and walk all the way back to the truck before noticing that he hasn't followed. He's leaning toward the tree for some reason.

"You coming?"

"I'll be there in a second," he says. "I ought to clean up all these casings. That's why we have the reloading gear, right?"

I have no idea what casings are, but I'm beginning to care about things I paid no attention to last week. Guns usually trigger nightmares of the night Dad died. But when I climb back into the truck and close my eyes, I don't think about the freckle nosed man, or my dad in a pool of blood.

I think of greenish gold eyes, and arms around my waist. And I smile.

CHAPTER 13

"What made you smile, sunshine?" Springs creak as Sam plops down on the truck seat.

I open my eyes and shake my head. "Nothing."

"Okay then." Sam turns the engine over, and puts it in gear.

I glance around, my eyes caught by the Cracker Barrel sign again. Maybe it's a supply depot. Maybe it refers to cracking barrels open. "Where are we?"

"Close to Beaumont, Texas," Sam says. "The Marked attack set us on a strange trajectory, but we've made it to I-10, so we're back on track."

Trajectory? I can't believe I thought he was dumb. "I still can't figure that out. Two large attacks in twenty-four hours. Bizarre, right?"

"They were looking for something the night they attacked Port Gibson."

"Really?" I ask. "Any guesses as to what?"

Sam shrugs. "We don't know exactly." He glances at me and then looks back at the road. "Fairchild's going to kill me for bringing you down here unless we return with a cure. I really hope your dad made one, and we can find it."

"Me too," I say. "For my aunt and everyone else."

Sam glares at me. "Just say Wesley."

My eyes fly wide. "It's about more than just him."

"Fairchild's son is Marked, but if we don't find the cure. . . this is bad. I should've circled back around to Port Gibson."

Regret. That's a feeling I understand. "Don't worry, I'll tell everyone it was my fault. I take full responsibility, you know. Like you said, you were protecting me."

Sam snorts. "I feel so much better knowing the minor in my charge will defend me. Thanks, but no thanks."

I scowl. He's acting like I'm a baby. "I'll explain I was out on the road when the Marked attacked, and you had no choice but to keep me safe."

"After defending you, then what? You held a gun to my head while I drove you in Port Gibson's emergency truck all the way down to Galveston? Maybe I should claim I couldn't overpower you." He shakes his head dismissively. "I don't need your help. I can handle Fairchild."

"Will you be in a lot of trouble?"

"I'll be lucky if they don't throw me in jail."

Guilt eats at me. "They won't do that, right? My uncle told you to protect me."

"And I hauled you off across Marked territory and down to WPN country. Even if they don't toss me in jail, I won't keep my job. I'll be sent back to the DecaCouncil for a hearing."

"Your dad's in charge though, right? So that's good."

"No." He shakes his head. "It's not good, but it's also not your problem. I'm a big boy. I make my own decisions, and I can handle the consequences."

Talking about the repercussions back home doesn't put either of us in a great mood. Sam's quiet for the next few hours, rebuffing my every attempt at conversation. I press my nose to the glass, sulkily counting trees.

"Should we stop for lunch?" I ask.

"No. Defense rations are fine. There should be some jerky and crackers in the glove compartment. I don't want to stop before we reach the island."

"Ok."

I fish out the last two granola bars and hand them both to him. Even with Sam in a funk, I marvel at the ease of our simple contact. Our fingers brush as I pass them to him. He doesn't shy away and he hasn't bothered putting on gloves. Which is strange.

"Why aren't we wearing gloves?"

He looks at me, a smile tugging at the corners of his mouth. "We're blending in, don't you think?"

"What do you mean?"

"Well, your hair's down."

I even scrunched it this morning, using the rearview mirror from the truck to fix the curls with a little water. He reaches up, pulls on a ringlet, and then lets go. He watches it spring back up before returning his gaze to the road. "It covers your forehead. You could be Marked."

I hadn't even really noticed when we woke up that morning, but his hair's down, not pulled back in a ponytail like usual. I mean, I noticed but I hadn't thought about why. This Sam's so different that individual oddities don't stand out.

"We're blending in so if a Marked kid sees us, they'll assume we're one of them. That's why you stopped wearing gloves."

"What did you think?" When he glances my direction, he looks confused.

I feel ridiculous again. Of course he wasn't leaving his gloves off so he could touch me. I'm such an idiot.

The truck slows down, and I ask, "Why are we stopping?"

"Something's wrong," Sam says.

I look at the dash. "Yeah, we're out of gas."

"Right. Duh."

He pulls the truck over to the edge of the road and hops out, leaving the door hanging open. I notice it's much warmer here than in Port Gibson. We should've opened the windows and enjoyed the fresh air.

With the door open, I hear every curse word Sam utters.

"What's wrong?"

He swears more, and louder.

"Sam?"

"I forgot the gas cans, okay? I hid them last night and didn't remember to put them back in the truck." Sam kicks a rock and it flies into the thicket beyond the road.

I rack my brain for a solution. I remember something from our section on cars during Defense training. "Can we siphon some out of other automobile tanks?" I gesture at the cars on the side of the road, and parked in front of businesses around us. I feel pretty good about my idea. I paid attention during that part of Defense. We're in the middle of some-place with lots of houses. "Where are we? It looks like a city."

"We're past Houston proper and into the sprawl beyond. It was a really big city Before."

"Great, lots of houses, lots of cars. Let's find some gas."

"Ruby, I appreciate the idea, I really do, but most of these cars were abandoned after they ran out of gas. Even if we found one with gas in the tank, you can't siphon gas from any old car. Once it sits for a while, the gas is garbage. Among other issues, since it's muggy and humid here, water forms on the walls of the gas tank and drips down into the tank. That renders the gas useless inside of a year or two. Ten years later? Forget it. Why do you think there are so few functioning cars left on the roads? The abandoned ones are all trash without weeks worth of work. I drove off and abandoned all the gas for the trip to the island, not to mention our return trip. We're screwed." He kicks the tire.

"Well, where are we exactly? I mean like, how far is Galveston from here?"

"I think we're almost to League City. Everything we've passed looks abandoned, but it might not be. We're technically in WPN territory, which is why these roads have been so good." He points. "See there? Someone repaired that pothole. If WPN sends maintenance crews out here, I really don't want to be here longer than I need to." He clenches and unclenches his fists. "Not that we have a choice. We're going the rest of the way on foot."

I unzip my mostly empty backpack and start shifting defense rations into it.

"What are you doing?"

"Offloading," I say. "What does it look like? Unless you intend to lug three enormous duffel bags full of stuff around for the next few days?" I raise my eyebrows at him. His face may be thunderous, but he doesn't scare me.

"I don't have a monopoly on sarcasm, I see."

After a minute more of pouting, he leans down and starts helping. I'm happy to see him pull a backpack from behind the seat of the truck. It's much larger than mine, but it'll still be easier to carry than the cumbersome duffel bags.

It's hot enough that I peel my coat off and roll it up. The down jacket actually compresses nicely. I tie it to the straps at the top of my backpack.

Sam takes his jacket off, too. He hasn't packed much in his bag yet when he hands me the gun I used that morning, along with a very heavy box.

"You need these. Make room." After I take them, he holds out a gun holster. "Put this on so you can reach it quickly, and put the extra bullets in your bag. I know they're heavy and I'd carry them for you, but you'll probably only need them if we get split up. Without ammo, that gun's nothing more than dead weight."

"I'd rather have tranqs."

"We only have one tranq. Would you rather I use the real one? I thought you wanted non-lethal force whenever possible."

"I don't want to shoot anyone."

"I don't want you dying," he says. "Better you shoot someone than die yourself."

I shiver and he puts his hand over mine. "I don't think we'll get separated, but I plan for contingencies."

I don't say anything as I shove the bullets to the bottom of my bag. I try to put the holster on but can't figure out what goes where. It has a lot of straps and clips.

"Um, that goes under your shirt," he says, avoiding eye contact.

I clear my throat so he glances my way, and I raise one eyebrow. "You'd like that, wouldn't you?"

"I'm trying to avoid awkwardness, but I'm actually not kidding. See?" He lifts his shirt a few inches to show me some similar black straps. I'm supposed to be looking at the holster and the inch of steel from his gun, but the line of his abs as it disappears into the waistband of his cargo pants eclipses the rest. My breathing becomes shallow, and I want to giggle for some reason, which is stupid. It's only Sam. I've known him for years. Why does two inches of his skin suddenly bother me?

I snap my mouth shut when I realize it's dangling open.

"You really do need to put it on under your shirt or it defeats the whole purpose. Accessible, but hidden." He leans over and touches my lower back lightly. "The gun should rest here so it's not immediately obvious you have it."

"Sure, whatever." I wad up the holster and stuff it into my backpack with the ammunition.

He grabs my wrist. "I insist you put it on. I'll turn around while you do, of course."

"I don't think I can put it on without seeing how it fastens first."

He looks at me for a moment. Without warning, he reaches down and peels his shirt up and over his head.

Forget about his abs. He has the most beautiful chest and arms I've ever seen, not that I've seen many. Almost no hair, and lots and lots of beautiful skin. How does he have such a great tan in February?

"Ruby?" I tear my eyes off his chest and look up at his face. His eyes sparkle, and I'm terribly afraid it wasn't the first time he said my name.

I blush. "It's a lot of straps. I can't figure out how they all fit together."

Because that's what distracted me. The holster, not the skin, and the muscles, and the abs. The holster's confusing, not my feelings.

"It's not that hard. It goes like this." He tugs and the black straps crossing his back shift. He has two straps, one crossing from each side. They hold two guns apiece, for a total of four firearms strapped to his torso.

"Mine looks different." I'm great at stating the obvious today.

"I can put it on for you if you want. It's hard to buckle if you're not used to doing it—even the single holster."

Fine. He'll put it on for me, huh? I don't warn him, either. I yank my sweater and shirt off as abruptly he did.

His gasp is very satisfying. He's as unable to look at my face as I was. The whole thing's stupid, since we're not showing any more skin than if we were swimming. It's all about context, though.

We are definitely not swimming.

I shake the holster at him. "I thought you were going to help me with this."

He looks up at my face and nods. "Right, yeah." He grabs the holster and loops it around my shoulders. He spins me around and hooks it all up from behind. I have to give him credit. He doesn't touch me a single bit more than necessary and his fingers never linger.

If I'm being honest, it's a little disappointing. So is the fact that when I turn around, he's already put his shirt back on. Adding insult to injury, he's facing away from me, and already back to packing his bag.

I reluctantly pull my shirt back on and yank the light sweater down over my head for good measure. I'm not entirely sure I'll be able to get to my gun easily now, but at least no one will see it. It's not like I have any intention of using it anyway. I pull on my gloves since we aren't in Marked territory anymore. Plus, it may be warmer than it was at home, but standing shirtless cooled me down quick.

We finish packing in silence. Sam takes the lion's share of the food, all of the weapons and almost all of the ammo over my half-hearted protests. I'm glad when he pulls two largish blankets out of somewhere. The temperature's already dropping and the sun hasn't even dipped below the horizon yet.

"Where to now?"

He starts walking in the direction we were driving. "We actually made good time, even with the unplanned detour north. We're almost halfway between Houston and Galveston, about ten miles from League City. See?" He points at a sign that's almost been swallowed by vegetation. It reads: League City 8.

"So in Defense, eight and ten miles are the same? Seeing a little more why you didn't choose Science."

He laughs, which is weird because my joke wasn't that funny. Somehow that improves my mood.

"Fine." He snorts. "We're eight miles away. Better get going."

"Hey, I'm not a defense prodigy. Two miles is a lot to me."

His face softens. "We don't have to go the entire way today. We'll see how far we can get in the next hour or so before full dark. Keep your eyes open for a good spot to spend the night." He tosses me a flashlight, and I scurry to keep up.

"I think my size is about to become a real nuisance," I mutter. I'm pumping my legs as fast as I can, but I'm taking almost two steps to every one of his. It's not sustainable.

"Don't worry, sunshine. If it comes to it, I really can carry you."

"That's hilarious. You're gonna carry me, my bag, and your pack?"

He shrugs. "You weigh about the same as my backpack. I've carried more."

He's kidding. I'm pretty sure he is.

CHAPTER 14

We haven't gone far when my right heel begins complaining. Loudly. I tell it to shut up, of course, but it doesn't listen. I will ignore it, because I don't want Sam to notice and get frustrated with my ineptitude. I'm proud of how I keep walking exactly the same, in spite of the pain.

"What's wrong?" Sam glances at my foot.

His observation skills annoy me. "Nothing."

"Then why are you limping."

"I'm not." I bite my lip and keep walking, without a limp.

He stops.

I continue on for a few yards more, then stop and roll my eyes. I huff. He still doesn't catch up or say a word, so I turn back. "What? My heel hurts, that's all."

"That's all for now. We've gone two, maybe three miles. We have more than thirty to go before we reach the bridge to Galveston Island. It's not a significantly long way, but if you hurt yourself, I really will have to carry you. While you don't weigh much, we have supplies to consider. I think carrying all of it would put me at a severe disadvantage on a tactical mission."

"It's fine." I scowl. "You won't need to carry me, okay? I promise."

Sam pulls his backpack off and looks in a side pocket. He walks over and crouches down to tap my foot. "Sit down so I can look at this."

"Oh, come on Sam. It's a blister. What are you going to do for a blister? You're a medic now?"

He looks up at me with one eyebrow raised, totally undeterred by my barking and snarling. I finally sit. He starts to take my shoe off, but I yank my foot away, glare at him and finish unlacing it myself. I yank off the shoe followed by my not-so-fresh sock. Wonderful. Two-day-old sock smell hits my nose and I want to cry for some reason, which is strange because it's not like Sam's socks would smell any different.

I hold out my hand.

"What?" He pulls a ten inch hunting knife out of his boot.

"Just give me whatever your miracle fix is for a blister." I point at the reddish spot on my heel. "I'll put it on myself."

"You got bristly in a hurry. Note to self. Cranky when injured."

I slug his shoulder, which hurts my hand and he doesn't even budge. I want to punch him harder, but I'm guessing the result would be the same.

He puts his knife back in his boot and hands me a sheet of thick, fuzzy pinkish fabric with plastic on the back. "That's called moleskin. Go ahead, Sunshine. Rip off a hunk with your teeth and slap it on there. Or did you want to try a go with my knife?" He gestures at his boot.

His serrated hunting knife, seriously? I'd slice my hand off. I doubt his magic moleskin would be as helpful for a blood-spurting stump.

I bite at my lip for a minute and then lean over and pull out the scissors I brought, proud I'd thought to bring them. I cut a neat circle out of the fuzzy stuff and start to peel the plastic off the back.

Sam's hand stops me. "Cut another hole in the center of that one. Moleskin isn't like a normal bandage. If you put it directly over the blister, it'll rub more, exacerbating the issue. You need to put a piece or two around the blister so it relieves pressure on the spot that's rubbing."

I follow his directions. By the time I finish, he's put away the rest of his first aid kit, including the remaining moleskin. He waits a few dozen feet up the road, his eyes scanning the horizon. It's cooled down in the last few minutes, and I put my coat back on before hurrying to catch up. Even moving at a brisk pace, my foot doesn't smart anymore.

"That feels a lot better, thanks. Sorry I got bristly and hit you."

Sam frowns. "You hit me? When?"

"On the shoulder, you don't remember?"

"Oh. Right. Uh-huh."

He didn't even notice I hit him. I'm like a tantruming toddler. Ugh. "Well, anyway, thanks."

Sam responds with a nod. The temperature's not the only thing that's gotten chilly.

We walk on and on along a large road with consistent scenery. Brownish brambles cover most everything around, but I can make out old street signs now and then. The ones along our route prominently display the number forty-five. I should be preparing to see our home, thinking about Dad's office and the safe, or maybe trying to recall details. Instead, I can't stop staring at the knocked over, rusted, and vine covered signs. The sprawling weeds cover up so much death and devastation on either side of the road. Houses built close together in neighborhood after neighborhood. Stores and stores and stores. Clothing, hair care, repair shops, all empty and abandoned.

I was so caught up in my own tragedy, and so isolated from the world eleven years ago when the Marking took place, that I missed most of the vast, horrifying reality of Tercera. I haven't ever really thought too long or hard about how many people must've died, or how much wasteland was left behind. I never looked around at the world outside of Port Gibson, never confronted the skeletal remains of Before.

As the sun sets, I think about how the monumental death toll is tragic, but not really the worst part. I was inconsolable when my dad died, but for a long time after, I was pretty numb. It's not the trauma from the initial death of a loved one that wounds the living. It's every single day after that, the days that pass, and pass, and pass. The light didn't go out of the world when it went out of my life. And no matter how much it feels like it shouldn't, time goes on. Life does too, and the one you care the most about just isn't a part of it anymore.

Muddling on alone hurts. I wanted to tell my dad about everything ten years ago, but I couldn't, not anymore. He never heard about my ideas, my thoughts or my accomplishments. I rarely wish I could tell him things now, but when I do, it's more of a dull ache than a sharp pain. What really guts me now in a way the sharp pain at the beginning never did is how time eats away at my memories and erodes the loss. Like moths gobbling up my aunt's crocheted shawl. What hurts the most is that *I don't hurt anymore when I think about him.* My memories of Dad are fading, and once they're gone, he's gone forever.

Who am I without my dad?

I walk past a beautiful neighborhood, full of large homes on enormous lots. Even here, even these stately mansions are being swallowed whole by trees, grasses, bushes, vines and weeds. Exactly as Tercera swallowed up all the people.

Millions of people, billions, all gone now. There's nothing left of them, their lives snuffed out. No one remembers them at all. The last rays of sunlight disappear, and I can't see the houses anymore at all.

Even knowing the magnitude of the epidemic, if a genie made me an offer: save the world, or save your dad, I'd probably trade all of them to get him back. At the end of the day, I don't know any of them, and I love him still.

Humans are crappy when you think about it.

"Hey, I think I see a decent spot—" Sam pulls up short. Suddenly he's standing right in front of me, grabbing at my hands. "Hey, what's wrong?"

I realize tears are rolling down my cheeks. Big, fat, girly tears.

"Nothing," I say, my voice depressingly wobbly. "I didn't realize how awful the world outside of Port Gibson really is. All these people are gone."

He pulls me against him and strokes my hair with one hand. "You haven't been out much."

I sob against his shirt until the tears dry up, but even then I don't pull away. It's been a long time since I felt safe. Finally, I push back, and wipe my cheeks with the side of my hand. "So where's this place you saw somehow, in the darkness?"

"Over there."

I squint in the dim light at a complex of buildings surrounded by a cracked and broken concrete parking lot. I follow as he veers away from the main road and toward a largish building. As we draw near, my flashlight reveals a sign that reads, "Happy Feet Floors." It fell sideways sometime in the past ten years and now dangles at an angle, but the store looks mostly intact.

Sam smashes the glass on the front door with a hunk of concrete, and shakes glass shards off his jacket.

"Why this particular place?" I ask.

"It was getting dark enough that visibility began to suffer. This looked like our best bet."

"Why's it the best?"

"Why a business, you mean?"

"I guess, yeah. One of those huge homes would've had nice beds and sofas, but we're smashing the door on a flooring store."

Sam reaches through and flips the lock. He tugs on the doorknob, but it doesn't work, probably because it's stuck. Sam jostles it, knocks some vines out of the way and tugs again. Finally, it creaks open.

"Most people died at home, Ruby." He steps through, motioning for me to follow.

Oh. Right. Gross. I hadn't thought about that. It made me think more of Rhonda for going on all those scavenging trips. How depressing.

"When I'm looking for a place, I look for businesses with intact windows and doors, bonus if they're covered in vines. Flooring stores frequently have piles of carpet. Not as nice as a bed, but better than concrete, dirt or tile."

Sam finally clicks on his flashlight, a brighter beam than mine.

"You check that way." His light motions right. "I'll check left. Look for a decent spot for the night. Check walls and ceilings for animals. Locked front doors don't exclude animal inhabitants."

I shudder. "What's likely?"

"Middle of winter? Mostly den critters. Raccoons, foxes, skunk. Coyotes or bobcats would be the most irritating."

"Skunks? Really?"

I haven't gone ten feet when my light encounters something enormous and I scream.

After all the death and horrible sadness I've encountered,

I shouldn't be scared of a cockroach. But I've never seen one this size. It could eat a small dog and still be hungry, I swear it on Dad's grave.

Sam rushes over like I'm in peril for my life, and within one second, his gun's trained on the cockroach. I kind of wish he'd pull the trigger.

"A bug? All that noise for a bug? If you're scared of insects, you're in for a rough trip. Texas creepy crawlies come super sized." He turns back the way he came, and I follow, not even a full step behind.

"Ruby?" He stops and I bump into him. His hand reaches out to steady me, circling my waist.

"Yes?"

"You aren't going to check that side, are you?"

"Nuh-uh. No way."

"You're seriously scared of cockroaches?" He holsters his gun.

"It's *dark* and that thing was bigger than a dog."

Sam snorts.

I forget about the bugs. His hand on my waist and his breath on my hair demand all my attention.

Neither of us moves at first, but I slowly sway toward him in the dark. His left arm tightens around my waist, and the hand holding his flashlight drops down to circle my waist from the other side, his fingers nearly meeting.

A tingle zings up my spine and transforms into a shiver that has nothing to do with the cold. I turn my face toward him reflexively, like a flower to the light, but I don't worry because he can't see me in this darkness. I only know I'm facing him because his voice came from this direction. I lean even closer to the warmth of his broad chest. The blackness is freeing somehow.

My kiss with Wesley springs to mind unbidden. I'd been giddy waiting for that, and impatient, even scared. I don't feel any of that now. It's like I'm standing on the edge of a cliff and I don't know what might happen if I step off. Will I fly to the clouds, or fall and shatter? After my repeated stupidity over the past few days, I fear messiness in my future. But there isn't a seatbelt to be buckled, not this time. There's only Sam and me under a cloak of darkness.

Sam's breath on my face tells me he's leaning toward me. He's so tall, it ruffled my hair before. My heart stutters, and I reach a hand up to pull him closer, but he tenses and straightens before I can.

"What was that?"

He steps away quickly and quietly, and a bucket of ice water wouldn't have shaken me more.

Sam invented a noise to escape? I'm glad for the dark, because I'm blushing right down to my toenails. This is so much worse than the seatbelt. I leaned into his chest! He must think I'm a total moron.

Until I hear it, too.

An engine growls in the overgrown parking lot. The sound grows louder and louder and then quieter again. Finally, it cuts off entirely not far past our building. Sam didn't make anything up. I exhale with relief.

I shouldn't feel relieved, of course. A roaring engine outside our location a few scant miles from WPN, is much, much worse than a cockroach.

I surprise myself by pulling out my gun. I maneuver my way over to where Sam now stands near the front of the store. I keep my flashlight angled toward the ground, but even with the filthy front windows, there's enough moonlight to make out his shape. I lightly touch his back so he'll know I'm there, and he doesn't shift a hair. He probably heard me come up behind him since my version of quiet and his aren't quite the same. I'm not shocked the gun in his hand is much larger than mine and most definitely not a tranq.

He leans close and whispers in my ear. "Stay put. I'm going." His hand finds mine and clicks off my flashlight. "No lights, and no screaming, even if a cockroach proposes marriage."

I muffle a laugh. "If I come, I might help."

There's just enough moonlight for me to make out his expression. Incredulity doesn't suit him. Okay, maybe it does, but I don't appreciate it.

"You said I was a decent shot." I hate the petulant tone in my voice.

"I can't deal with them effectively while worrying about you." His hand touches the side of my face.

Worrying about me like he'd worry about a child? Or something else? I sigh. "Fine."

I'll sit in here alone while creepy cockroaches crawl all over me, and Sam's who knows where, watching people do who knows what. I shudder.

He starts toward the door, and I try to stay put, but my body follows him automatically.

He turns back abruptly. "If you come, it could ruin everything."

A bullet could not have halted me more effectively. I turn back and flee into the dark, dank store, stumbling over rugs and carpet, but not stopping.

I finally reach a wall and lean against it for a few minutes, still smarting from Sam's reprimand. When I don't hear anything, I take a step to the side. My knee bumps something. It's so dark I can't see my own hand in front of my face. I could walk right into a badger den. No lights? Yeah right.

I hold my shirt over my flashlight so it shines dimly into the room in front of me. I should at least be able to use it to find somewhere to sit so I can wait patiently. And wait. And wait. I don't know how much time passes, but I figure something out.

Waiting sucks.

The longer I wait, the more my boredom morphs into worry. What if something happens to Sam? I don't want to ruin anything, but what if things have gone wrong? What if he really does need my help? Wouldn't it be awesome if I saved him after he'd been such a jerk about it?

I wait a little longer and listen as closely as I can. I don't hear a thing. I look at my watch. It's almost nine o'clock.

Knowing the time isn't helpful because I hadn't looked at it before.

Twenty minutes later, I can't wait another second.

I stumble toward the front of the store and shut off my flashlight before I leave. I might not move inhumanly silent like Sam, but I'm not so loud I'll give myself away. I grumble (quietly) to myself as I walk. I wish I'd seen the car so I knew where to go, but then there aren't many cars on the roads these days. Surely I'll spot the only one in running condition.

I walk a few yards past our little floor store and continue beyond another tiny building too. What if Sam really is in danger? He could be hurt or dying. Panic rises in my throat and my legs pump faster. I need to find him.

I worried about spotting the vehicle, but when I round the corner, it becomes obvious. A van's parked in front of the entrance to a large building and it's in decent condition. The paint's patchy, but there's no rust. The real giveaway is that something drips from underneath it, puddling on the buckled pavement. The van doesn't really draw my attention however, thanks to the lights shining out of the adjacent building. At least I know where Sam went.

I circle around and creep up slowly from the south, keeping close to the side of the building all the way to the entrance.

Unfortunately, the entire front of the building's made up of windows. I recognize why when I read the sign. It used to be a grocery store, which really sucks. There's a lot of accumulated debris in front of the windows, including several creeping vines, but they won't block my movement if I walk past.

Two men with guns talk to each other in the front part of the store. The shorter man's belly hangs over his pants, which is rare these days. His red hair pokes up every which way. He walks back and forth in front of two big boxes. The taller man gestures angrily, and I realize they aren't boxes at all. Two people are tied to chairs. They're too far away for me to make out details.

The light radiates from two gas lanterns, and the movement from the men waving their hands around casts strange shapes across the occupants of the chairs. One of the people tied up is bigger than the other, but big enough to be Sam? I doubt it, but I can't be sure from this far away.

I try to listen, but I can't make out much. The sound I hear comes from a broken window a few feet away from me, near the center of the store. Since they're located in one enormous room, I catch intermittent phrases depending on where the speaker's standing. Something about cleansing, or maybe cleaning? Mention of a waste, but a waste of what?

This is pointless. I have no idea what they're saying from here. Unless I move closer, I can't figure out whether Sam's in trouble. It's a risk because they have guns and two captives already, but I'm armed too, and they don't know I'm barely competent. I click the safety off my twenty-two, and creep toward the broken window.

I forget one critical thing when I begin creeping toward the window. Grocery stores had automatic sliding doors. In my defense, the gas lights didn't indicate the building had power. I should have thought of it anyway.

The doors slide open when I approach, which immediately alerts the guys with guns to my presence. So much for the element of surprise. I leap to my feet, gun pointed outward.

"Put the gun down." The portly redhead points his gun right at my face.

Mine's aimed at him, too. I think. We stare at each other, my hand trembling. The same image comes to my mind over and over. My dad's face when he was shot. Surprise, pain, fear. I want to save Sam, but I can't do that to another person. I can't fire this gun. Lucky for me, this guy doesn't know the truth or he'd already have fired.

I let my dad down ten years ago. I let Wesley down last week. My uncle had so little faith he left without me, and sent Sam to babysit me. All I ever do is disappoint the people I love. I want to do better, but I can't shoot someone to do it.

I lower my gun and set it on the tile floor.

I'm lifting my hands in the air when two loud shots ring out and both men drop, blood pouring from identical holes in their foreheads. Who shot them? Both shot clean in exactly the same place. I think back to the clearing that morning. It feels like days ago.

I glance behind me at Sam. Of course it's him. He holds his gun out in front of him while advancing toward me slowly. I turn back, eyes drawn against my will to the two people he shot. The two lives snuffed out like candles right in front of me. Neither of them even twitch.

"They might not have shot me." I'm too shaken to be properly grateful.

He doesn't respond. He's too busy scanning the inside of the building.

"I mean thanks for saving me, but did you have to kill them?"

"Yes." He bobs his head toward the corner of the large room. "They were about to kill those two, but more importantly, you don't wound someone aiming a gun at someone you care for. In that instance, you always shoot to kill."

He shot them in the head because of me. I close my eyes and try not to cry. Everything I do is wrong.

A whimper from the corner draws my attention. The people on the chairs are gagged, their gloved hands bound behind them. One of them's wearing a bright red, knit cap with a golden puff ball on top.

I gasp.

Now that I'm closer and not in imminent danger, I recognize the hat. I circle around the two of them and see familiar faces, too. Sam didn't just save me. He saved Job and Rhonda as well. I run toward them, intent on removing the ties and gags so I can ask what they're even doing here. I'm only a pace away from them when Sam yanks me back.

"Ruby, no."

I look up at him. "What?"

He doesn't explain, but the sorrow in his eyes worries me. I thrash against him and smack at his chest with my gun. Why won't he release me?

He growls. "That safety better be on."

I click it on and thinking about a possible misfire calms me.

"Put me down so I can free them."

He turns me around, but keeps one hand on my arm, shackling me against his chest. Job and Rhonda's faces mirror Sam's stoic one.

I finally notice it high on their foreheads. Oh, no, no, no. Heaven and earth and everything in between, no. Not them, too.

They're both Marked.

CHAPTER 16

I'm cursed.

My dad created Tercera, and I let him die before he could perfect the cure. Now everyone I care about is contracting it, one by one. I sink to my knees a few feet away from the closest thing to a brother and sister I've ever known. They look fine, but now they're dying slowly, just like Wesley, just like their mom.

"What . . . How . . ." I don't know what to say.

Muffled sounds remind me of their gags. I start forward to release them, but Sam's hand stops me again. "Gloves." He's wearing them, and I'm not. I left mine back at the carpet place with our other stuff.

He walks around behind them and pulls the wicked looking knife from his boot. With a flick of his wrist the jagged edge meets the fabric and Rhonda's gag falls into her lap. Job's is only a second behind.

"Thank you so much, Sam," Rhonda says.

Sam cuts the ropes binding their hands and feet next.

"Seriously man, great timing," Job says.

"What are you doing here?" I ask. "And why were they going to kill you?"

Rhonda stands slowly, stretching. "Mom and Dad left, and then you and Sam left too. Port Gibson was in an uproar."

"The Marked attacked a second time, right after you left," Job says. "The pressure's on for a cure. Dad had some motorcycles stashed in case of emergency. Rhonda knew where they were kept. We thought we'd pass you on our way down. It's pretty easy to make good time with motorcycles. Easier to avoid potholes. I guess we passed you without knowing it?"

"How did we miss you?" Rhonda asks.

Sam sighs. "Ruby didn't convince me to leave until we caught what must have been the north end of the second Marked attack. A whole bunch of them had guns on us. We started out north and headed down a roundabout way."

Rhonda nods.

"So, what happened?" I ask. "How'd you get—"

"Caught?" Job asks. "We couldn't figure it out at first either, but WPN must lay trip wires on the roads in from Marked territory so they know when someone crosses. It's the only thing that makes sense. They set a trap and we fell right into it."

I meet Sam's glance and know he's thinking the same thing as me. How'd we make it through?

"Where were they?" Sam asks.

"A few miles from here," Job says.

Our bad luck might not have been so bad after all. Our truck must've run out of gas before the wires.

"When did they catch you?" I ask.

"Early this morning," Rhonda says. "How'd you guys find us, anyway?"

"Pure coincidence," I say. "We heard the van. Why'd it stop here?"

"To refuel," Job says. "They're using this place to store supplies for the . . . did you hear them? What they're planning?" He rubs his wrists where the ropes were. They look raw.

I glance at Sam, but he shakes his head.

"Hear what?" I ask.

Rhonda says, "World Peace Now plans to exterminate all the Marked in less than a month. They're calling it the Cleansing. We knew the hormonal suppressants were failing, but what we see as a tragedy, WPN views as a threat. Apparently the Marked asked them to perform marriages for the ones who become pregnant after suppressant failure. Many want to get married before the babies are born."

"Babies?" My stomach turns. "Wait, is that how you got Marked? From kids who came for a wedding?"

"Huh?" Rhonda asks. "No, I haven't seen any."

"Then how—"

Job smacks his forehead. "Duh. They wouldn't know."

"Wouldn't know what?" Sam raises one eyebrow.

Job holds his hands out to me. His fingers are red. I glance up at his head. Where he smacked it, his rash looks strange, blurry.

"But why?" Then I understand. Sam and I left our gloves off and let our hair down. They took the same idea one step further. I reach over and rub Rhonda's forehead myself, and Sam doesn't stop me this time. My fingertips come away reddish brown.

"Of course," Sam mutters.

I feel such an overwhelming sense of relief that, although I don't find the situation very funny, I laugh. Grief, fear, and exhaustion do funny things to me.

"Sorry, I forgot all about that," Rhonda says. "I'm so glad

we found you. We were hoping to catch you before you reached the island."

"*You* found *us?*" Sam raises one eyebrow.

Rhonda rolls her eyes. "Details."

"I can't believe you let those idiots get the drop on you." Sam shakes his head. "Pitiful."

"Now we'll have two sets of eyes watching out for stuff," Rhonda says. "It won't happen again."

"No," I say. "You two have to head back."

"What?" Job asks. "Why?"

"Because," I say. "When I saw you, gagged and tied, about to be shot, and then again when I thought you were Marked." I inhale deeply because I finally understand Aunt Anne's position. "I can't do this with you guys along. I need to know someone's safe back home, not risking their life to find this cure."

"It's a tactical op," Rhonda says. "You can't run a tactical op without someone to provide cover. You need me."

I'm resolved. "No, there's me and Sam. It's enough. If he can't get me in, an extra person won't make a difference."

"That's not true," Rhonda says. "Sam knows it isn't. I'm excellent at CQC. You'll need that."

At my blank stare, she sighs.

"Close quarters combat, and I got top marks on Advanced Combat Marksmanship too. I've done several operations, and I remain level headed under stress. We partnered on several ops together and we were like peanut butter and jelly. Sam's better with me along, right?"

Why's she asking him? I'm the one going for the cure, and I'm the one who can get into my dad's safe. I turn toward Sam, my jaw set, my eyes flashing. "We don't need them with us, right?"

"We shouldn't make this decision here," Sam says. "Maybe before we make travel plans, we should all eat dinner. It's easier to think rationally with something in your belly."

I want to smack Sam. Except, I know from past experience it would only hurt my hand. "Are you saying I'm irrational?"

Sam sighs. "We all are. Let's get out of here before someone sends in back-up to check on these two."

I didn't realize I was such a burden to everyone around me. I fume.

"I'm starving," Job says. "I'd love to eat, most anything really."

My head hurts and my hands shake. All I've eaten today is a granola bar and walking ten miles didn't help. I glance at the two dead bodies, and the rows and rows of shelves full of weapons and ammunition. It looks like an armory, not a grocery store.

Sam crosses the room and walks down an aisle. He picks up guns and then ammo, his face like a kid in a candy store. He's got a lollipop in both hands, only his lollipops kill people.

"Really Sam?" I ask. "You don't have enough already?"

"I didn't pick what we brought," Sam says. "I got stuck with whatever was in the truck cache, plus my own normal handguns. This is a miracle sent to prepare us to retrieve the cure. We'd be stupid to ignore it."

I roll my eyes. "I thought we were in a rush?" I gesture at the dead guys.

"Yes, we'll be quick." Rhonda grabs two weapons herself, and tucks them into a holster, already concealed under her shirt. She selects a third for Job.

"What about me?" I ask.

Sam frowns. "You've got one. That's plenty."

I try not to pout when we walk outside to the van. A

single key protrudes from the ignition. Job twists it and the engine starts, but the gas gauge points to empty.

"Did they say where the gas was stored?" I ask. "We could take this the rest of the way."

Job shakes his head. "We can't take the van. It's not safe."

"We didn't see their trip wire, even on a motorcycle," Rhonda says.

"Sloppy," Sam says. "But even if we avoid wires, they could have video feeds, trackers in the van, or sweeping patrols. And if we avoid those, the van still ties us directly to these two."

Hello WPN, we killed two of your men. Can we pop inside for a moment to steal a cure from your island? We'd like to heal the thousands of people you're planning to massacre.

"We're only thirty miles from the island." Rhonda reaches into the van and rummages around. "Grab anything we can use and we look for a place to sleep. We'll reach the island late tomorrow night if we leave at first light."

Sam's lack of input tells me he wants Job and Rhonda to come.

"Ruby?" Job asks.

"I don't want you two along," I say. "But I thought we agreed to eat first."

"Yes," Job says. "We did."

"But while you're thinking about it, consider your boyfriend," Rhonda says.

I gulp. I think Sam wants them to come, but how can she know that?

Rhonda puts an arm around my shoulders. "I know you're worried about us getting Marked, or killed, or whatever, but if our help gets the cure, Wesley can come home."

Right. When she said my boyfriend she meant Wesley not

Sam. Of course she did, because Sam and I aren't anything. We haven't even kissed.

I think about when Wesley kissed me, and my fingers fly to my lips. I'd sort of shut down that whole line of thinking when I realized I wasn't Marked, but what if we actually find a cure? I don't want to risk Job and Rhonda, but I do want Wesley back, and my aunt. Rhonda hasn't mentioned her mom, which means she probably doesn't know. I should tell her, but if she's this determined to go without knowing . . . I don't want to make it worse until I've decided whether to bring them.

"I'll go get our stuff so we can leave." I turn toward the floor store. I need to think without anyone badgering me, without anyone telling me what to do. It's my dad's cure, and my dad's lab.

I'm almost to the vine covered doors when I notice it. I don't hear anything, but I feel something, or more accurately, someone. "Sam?" I spin around and see him, standing like a statue in the moonlight, as gorgeous as any carving I've ever seen.

"I can grab our stuff. You didn't need to come." Except that's completely false, I realize. I can't even lift his bag.

He shakes his head.

"What's wrong?" I ask. "Are you mad I came after you? I'm sorry I did, but I thought maybe you were hurt."

"I knew you would eventually. It's just hard for me. I have to keep you—" He stops.

"Keep me what?" I ask.

"I promised to keep you safe." He looks at the ground and digs at a weed with the toe of his boot.

I can barely make out his face, but I think he looks torn. Upset, even.

I walk toward him. "There's something else going on in there." I tap his forehead. "What aren't you telling me?"

"It's nothing."

"Is it Rhonda? Is that why you're being strange all of a sudden?" Anger bubbles up in my chest at the thought. One minute he's leaning toward me in the dark, hands around my waist. The next he's barely talking to me. The only difference is Rhonda and her insistence she be the peanut butter to his jelly. I love Rhonda, but I want her safe at home, not here with me. And Sam.

Is her safety my real reason for wanting her to go home?

"Why do you keep asking about her?" he asks. "Does it make you feel better?"

"What?"

"About him?" he asks.

I have no idea what he's talking about. "Him? Him who?"

He turns away.

"Welcome back, monosyllabic Sam. For the record, I didn't miss you."

Sam grunts, and I think about what he said. Does it make me feel better about 'him'? The only person he might mean is Wesley.

"Are you mad I want to save Wesley? Because that's freaking ridiculous. He's dying, and I haven't seen him since . . ." I was going to say since he kissed me, but I snap my mouth closed instead.

"Since what?"

"You did mean Wesley?"

"No, of course not." He paces. "I haven't given *him* a second thought. He's nothing to me." He paces more. "But your aunt's Marked and Rhonda and Job don't know. You don't want them to come, but they have a personal interest in that cure."

"I don't want them to get Marked, too!"

"Until Rhonda tells you it's more likely that we can save *Wesley*. Then you change your mind."

"It's not like that." Except it kind of is. "If I tell them about their mom, wild horses won't be able to drag them home."

I look up at him, the sharp lines of his face so pristine and perfectly symmetrical in the moonlight that I almost can't stand it. His mouth hovers mere inches from mine. How did I find Wesley good looking? No one compares to Sam. He mumbles something I can't hear.

"What?"

"If Rhonda might keep you safe, I want her along."

"You do want them to come?"

He frowns. "Not for Wesley."

Is Sam jealous? I grin. "You don't like him."

"No," he says. "I don't dislike him. I don't care about him at all. I like someone else."

His hair falls around his face in soft waves. One arm moves behind me and pulls me close. The other cups my cheek as his lips move closer, slowly bending toward mine. My lip trembles, but I don't even consider biting it. It should feel wrong, wanting Sam this way, when Wesley's in mortal peril. But how can an anchor for my world be wrong? Sam's arms surround me, and his face hovers above mine. For the first time since my dad died, in this moment, my world feels exactly right.

"Ruby? Sam?"

Except that.

Job's voice slides like an ice cube down my back in July. Sam almost shoves me over in his haste to put space between us.

"Her eye," Sam says.

"What?" Rhonda, a step behind Job, looks totally lost.

Sam clears his throat. "Ruby got something in her eye. I was checking it out, but it's hard to see out here. At night."

Lame. No way they'll believe that. It's seriously dark, for

one thing, so he couldn't possibly have thought he'd see anything in my eye.

Worst excuse ever.

Except they buy it. I'm a little offended no one suspects that Sam meant to kiss me. This time I'm positive he did. No seatbelts, no darkness filled with giant cockroaches, and no WPN vans.

"Are you okay?" Rhonda asks.

I blink a few times in case they see better than me. "Sam got the dust out."

"Good." Rhonda pats my arm as they walk past like nothing's out of the ordinary.

Job asks, "So do we stay the night here?"

"Bad idea," Rhonda says. "It's too close. If someone comes looking for those two, they'll find them and start searching from there. They can't check everything, but we need to be further than this."

Sam and I grab our bags without delay, and we hike along the road in the dark looking for someplace close, but not too close. It gives me time to think, and I realize I need to tell them. Nothing good comes from deceit.

"There's something you need to know, guys."

Job stops walking. "What?"

"Your parents left right after the attack for a reason," I say.

"Dad's Marked, isn't he?" Job asks.

Sometimes I forget how smart he is. "No, but your mom is."

"We figured," Rhonda says. "They left without warning in the middle of the night? Why such urgency, after ten years?"

Job sighs. "A huge Marked attack, both of them on the front lines, and an early morning departure without even a check in?"

Tears glisten in Rhonda's eyes. Suspecting and knowing aren't the same. I can't send them home now, knowing exactly how they feel. They know the risk, and they want to come anyway.

"Fine," I say. "You can come."

Rhonda hugs me. "We'll make it through this and out the other end. Then you can marry Wesley in a big, puffy white dress, and run Port Gibson together like you always wanted."

I roll my eyes and squeeze Rhonda's hand. A second later there's a loud crash up ahead. I'm pretty sure Sam broke a window.

"What're you doing?" Rhonda asks.

Sam growls. "If people are looking for us, I want them to have some places to search."

"You could've warned us," Rhonda says. "That scared me half to death."

"Sorry."

He doesn't sound sorry. If I had to guess at his expression underneath the garish shadows from his flashlight, I'd say Sam looks pissed.

Which makes me smile.

CHAPTER 17

We walk one way for half an hour or so, smashing windows periodically, and then we turn around and walk another direction before backtracking and smashing more windows. We do this three times before we walk along a road without touching anything. By this point my blister's smarting again. I resist the urge to kick every tuft of grass and throw every rock I stumble across.

Eventually, Rhonda and Sam both agree to stop at a church across the big road Sam and I travelled along initially. Christus Lutheran something or other. Rhonda walks up to the front doors.

"It's kind of a shame." She shines her flashlight on the front doors. "Smashing up all this beautiful glass."

"Don't smash the front," Sam says. "Let's use a side door or window. They'll be less likely to search if the building appears untouched."

We follow Sam's lead. He wanders around a labyrinth of back doors and windows before choosing one. He wraps his hand in his jacket and knocks the glass out of the window. Then he shakes out his coat and lays it down over the jagged edges before climbing over. I scramble through after him, grabbing the arm he extends to lift me through and set me down. After I make it over, he picks up his coat and shakes it off.

"There's still glass." Job points at the sharp edges.

"Use your coat." Sam grins and walks off into the depths of the church.

It's black as pitch inside. I shuffle along until I slam my shins on something hard. I shine my flashlight down belatedly. Pews. Of course.

Sam reaches my side instantly. His glove-free hand slides over mine, interlacing our fingers. "Stay close."

Butterflies fill my stomach. He didn't take off his glove to blend in tonight, not inside a cold, dark, church.

I let him tug me along, happy to be near him.

He releases my hand when Job and Rhonda approach and shines his flashlight around the room. "This is as good as anywhere. Sleeping up on the pews will be warmer than on the ground."

"Sure." Rhonda holds her flashlight in her teeth and pushes two pews together, so they face one another, making a larger space.

"What're you doing?" I ask.

"Making us a spot. The boys smell. Go find somewhere far away." She wrinkles her nose at them.

Sam walks over and hands me a blanket. A thrill runs up my arm when his hand brushes mine.

"Thanks."

"You're welcome," he says, so softly I almost don't hear him.

Apparently boys can be taught.

Sam opens some cans of stew and passes them around. Rhonda places the flashlights at intervals facing outward to provide a little bit of consistent light for our meal. We perch on pews to eat. Even now, hours later, I can't quite get the image of that cockroach out of my head. It occurs to me while we eat that cockroaches are as likely to be on a pew as on the floor. I shiver involuntarily.

No one speaks once we have food in our hands. Sam was wrong about the stew last night. It was much better warm. I try to ignore the blobs and swallow, but I've got several bites left in my can when the hunger pangs stop and it's hard to force the rest down. Sam opens another round of cans, which Rhonda takes, but I decline. I barely finished the first. Sam shrugs and eats the one he offered me himself.

Rhonda asks, "What's the plan for tomorrow?"

"Depends," Job says. "What do we know about World Peace Now?"

"Not much." I tick a few things off on my fingers. "They're planning mass murder, so they must fear the Marked. They live in some kind of communal religious compound."

"They're trying to repopulate the earth with Godly people," says Job, "They think Tercera was God's plan to cleanse the earth of the wicked, per our captors from earlier."

"Then why fear infection?" Rhonda asks. "If the Marked are still here, isn't that part of God's plan, too? And if only the wicked get wiped out from Tercera, how's it a threat?"

"A tool can be turned on its owner, or so they say." Job finishes his second can of stew.

"Good dinner Sam, thanks." Rhonda leans over and pats his leg. "You can always count on good old Defense provisions, right? I thought I'd get a break from them on this trip. I thought we'd be scrounging, but we needed to hide, and I'm hungry enough I don't care." She laughs.

"It was better last night. Ruby caught a rabbit."

"A bunny?" Rhonda turns to me with an incredulous look on her face. "You killed a bunny? You always let them go."

I blush. "Sam killed it."

"Ruby caught it. And she put some..." Sam rubs his fingers together, "some little leaves and stuff in the stew, too."

"Well, aren't you quite the little traveling homemaker?" Rhonda snickers. "What exactly did you add?"

"Basil and thyme," I say. "Nothing fancy."

Rhonda raises one eyebrow. "Where'd you even get those?"

"I brought some dried herbs with me. I'd put more—"

Rhonda's laughing too hard to hear me.

"Why's that so funny?"

"Only you." Rhonda wheezes. "Only you would bring dried herbs on a mission."

I frown.

"Your cooking skills may finally be appreciated before too long," Rhonda says. "When we get the cure and you get your boyfriend back."

My face turns bright red.

"Is he her boyfriend, or not?" Sam asks.

"Wesley's Marked," I say.

"Until we get a cure," Sam says. "What then?"

"I don't know." I look down at the ground.

"Ruby's loved Wesley for years." Rhonda smiles. "She didn't realize he was pining for her, too. It was about the cutest thing I've ever seen. Sometimes I thought about telling one of them, but it was too much fun to watch. Now, with him being Marked, it's a little Romeo and Juliette-esque."

Sam asks Rhonda. "What'd you bring?" He grabs for her bag and she snatches it back. They shove each other around a bit, both laughing. Finally, Sam gets it away from her and opens it up. "Jerky, smart. Crackers? Really? That's it? I'm disappointed."

"I was in a hurry, okay? Besides, I don't do the trading for the family. Ruby handles all that. I had to make do with what I found."

I bite my lip.

"I did have some other stuff, but we already ate it. Soup, noodles, rice. We boiled it when we had a fire. We're too close now, so I saved this stuff for the end."

"All right," Sam says.

"Besides, for a normal person, your stew's too heavy to carry. I couldn't have lugged it this far."

"We didn't plan to leave," Sam says. "We got what was in the truck."

"You don't have to worry about things being heavy. You're built like a bear." Rhonda pats Sam's arm again. I tear into my poor, innocent lip. I love Rhonda, but if she keeps touching Sam, I might claw her eyes out. I have no right to be angry. It's not like Sam and I are . . . well, anything. I'm not even sure he really likes me. We have chemistry maybe, but it's not like he's kissed me. He drops my hand like it's on fire when anyone else is around.

And anyway, I'm not sure I like him like that.

The exhaustion from the day crashes over me in a wave. I consider curling up right where I am. Sam looks my way, but I can't read his expression. Everything's confusing.

"Let's figure this out," I say. "I need sleep. We walk to the bridge to Galveston, and look for a boat. The water in the West Bay's calm. I've been fishing out there with my dad. I could point out the building we lived in from the coast; I'm pretty sure."

"Why risk stealing a boat when we might not have to? Why don't we walk up and tell WPN we want to convert?" Rhonda asks.

I shake my head. "There's no guarantee they'll believe us. And if we get in that way, how would we escape?"

"Those are good points," Sam says, "but if we go in tactically, we're more likely to get gunned down. If they welcome converts, that's our best bet."

I snort. "So we waltz up to the front gate and tell them everything? While pretending that we love God and want to join their loopy compound?"

"I'm with Ruby," Job says. "We aren't even active Christians. We don't know enough about WPN's beliefs to fill a thimble, much less convince them we believe too. We're better off playing to their fears. We say we approve of the Marked attacks if they ask, and suggest they should find the cure in case any of the righteous get sick in the cleansing they have slated."

"We walk up, say, 'Hey by the way, we know about your plan to massacre the Marked kids, and guess what? We wanna join you?' They'll know we killed their guys and shoot us in the head," Rhonda says.

"I prefer my head hole free." Sam smiles. "Maybe we don't tell them we know about the Cleansing. Job's right that we play to their fears, though. We tell them we hate the Marked. We think they pose a threat and want to eliminate them. The Unmarked kicked us out for taking radical but necessary positions. We heard WPN understands. No religion, just half-truth."

"Not a bad plan," Job says. "We tell them the Marked killed our family and we're pissed."

It's not even a lie, not really. I try not to think about Aunt Anne or I get weepy.

Rhonda and Sam nod. This could go any which way. We have no idea how they'll react to any of it.

"We should make that our fall back," I say. "First, we scope out the island. If there aren't guard towers, we try to sneak around in a boat."

"What's with you and floating?" Rhonda asks. "If we want to go in tactically, we cross the bridge."

"They'll have it under guard," I say.

"I don't wanna rely on something that one bullet might sink." Rhonda scowls.

"What's the big deal?" I ask. "You can swim."

"Sharks," Rhonda says.

I roll my eyes. "They leave humans alone."

"We had this substitute at school once who didn't want to do anything. She made us watch tv and the week she was there, some channel played this terrible marathon program. Shark Week."

I lift my eyebrows. "And?"

She shudders. "Boats are out."

"So we go in tactically, and if that fails, we tell them why we're there. That gives us options."

Rhonda sets her jaw just like her mom. "What do you guys think?"

Sam shakes his head. "I'm more afraid of this discussion than a sea full of sharks."

Job snorts. "Ruby's plan makes sense. Investigate and go from there. We can always come clean if sneaking in doesn't work."

"Except then they can't trust us." Rhonda shakes her head.

"Bullets do kill sharks, you know." I walk over to Rhonda's pews and toss down the blanket Sam gave me.

"Most guns don't work once they're wet," Rhonda says.

I set my gun on the pew next to my backpack, safety on. "So we keep them dry." I pull my little blanket out of my bag to use as a pillow and lay down fully dressed.

Job pops his head over my pew a minute later. "You okay?"

Job's presence means Sam and Rhonda are alone together. Probably flirting. The two perfect physical specimens in the room, reminiscing about their shared Defense training. Complimenting each other's skills. Rhonda's telling Sam he's super strong, like a battering ram, and rubbing his arm. Gah.

Job's being sweet, so I try to appreciate the gesture. "I'm fine, just tired."

"Long day, huh?"

"Yeah, I need some sleep." And he needs to get back over there to chaperone.

He looks at me for a moment, but I don't back down.

"Message received, little sis. I'll buzz off, but I wanted to make sure you weren't lonely. I know Sam can be reserved, but you're with family now. Everything's going to be okay." He kisses my forehead.

He's a good guy. "I'm glad to have your help, Job." He squeezes my hand and walks back to help Rhonda and Sam clean up. I sigh with relief.

I drop off to sleep quickly, but I wake before anyone else as a result. I don't need an alarm clock or even sunlight, thanks to a very helpful cockroach perched on my nose, antennae twiddling. I consider it one of the crowning achievements of my life that I don't scream. I swat it away and shudder violently. Rhonda shifts when I crawl out of the pews, but she doesn't wake up.

I grab my bag and walk convulsively outside. I feel a little better after I pee and brush my teeth. I'm headed back inside when I see Sam standing by the door, his arms crossed over his chest.

"What are you doing?" I raise one eyebrow.

"I had third watch, so I heard you leave. I figured you wanted to be alone, but I came out to make sure you were safe."

Great. Guy with supersonic hearing just listened in while I peed and gargled. At least I didn't scream over that gargantuan bug. I hope he noted my bravery.

"I didn't know there were watches."

"We left you out. You looked pretty tired."

"Thanks." I try to duck past him, but he grabs my arm.

I feel a question coming that I'm not ready for. I deflect without thinking. "If you need to borrow some toothpaste, you don't have to manhandle me. Just ask."

"Believe it or not, I have my own, standard issue. It's more powder than paste, but it does the trick."

"Need me to check for you?" I say, flirting like an idiot.

"No."

The bottom drops out of my stomach. What's wrong? Yesterday he seemed playful. Into me, maybe.

"Morning, guys." Job pushes past us. "We really need to get going if we're going to reach WPN in one day. Also, I'm starving. You got any food left, Sam? Rhonda's been passing out dry oatmeal, which is gross, but I think she's nearly out."

Sam leans close and whispers in my ear. "You have to talk to me eventually." His breath really is minty fresh. Why's he upset? Interruptions, or something else?

I'm not sure I want to know. I push past Sam and back into the church, eager to escape the unknown, even if it's only a reprieve. Light streams through the upper windows in the church, rendering flashlights unnecessary. Sam follows me inside and pulls more food from his magic bag. He shares out some kind of hard biscuits and dried fruit in little plastic packages.

"Wow, MREs." Rhonda laughs. "Meals rejected by everyone."

I take a package. "Are they that bad?"

Rhonda nods. "So bad. Everyone in Defense hates them."

Sam's face relaxes. "Meals rarely edible."

Rhonda smiles. "Meals rejected by the enemy?"

"Morsels, regurgitated, eviscerated." Sam taps his on a pew and it makes a knocking sound.

The corner of Job's mouth turns up. "Eviscerated? Use that in a sentence."

Sam shadowboxes Job in the gut. "I'll eviscerate you for mocking me."

Job doubles over in feigned pain. "No need to disembowel me. I didn't think you knew complicated words, that's all."

Rhonda pats Sam's arm. "Sam's smarter than me. I think he wants people to assume he's dumb."

Sam shrugs. "I just don't care what people think."

Rhonda sighs. "Their dumb remarks annoy me, but if you don't care, I guess I shouldn't either. Thanks for breakfast."

I grit my teeth and gnaw on my biscuit. They're right about one thing. This food sucks.

Rhonda and Sam keep joking around like they're best friends. Not to be petty, but Rhonda already has a twin. Everyone in the world can't love her best. I busy myself with preparing to leave so no one will notice I'm sulking. I'm the first one done eating, the first one with my laces tied, and the first one with my bag packed. Of course, Sam's ready seconds after me. A few minutes later Job's got his bag in hand, eager to leave.

"Where's Rhonda?" I didn't see her leave.

"She found a bathroom." Job rolls his eyes. "Apparently there's even a mirror."

My hair must be a nightmare. I desperately need an excuse to head in there. "I'll try to hurry her up."

"Girls." Job shakes his head.

I bumble down the hall, knocking into walls and benches. I should've brought my flashlight. The main sanctuary had windows, but the hallway doesn't.

"Rhonda?"

"Over here."

She has her flashlight out.

"Wow, you found a mirror?" I feign indifference. "I'm scared to look. I probably look like Medusa."

"Actually, your curls look great," she says. "It's too bad the

Council makes us keep our hair in braids. Yours looks way better down."

I peek around her shoulder. She has mascara. Scratch that. She has an entire make-up bag. Why in the world would she put on make-up out here? She wasn't wearing any yesterday.

I can only think of one reason. A big, gorgeous ox of a reason.

Rhonda already has a lot of things I don't. Straight, smooth hair. Big dark eyes. Fitted, tough looking clothes. Knee high boots. Amazing skills. Athletic ability. Height. And most of all, a banging rack. Does she really need to widen the chasm?

"What're you doing?" I narrow my make-up free eyes at her.

"Just putting on some mascara," she says. "No biggie. You're blonde, so you understand. If I don't put on mascara, my eyes disappear completely."

Light. Keep it light, Ruby. I love Rhonda, maybe more than any other person in the world. If she likes Sam, I should be happy for them, because no one on Earth would choose me over her. I need to think of a way to shift the conversation that doesn't give away how I feel, but encourages her to be honest with me.

"Do you like Sam?" The words tumble out. So much for broaching the subject smoothly.

Rhonda shines her flashlight in my face. I'm like a deer about to be hit by a semi-truck.

"Do you?"

I clear my throat. "Why else would you be putting on mascara in the middle of nowhere?"

"You do." Rhonda shifts the flashlight so it's not blinding me anymore. Of course, I still can't see anything. Retinal burn.

"That's why I kept pushing Wesley, you know."

"So, you do?" I hate that my voice wavers.

"I've liked him for years, Ruby."

I want to puke, and ball up my fists and hit the wall, and collapse in a heap to cry. I can't compete with Rhonda. I don't compare to her for one, but liking someone she likes will break me. If Sam bizarrely did like me, it'd upset me because she'd be sad. When he likes her, I'll be angry and petty. It's a lose-lose.

"You gave up on Wesley already?" Rhonda asks.

"No, but maybe I'm mad at him for almost Marking me. I don't know. Ever since we came on this trip, Sam's been . . . different."

"It's the first time you've ever been around him, just the two of you. He's pretty intense," Rhonda says. "People don't slow down to notice."

I nod.

"I'm not glad you like him," Rhonda says, "but I get it. And—"

"And what?" I ask.

She exhales and clicks a button on the flashlight. The base lights up and low light bathes the small room. "He doesn't like me like I want. He never has."

"How do you know?" I ask.

"Because I do, okay? We've talked about it."

I'm completely floored. Rhonda's perfect. "He's crazy."

Rhonda shrugs. "It is what it is. If he likes you, I'll be happy for you, I swear. But Wesley? I can't imagine he'll be pleased if he gets cured only to come back and find you and Sam together." Rhonda pokes me. If she's teasing me about it already, I hope that means we'll be okay.

"If we can cure Wesley, he'll forget all about me in his joy at having his life back."

Rhonda shakes her head. "That boy thinks you hung the stars."

I look at the ground. "I don't know how I feel about him anymore, but unless we find a cure it's irrelevant anyway."

"How does Sam feel about you risking your life to save Wesley?"

I shrug. "I don't think he loves it, which is why—"

"His tantrums whenever Wesley comes up are a good sign."

I shrug. I should feel excited that someone else noticed, but I feel sad instead. Or maybe guilty. "The boys are ready to go. You almost done?"

Rhonda puts on one more layer of mascara and shoves it into the bag. "Yep."

"Actually, I'm blonde too," I say. "Mind if I borrow the mascara?"

"Like you need any help." She rolls her eyes.

My jaw drops. "Are you kidding? I look like a ten-year-old boy."

"You're ethereal, innocent, and delicate. I'm like a she-man. . . Job with boobs."

Laughter erupts from my belly, filling the small space and reverberating. She's as far from a she-male as possible, but the image of Job with boobs? Priceless.

Rhonda places a hand on my arm. "I'm not upset you like Sam, because who doesn't? If it has to be someone else, and believe me it does, I'd rather he end up with you than one of his fangirls."

Every year after the seventeen year olds Path, the Council reassesses each settlement's needs. Port Gibson gets transfers, mostly new adults, but some older people too. For the last few years, Sam's acquired a gaggle of doe-eyed followers after each transfer. I didn't even like Sam yet and they annoyed me. I can only imagine it's worse if you work with him . . . and have feelings for him.

I put my hand on her shoulder. "I'm sorry, Rhonda."

She sighs melodramatically. "Honestly, it's fine. The more I think about it, the more it makes sense. You're different enough to be interesting, and maybe you appeal to his desire to save people."

That stings a little, but I try to shake it off.

"You okay?" Rhonda asks.

"I'm fine," I lie. "Just thinking about going back to my dad's old lab." Which actually depresses me, which is what sells it.

"You were so young," Rhonda says. "Will you really recognize where you lived? Were you actually right on the beach?"

"Our condo was right by the water. It should be easy enough to reach by boat, if the building's still standing."

"Why wouldn't it be standing?" she asks.

"Hurricanes are pretty common in Galveston. It's been ten years. Who knows whether it's even there anymore, and if it is, what kind of shape it'll be in."

"Yeah, so even if your dad had a cure, this is still a long shot. Understanding my parent's reticence a little more."

"Even if we do get past any WPN guards, and the building's standing, we don't know if the safe still works, and whether or not my blood will open it," I say.

"Where's it hidden?"

"Only my dad and I knew."

Rhonda's perfect eyebrows draw together. "And?"

I should tell her. If something happens to me, if anything goes wrong, she might need to know.

"You're going to be fine," Rhonda says, "but it's better safe than sorry. Especially with the location of the cure for a virus that wiped out almost everyone alive, for instance."

She's right. "It's behind a bookshelf in his home office. It's about three shelves up on the right side, but you won't see it without opening it. Even if you remove the books, it's hidden by the seams of the woodwork in the bookcase."

"Okay."

"It wasn't opened with a key or a combination or anything else. My dad had this Eiffel tower clock mounted on a built-in-desk next to the bookcase. He pricked his finger on it and some little mechanism inside registered his blood. If it was his, a wall safe opened. I asked him once why he'd want something that hard to open. He told me it was only for things so important he was willing to feel pain to keep them safe."

"You think your blood will work?"

"In his journal, Dad wrote, 'She can always find what she needs.' What else could that mean? I must be able to reach the contents of his safe."

"Why'd he tell a six year old, if it was a secret?"

"I saw him open it," I say. "By accident. Some books fell out of the bookcase when a little door opened up behind them, and one fell on my foot." I look at my feet now, so much larger than my little bare feet when the book landed on them.

Rhonda asks, "What was in there?"

She's probably hoping I saw a vial labeled 'the cure' or something, but I couldn't even read great then. "All I saw were papers."

And my mom's wedding ring. Dad told me I could have it when I was old enough. That doesn't seem relevant, so I don't mention it.

"That presents a problem." Rhonda taps her lower lip with her flashlight.

"Why?"

"After you went to bed, we kept brainstorming. We

thought maybe Job and Sam and I could go in, and you could stay with the supplies."

"You planned to leave me waiting, with no idea whether you even made it in alive?"

"It sounds terrible when you say it like that."

I lift one eyebrow. "How did you mean it, then?"

"We'd need our gear to get back home safely."

Rhonda hears how pitiful it sounds once she says it aloud and she winces.

"So I'd be, like, watching the bags?" I raise both eyebrows.

"Now I think about it, maybe you do need to come along."

"Yeah, maybe so."

"What if something happens to you?" she asks.

I raise one eyebrow. "Like what?"

"Anything. You could be injured, or detained." She doesn't say I could die, but that's a possibility too. "We should have a contingency. That's all."

"Like a blood sample?"

"Maybe."

"I don't want to get ditched. I'm not a little kid."

"We really do need someone to watch our stuff. Besides, me and Sam and Job can all offer to join their Marked elimination team if they catch us. You aren't a good enough shot."

"How do you know?" I ask. "Sam gave me a lesson and I did okay."

"He's the one who told me that. Last night."

Something's pushing on my chest and it's hard to breathe. They talked about me last night and Sam said I'm a lousy shot? "Fine, then. I guess you have *almost* everything you need from me."

I pull my sleeping pills out of my bag. I dump them out of their little glass bottle and into my jeans pocket. I've been so afraid to be groggy lately, I haven't used them at all. I pull out my scissors and slice the pad of my thumb before Rhonda can protest, pressing it over the top of the bottle. I squeeze for quite a while before it looks close to full.

"I don't want to be left behind, even if you all think I'm a liability. But if we get separated, I'd hate for the mission to fail." I think about my aunt, and about Wesley. "I doubt you'll need that much, but it would really suck to get there and not have enough." I shove the stopper in, and push the vial into her hand, warm and gross looking.

She takes it and traps my arm while she pulls gauze and tape from her bag. She wraps my thumb tightly without saying a word, then squeezes my hand.

"I'm not sure how long this will be good," she says. "But it should last longer since it's cold outside. We better get moving." I realize I'm blocking her way out.

I catch sight of my face in the mirror. I do look young and innocent like she says—the face of a little girl. It pisses me off.

I step back, but throw one hand out. "I still need that mascara."

"Sure." She hands me her whole bag and walks away.

CHAPTER 18

The guys don't notice my makeup when we emerge, or if they do they don't comment.

Rhonda notices, though. "What's with the Mark on your head? We're past Marked territory."

I walk over to Job, dip my fingers in Rhonda's pot of foundation and dab at his forehead, creating tiny bumps in the right configuration. His eyes widen, but he doesn't stop me. I rub blush over the bumps to turn them pink and then carefully dab with the edge of my damp shirt to wipe off the excess.

"What're you doing?" Sam asks.

I turn to him. "You and Rhonda are next."

"We're headed for WPN," Job says.

"It'll be pretty easy to tell, once we get close, which group we're dealing with. You told me yourself, the Marked travel down here to ask for WPN to marry them. We can always wipe the Mark off if we need to, but we can't put a fake one on once we're spotted. If we run into WPN, we can claim we're here to be married."

Rhonda balks. "We didn't have time to wipe it off with the

WPN patrol. They didn't offer to marry us either. They almost killed us because of it."

"They were idiots," Job says. "The fat one even said that King Solomon would've wanted us brought to him for questioning."

"Besides, we know better this time," Sam says. "If it's WPN, we can wipe immediately."

"Wait, who's King Solomon?" I ask.

"The idiot leader of WPN apparently started going by king sometime in the last few years," Job says. "He did warn the world about Tercera before anyone knew what it was, and he negotiated the government into handing over everything valuable to him. He's sort of their ultimate leader. Maybe it's not an inaccurate title."

I gesture for Rhonda to crouch so I can apply her Mark. "If he's some kind of absolute ruler, why didn't the two WPN guards follow his commands?"

"They were too scared of becoming infected themselves. Apparently they were wicked enough they didn't believe God would protect them." Rhonda shakes her head.

"Do they really think God decides who contracts a virus?" I ask.

"The man who saved them tells them that," Sam says. "You can Mark me next." He steps toward me, but I think about him telling Rhonda I'm a sucky shot. I imagine the two of them laughing at my ineptitude. Sam wanted me to stay and watch the bags while the three of them forged ahead.

I shove the bag at Rhonda and walk away. Let her Mark him. I don't want to be anywhere near him.

They catch up with me before I reach the main road. Sam and Rhonda insist on slogging through the vegetation growing profusely alongside the road to avoid creating footprints WPN patrols might notice.

With my short legs, I warm up pretty fast trying to keep

up with them. Even Sam eventually works up a sweat. He and Job peel their shirts off an hour or so into our brisk hike, but I'm not complaining. It greatly improves my view where I bring up the rear.

After a few hours, Rhonda takes the lead. Sam pulls a shirt on over his head and drops back by me. I wonder why he passes control off to her. It's unlike him.

"You okay?" he asks.

"Sure. And in case you're wondering, I'm not panting, just breathing heavy, which isn't the same."

He smiles. "If you need a break, we can take one."

"I'm good, thanks." I make a concerted effort to leave my lip alone. Rhonda gave me chap stick earlier, so it feels much better. I don't want to backslide.

"We should be about a third of the way there, so that's good news." He hands me some water. "How's the heel?"

"Fine." It annoys me that he walks along so effortlessly, while I practically have to jog to match his speed.

"Now who's uncommunicative?"

"Look," I say, "don't try to talk to me while I'm struggling to keep pace with three giants, okay?"

"We're hardly giants, and we slowed down. You didn't notice?"

"No, probably because slow for you is still fast for me. You're all over six feet. Giants take giant steps."

"Rhonda's not quite six feet, or I don't think so."

"Close enough. I barely top five, which is probably why I'd be so great at watching bags." I'm tired of talking at this point and growing crankier by the minute. My heel's been stinging for over an hour, not that I intend to tell Mr. Amazing, especially since they've already slowed up for me.

"About that," he says. "I wanted to apologize. Rhonda and Job want you safe, just like me, but it's not fair. I know that."

"It's not." I huff.

"Plus, I was being kind of a jerk earlier and I wanted to make sure you weren't mad. We haven't talked about it but —" He tenses up, a deer sensing a hunter.

That's not right. No one would ever characterize Sam as any kind of prey. He's far too eager and much too dangerous. A panther scenting another cat, maybe.

He jogs ahead and taps Rhonda's arm. She and Job stop walking. I notice Job put his shirt back on, too. I stand on my tiptoes to see what lies up ahead. A large road branches off from the one we're walking alongside. Some kind of expressway, judging by the signs.

Job points and shrugs as if to say he isn't sure how much further. Sam holds up five fingers and makes an unintelligible swooping motion. Rhonda taps her arm and points another direction. I give up on trying to interpret. How the flip do they all know some secret hand language?

I walk as quietly as I can to where they are and stand utterly still, waiting for something to be decided. Eventually Sam breaks away from the pow-wow and motions for us to follow. He screws on his silencer as he walks, and Rhonda does the same. I reach under my shirt to pull my gun, but Rhonda shakes her head vehemently. When I pull it out anyway, she walks near me and whispers in my ear.

"We don't want friendly fire, plus you don't have a suppressor. Sam and I have this under control. Get yours out if you see Job draw his. Emergencies only."

They think I might shoot one of them! I pretend that doesn't smart. We leave the road we're on, the Forty-five something, and follow the expressway. The raised road we were walking along disappears from sight and I relax, assuming we're home free.

Until I hear a familiar sound, the whooshing that accompanies shots from a silenced gun. A muffled thud follows, and I turn toward the sound. Someone falls from a nearby tree and his gun slides from his gloved hand when he hits the ground. I whimper involuntarily at the sight. Sam glances sharply my direction, and I make as apologetic a face as I can manage.

Sam scoops up his gun with a gloved hand, releases the clip and throws the gun and clip in opposite directions. I avert my eyes from the fallen man as we jog around him and continue down the road. Sam, Rhonda and Job run even faster now, jumping over tree roots and ducking under branches easily. I scramble and trip and stumble, moving as quickly as I can, but I fall farther and farther behind. Sam looks back intermittently, probably to make sure they don't lose me completely. Within a half mile, I bring up the rear by a fair margin. Sometimes, I lose sight of them entirely.

Which is how I avoid the net that drops from a monstrously tall live oak tree to pin the other three to the ground.

I'm the worst person to have avoided it. Sam would've freed the rest of us in two minutes flat. I pull my gun, aiming at the half dozen people advancing on the drop site, but they're armed too.

The net looks heavy, made of old rope almost as thick as my wrist. It knocks Rhonda, Job, and even Sam to the ground. Sam's gun rests on the ground a few feet from him, on the other side of the net. Rhonda kept hold of hers, but she has the same issue I do. There are too many of them. She still might have been able to do something if she hadn't landed flat on her face. She's struggling to push up on her knees when one of our attackers speaks.

"Weapons down," says a thin man with black hair and an angry red scar crossing his left cheek. He's skinny, like unhealthy, emaciated, and bony. Next to Scar stand two girls, one thin, one thick. The large one, with a reddish complexion, holds a shotgun. The other girl, lank hair drooping down into her face, holds a bow, an arrow notched and pointed at Rhonda.

Rhonda lowers her weapon to the ground and Scar kicks it a few feet away. I'm ten feet from everyone else, far enough to shift my gun until it points at Scar, since he seems to be the leader. I glance at Sam for direction.

He shakes his head tightly. What does that mean? Put it down? Don't? I left Defense before the class on non-verbal communication.

"You might get me blondie, like your buddy got Dax," Scar says, "but my friends'll take you out afterwards. Tweak is awesome with her bow. We'll shoot the rest of you too, just cuz you pissed us off."

It's Rhonda who saves us all.

"We're not the enemy," she says calmly. "Look at us. We're Marked. We didn't mean to hurt any of you. You scared us. We sensed you in the trees and thought you were a WPN attack team."

Scar squints at her and spits at the ground.

As a show of faith, I lower my gun. Sam manages to sit up and nods at me. Apparently, the head shake meant, 'Put your gun down, stupid.'

"You shot Dax. Why'd you do that if you were looking for us?" he asks.

"I didn't kill him," Sam says. "He was in a position of tactical strength. I clipped his shoulder to keep us safe, but he'll be fine. We ran into a WPN patrol earlier, and they were particularly eager to kill us. It made me jumpy."

"How do you know you didn't kill him?" Scar asks.

"I always hit what I aim for, even with a suppressor." As if on cue, a bleeding Dax stumbles up to us, gun outstretched. He apparently found the clip, or wants us to think he did.

"I don't care what you fools say," Dax says, "I'm shooting that one." He aims his gun at Sam's head.

I don't think, I react, jumping in front of Sam, blocking his body with mine. "You can't! I need him."

Scar's eyebrows rise. "You need him? For what?" He narrows his eyes and looks me up and down. "You don't look pregnant."

My jaw drops, and my eyes widen. "I most certainly am not!"

"She ain't even old enough to be pregnant," the beefy looking girl holding a shotgun says.

"I'm plenty capable of having a baby," I say.

Job, Rhonda, and Sam all stare at me, wide-eyed. This entire line of questioning has gotten out of hand.

"Look, I'm not pregnant. None of us—"

"Then what," Beefy asks, "are ya'll doing here?"

We don't know what to say. Do we tell the truth or lie? I scramble for a lie that might earn us forgiveness for shooting Dax. The suppressant's failing for some of them. If Marked kids are getting pregnant . . . and coming here for WPN to marry them . . .

Wesley told me once that if you have to lie, stick as close to the truth as possible. "We all got Marked in the last attack on Port Gibson—thanks for that by the way—and now we're dying just like you, only faster. Since WPN's the only religious group left, and we want a wedding, we heard they would do them down here."

Beefy squints at me, and then glances over to Sam and Job. "Who's gettin hitched?"

I sputter. I can't really say Sam and I are, and I don't want to say Sam and Rhonda are. Before I can respond, Sam says, "We are." He points at me.

I grin ear to ear.

Scar grunts. "Congratulations." He coughs and turns to me. "Are you sure, though?"

"Sure about . . .?"

"Sure you wanna get married? You could try the suppressant. It only starts failing after ten years or so. You could have a decade ahead of you. If you marry that guy, it's one or two good years, tops."

I want to scream. I got my period two years ago! Why does everyone think I'm a kid? I have make-up on! Since he's still holding a gun, and my friends are all trapped under a net, I stay calm. "I can't take the suppressant."

"Fine, marry the meathead. What do I care?"

"No one's marrying him. He shot me!" Dax waves his gun at Sam. "I don't care if he's one of us or not. He has to pay."

Scar shakes his head. "Calm down, Dax. He told the truth. He clipped your shoulder, and that's all. We can't shoot people for defending themselves."

"You have bigger problems anyway," Sam says. "The WPN patrol we ran into told us they're planning to eliminate the Marked population in a few weeks."

Scar raises one eyebrow. "Why would they do that now, after a decade of peace?"

"Let my friends out of the net," I say, "and we'll explain." This is getting ridiculous.

"Don't let them out," Dax says. "Not that one. He needs to pay."

"How about restitution?" I ask. "He'll give you a gun."

Scar growls. "How do you have so many weapons, anyway?"

"The WPN patrol that attacked us dragged us to one of their storage facilities," I say. "After we took them out, we took whatever we wanted."

"How bout you give us *all* them weapons," Beefy says.

"You aren't in charge," Scar says. "And we don't want to leave them defenseless if they're going to petition WPN."

I like Scar.

"But I think they can spare more than one." Scar motions

to Sam. "We'll let you out, but Dax gets a new gun, and so does each one of us."

Sam opens his mouth to argue, but I shake my head this time. He can deal with it. I saw him take several extra guns at the WPN warehouse. I'm not sure how many he has, but it's enough to share.

Dax leans over and picks up the gun Sam dropped when the net hit. "I'll take this one."

"No way," Sam says.

I glare at him. "It's fine, Dax. Go ahead." A raindrop plops on my hand. I glance up. It's overcast, but no downpour yet.

Beefy slings her shotgun around to her back and picks up Rhonda's. "This one'll work nice."

The girl with the dirty hair, I think Scar called her Tweak, picks up my gun and smiles. She's missing two teeth. "I've never had a gun. Does it work like a bow?"

"No stupid, it's way better." Beefy scowls at the skinny girl before turning toward Sam. "You better got another one, cuz you still owe Sean."

"I have another in my bag," Sam says, "but you'll have to release the net, or I can't reach it."

Scar, err, Sean, nods his head. Dax and Sean keep their guns trained on Sam and Job, while the two girls tuck their weapons in their waistbands.

"Does water ruin it?" Tweak asks.

"Does it ruin what?" Sean asks.

"My new gun. I ain't never had one, and it's starting to rain."

Sean snorts.

Sam says, "It won't ruin it, but you'll need to clean it well when you reach cover."

The lank-haired girl and Beefy cut the ties securing the net. Sam leaps free a nanosecond later, and helps Job and Rhonda extricate themselves.

"If you could tell us the quickest route to wherever WPN performs the ceremonies," I say, "we'd appreciate it."

Dax frowns. "I think they only do them on certain days." He glances at Sean. "D'you know when?"

Sean shrugs. "No, but they do them at St. Mary of the Miraculous Medal, I think." He pulls a walkie out of his pocket. "We've got a party here, Marked, looking for a ceremony. Over."

Static. Then a voice, crackly. "St. Mary's. Over."

"I know that," Sean says, "but when? Over."

"They might catch one today. Then not for at least two days. Over."

Sean nods at Sam. "Maybe y'all should hurry. You might get lucky."

"Not much luck for me lately," I say. "Or at least, not the good kind."

"Don't I know it," Sean says. "Marked this week, you said?"

I nod.

"It's a big orange building over on Ninth Avenue by a lotta schools," Beefy says.

Sean nods. "Ya'll got a map?"

"We do, thanks. We'll head that direction."

I glance at Rhonda. Her mascara's running, making her resemble a raccoon, but she's up and moving.

I swear under my breath. More than her mascara's running.

My hand flies to my forehead. It's wet, too. I catch Sam's eye. "Sweetheart, we better hurry. We don't want to miss them, but I don't want to get married sopping wet, either."

"Yeah, let's go."

But it's too late. Something in my voice must've alerted him, or maybe we were always doomed. Sean looks from me to Sam and then toward Rhonda and Job. He grabs his walkie. "They aren't Marked," he says. "I need backup."

Sam pulls two new guns so fast I don't see the motion. We're lucky he's not pinned under a net anymore. "You will let us go, or I'll do more than clip your shoulder."

Rhonda's got a gun in her hand again too, and she's facing off against the two girls.

"Who are you?" Sean asks. "Why are you really here?"

"We're just passing through. We mean you no harm, that's true," Sam says. "Don't make this into something bigger than it is."

"We've doubled our patrols lately," Sean says.

"Cuz we're looking for someone," Beefy says. "Someone that looks like that little girl, there." She spits in the bush next to me and wipes her mouth on her shoulder.

"I'm nobody," I say.

"Nobodies don't say that," Sean says.

There's a rustling in the brush behind us.

Before I can turn to see what the noise is, Sam pushes me behind him and roundhouse kicks a newcomer in the face. Our would-be attacker collapses in a heap, but at least a dozen more appear. Dax, Sean, Beefy and Tweak are aiming our own guns at us.

A tall man with mahogany skin and long black hair, clearly not on hormone suppressants, stands at the front with his handgun pointed at us. Sam holds a gun in each hand, one aimed at the tall black-haired man, the other aimed at Sean. I can barely make out the Mark on the tall man's forehead, but it's there. The Marked have us between a rock and an infected place.

Sam says, "You may get me, but I'll take all of you with me. That's not boasting. It's a fact."

"I believe you," the tall man says. "You look like you know

how to handle yourself, but it's an unnecessary threat. We have no quarrel with you."

I peek out from behind Sam, despite his efforts to push me back.

Sean lowers his gun. He doesn't want to shoot me, I can tell. His voice is plaintive, almost wounded, when he asks, "Why pretend to be Marked?"

"We mean you no harm," the man says to me, taking a step toward us. "In fact, we've been looking for you. You're the Promised. We welcome you."

The Promised? What in the world? They're out of their minds. The Marked must've heard about my dad's journal and somehow twisted that into me having the cure or knowledge of it. Ironically, their interference could prevent me from getting them the real deal.

"I'm sorry," I say, shaking my head. "I'm not the 'Promised' or whatever. I don't have any idea what you're talking about. I really am no one special."

"Oh you're her, all right," the man says. "They've believed for years you'd come if only they were patient. There've been legends about you, but we didn't know who you were exactly until recently. You fit the description perfectly. The boss knows someone who knows you himself, and he told me all about you. Bright blue eyes. Pale, thick, curly blonde hair. Thin. Gorgeous. Besides, who but the Promised would pretend to be Marked? Anyone else would be too afraid to be near us. It's you for sure, and we have our orders. The boss was clear. Bring you to him alive, no matter what. We recently found out your name. Ruby Behl, right?"

I gasp. That can't be right. Who's this boss, or the person he knows? What could he possibly want with me? How does he know me? It has to be related to my dad's work. It's too big a coincidence otherwise, and I don't believe in coincidences. Or prophecies.

"What? Who—" I say.

Although the man speaks to me, he keeps his gun trained on Sam. "Come with us Ruby. Don't resist, and we'll let your friends go. We've got no claim to the rest of you, as long as you don't fight." He gestures at Job, Rhonda and Sam. "We only need the girl."

Before I can protest that they have things all mixed up, a voice rings out, clear and firm. "You're wrong, all of you. She isn't your Promised. I'm Ruby Behl. See for yourself if I don't fit that description better. I'll go with you, if you let my friends go."

Rhonda.

Blonde hair. Thin. Blue eyes. Darker blue than mine, but apparently this boss didn't specify. Undeniably beautiful— much more so than me. With our hair pulled back, who would know Rhonda's hair isn't curly?

Rhonda's gaze slams into me like a ton of stone. "Go," she mouths the words.

I appreciate her sacrifice, but this feels all wrong. She has my blood, so she can access the safe. They were planning to leave me behind anyway, an hour ago.

All I have to do is tell them her hair isn't curly. They already suspect me. Before I can, Sam pulls me against him, my face turned into his shoulder. I push against him, desperate to expose Rhonda as a fraud.

Sam whispers. "They'll Mark you for sure. They're crazy. Rhonda knows what she's doing."

"They said you could leave," I say. "I'm staying."

Sam shakes his head. "We need you in Galveston. Rhonda told me."

Sam shushes me in time for me to see Rhonda walk across the boggy ground toward their leader. Two paces away, she pulls her gun out in one smooth movement. She holds it up and my heart flies to my throat. Who's she shooting?

Sam doesn't shift. He expected this, whatever it is. He pulls me away, but I resist. I need to know what's going on.

Rhonda puts the gun up to her own temple. "You'll let my friends leave now—right now—before you touch me. I won't trust you otherwise, and I'm dead serious that I will put a bullet in my head if you don't free them right now."

"No. No!" I scream, but it's too late.

Sam slings me over his back and runs. Job takes a few beats longer, but catches up to us within a few dozen yards. I watch Rhonda as long as I can, the rain sluicing down her perfect features, her eyes ablaze like a goddess, utterly unafraid. The tall, dark man watches us leave with a pained look, but he doesn't stop us. My thrashing finally stops Sam a few hundred yards away.

He finally puts me down when I almost slip out of his hands. His scowl makes me nervous, but I have questions.

"Why did she do that? Why are we letting her?" The rain falls in sheets, making it hard to see or hear.

"We have to keep moving," Sam says.

Job speaks, his voice dull and despondent. "We had to leave before they thought to detain us. They think you can't be Marked Ruby, which means they think Rhonda can't either. Once they're proven wrong, they'd insist on testing you."

I shake my head and water flies into my eyes. "But why? Dad's journal?"

Sam shrugs. "They're grasping at straws. The suppressant's failing and they're scared."

"We need to go back," I say. "They might shoot her when the Mark appears."

"It would appear on you, just like her." Sam doesn't break stride. "Her only hope now is a cure."

"Or I can go back and tell them I'm Ruby Behl."

The anger in Job's face pulls me up short. "She already sacrificed herself for you, so don't bother pretending to be noble now. It's too late. You're not a heroine and no one expects it."

A slap wouldn't have stung this badly. "I didn't ask her to lie for me. I didn't even want it."

"You could've fooled me," Job says.

Sam's shove sends Job sprawling in the mud. "You're a moron. I carried her off before they decided we were all a bunch of liars and Marked us all. I couldn't have passed for Ruby or I'd have stayed in her place. Ruby wouldn't have thought to threaten to kill herself so the rest of us could escape, but Rhonda's been trained to think that way. Stop acting like a baby and get moving."

When Job stands up, his backside coated with mud, he glares at Sam, but doesn't speak. In ten years, I've never seen them fight. It's my fault, just like everything else.

When Job stands still staring at his hands, Sam gets right in his face. "And if you ever talk to Ruby like that again, whether you're her brother or not, I'll permanently rearrange your face. We clear?"

Job nods, and starts running. The rain falls all around us, churning up mud, but otherwise, washing the world clean. Even Job's back clears off as time passes, but my mind can't be repaired so easily. Job's words haunt me. He knows I'm a useless coward.

All the rain in the world can't wash me clean. My sister willingly stepped into my place to die, and I let her. The raindrops repeat the truth over and over.

Coward. Coward. Coward.

They're right.

CHAPTER 19

We jog until my lungs burn, and then we jog more. On a normal day, I would've stopped. I would've thought I couldn't go another single step. Today I revel in the pain, because I deserve it. Daggers stab me on both sides, and when I try to breathe, I suck in water from the downpour. I cough and splutter and ignore the sharp pains in my sides, the blisters on my heels, and the tears leaking down my cheeks.

At least no one knows I'm crying.

I have no idea how far we run before I trip over a rock and fall. As bad as my wind pains hurt, they're nothing compared to the sharp spikes of pain in the heels of my hands where they make contact with the concrete. Blood paints the ground in streaks behind my palms, and I can't look away. On top of that, I'm not sure when in the downpour the bandage on my finger came off, but the blow to my hand reopened that slice.

Hands wrap around my shoulders and pull me up off the pavement. I'm expecting Sam, so when I look up at Job, my eyes widen.

"I'm sorry." He doesn't meet my eyes, and I pull away immediately.

I wipe my hands on my pants legs and immediately regret it. Pain shoots up my arms and I bite down on an involuntary sob. I force my feet to keep moving, until I hear someone clear his throat. Sam's staring at Job.

"Don't bother, Sam. It's fine." I kick a rock out of the way and press forward.

"Sam's not making me say anything." When I don't turn back toward him, Job grabs my arm. "I really am sorry. I shouldn't have said any of that. You aren't a coward. Rhonda did what she always does, she took the risk on herself. That's not your fault. That's hers."

"No." A tear rolls down my cheek, and I have renewed gratitude for the rain. "You were right, about everything."

"I meant what I said at the time." My heart breaks, but he plows on, oblivious. "But I wasn't mad at you, I was mad at myself. I've always been the smart one, the clever one, but where was that ingenuity when my sisters needed me? Why didn't I come up with a way for you two to escape and me to take your place? I stood there dumbly while they threatened you, and again while Rhonda stepped up. I couldn't save either of you. I just ran."

I look at him blankly, too numb to process his words.

"You're not at fault, Ruby. I'm the failure. I'm sorry for yelling at you, and for lying to myself. I took my shame, my inadequacy, out on you. Please forgive me."

I can't look at Job without remembering hikes in the woods, family dinners, jokes about molecules, the sound of his wheedling voice trying to convince me to do his chores, games we played that I usually lost, and pranks he planned. How could big, brave, smart Job think he's to blame?

I exhale. "I won't forgive you." His face falls, and he stumbles back. "I won't forgive you, because you didn't do anything wrong. We were all upset, and you did what you had to do. You ran so we wouldn't waste Rhonda's sacrifice, same as me."

Job smiles then, and even if it doesn't quite reach his eyes, it's a step. We run more slowly, and eventually that slows to a quick hike. We intended to infiltrate, or if necessary, petition WPN today. I knew they wanted to leave me behind with the gear, but Rhonda's capture set us adrift. No one takes charge, all of us unsure what to do next. The rain never lets up, and it feels like the earth cries around me when my tears finally dry up.

The deluge keeps my eyes down, so when I finally look up, I'm surprised that the bridge to Galveston Island looms a few hundred yards away. I can barely make it out. With all the rain, it's so overcast that nightfall barely registered, but the occasional star twinkles between the clouds.

"We should make camp here. Rest and recover," Job says, "and make a new plan in the morning."

I nod at Job, apathetic. The miserable cold, combined with the squishiness of everything on me, from socks to shoes to pants and even underwear, almost feels like penance. I haven't slept much in the past few days. It's actually odd I don't feel more exhausted than I do. I keep thinking of Rhonda, her blue eyes blazing, charging me to take things from here. It's my duty now to bring her the cure and make her sacrifice worthwhile. I have to believe she's still alive. Sean, at least, didn't seem like an indiscriminate killer.

We halt, facing the bridge to Galveston Island. The edges of the island are visible from where we stand, even through the rainfall. No humans are visible anywhere, although there are some buildings to our right, and a few more that branch out onto a tiny plot of land across a small bridge a few hundred feet before the main one. The one that leads to WPN's island capital.

Job's shaking visibly, whether with cold or sadness I don't know. "I'm going to look for somewhere to escape this rain." When neither Sam nor I protest, he walks off toward the small bridge. He pushes past the first cluster of buildings and drops from sight.

I slump to the ground, waterlogged and dripping head to toe. I pull my brush from my bag, and yank it through the knots in my curls, the ones I should've used to prove Rhonda's statement false. I was too spineless to show them when it mattered. The water from my hair sluices into my collar and runs down my back. I shiver. I've been freezing cold and sopping wet for so long, things have probably gone permanently numb.

I begin shaking uncontrollably, and Sam's arms encircle me from behind. He's so warm, so strong, and so good.

Far too good for me.

He's a better fit for Rhonda, who would be here if it weren't for me. I pull away. I'm a much better match for Wesley, come to think of it. The guy who's so careless he almost Marked me, so selfish he'd risk my life for a kiss. I slump alone in the mud, freezing. Somehow, even though I can't accept comfort from Sam, I feel better knowing he wants to provide it. He saw my weakness, and doesn't despise me for it.

Tears I thought were dried up completely leak down my face again. How he can tell in the rain that I'm crying, I don't know, but he leans toward me and cups my face.

"It's okay," he says. "We're going to get the cure, and Rhonda will be fine. She knew it had to be you, since you're the only one who can reach it. She told me about the journal entry."

I shake my head then, remembering he doesn't know I

gave her my blood. He doesn't understand. That's why he's being so kind. Fear slices me in half, and I dissolve into the mud. I want to let him believe the best of me, but I can't. He needs to know the truth. He needs to see the real me, even if he recoils in disgust.

"I told Rhonda how to reach my dad's safe at the church. It has a blood key, so I gave her a bottle full of my blood while we were there. That's why my finger's bleeding."

He pulls back in confusion. "What?"

"There's a safe in my dad's lab that has a blood key. That's why he said I could reach the cure. It must be in that safe, which is keyed to his blood, and presumably to mine too."

"See?" His eyes soften. "You need to be there. Rhonda did what she had to, to let you get there and open that safe."

"I gave her my blood, Sam. I shouldn't have let her take my place. The Marked knew my name."

"How long would your blood sample last? A day? Two? We have no idea what we'll find inside, or what reception we'll receive from WPN. Besides, what if you're wrong? What if some other little thing you know or remember ends up being important? It had to be you. Rhonda knew it too."

"She's Marked because of me."

"She loves you, Ruby. She wasn't afraid."

"I was. I always am." I hang my head. I'm so ashamed, so completely disgusted with myself.

Sam doesn't argue, but he reaches over and pulls me close.

This time, coward that I am, I let him. "Am I ever going to be brave?"

"You already are," Sam says.

"No, I'm not. I always chicken out."

He pulls back and looks into my eyes, but there's no judgment in his.

"You aren't a coward. Everyone's afraid," he says. "Even me."

"But you still do stuff—scary stuff—and you save people. You fight, always. I'm a total drain." My voice drops to a whisper. "That's why you wanted to leave me behind."

"I didn't want to leave you. I wanted to keep you safe. We're afraid of different things, Ruby. A guy with a gun doesn't scare me because I know how to deal with it."

"What scares you, then?"

Sam snorts. "You're changing the subject."

He's too smart, and it still annoys me. He squeezes me when I shiver.

"You're wallowing right now, and that's okay. It's a natural reaction." Sam shifts me around until I'm looking at him. "You figured out the whole cure thing after reading your murdered dad's journals. That took guts. I also watched as you calmed down all those kids the night of the Marked attack." He smiles. "And you caught that rabbit."

"The one I couldn't kill?"

Sam shrugs. "I said you're brave, not bloodthirsty. There's a difference. But even before that, you kept me from killing the Marked kids with your gunpowder idea. You distracted the WPN guys in the grocery store so I could save Rhonda and Job. You made us Mark ourselves this morning, which saved us today from death under a net. You've done a lot more than you give yourself credit for."

"I've done way more wrong than right."

"Stop." Sam touches my jaw with his hand. His eyes are full of compassion I don't deserve.

"I saw it." I blurt it out, because I can't keep my secret inside a moment longer. "I saw a man shoot my dad. A man with brown hair and freckles on his nose. Blue eyes, and a strong jaw. He talked to my dad first, talking and talking. Then yelling, so much yelling. My dad wouldn't listen to him, so he shot him, and I was there. I saw it all with a phone in my hand. I was too scared to call 911 because the buttons made a tiny beeping sound." I shudder. "I was too scared to save my dad's life."

Sam doesn't speak at first. He turns my face back toward him gently but firmly, whenever I try to look away. "You were only five." His brow furrows.

"Almost six. Old enough to know." I look down. "I don't deserve Rhonda's sacrifice."

He pulls me closer and jounces me until I meet his eyes. "No one blames you. Your dad's proud of you, wherever he is, probably up in heaven if it exists."

The rain continues to fall, its soft pattering the only sound I hear.

When Sam speaks again, it startles me. "You think you're worthless, so you act like someone worth nothing. You run and hide from scary things." He pauses, but before I can contradict him, he says, "The worst part is that when you run, you miss the good stuff."

"I don't run." I shake my head. "You're wrong."

"I'm not," Sam says. "Your dad knew you were hiding, right? When he got shot?"

"Yes." I can barely breathe.

"He knew, and he died protecting you. He didn't yell your name or ask you to make a call."

"I guess."

Sam's hand draws lazy circles on my back. "He sacrificed himself to keep you hidden and safe. Don't dishonor his actions by blaming yourself. You're only a coward if you keep shutting out the people who love you because of a tragedy a decade ago."

"What do you know about it?"

"A lot, actually."

"Like what?"

"My mom left my dad," he says. "I mentioned that before, but I didn't tell you what it did to him."

I realize something about Sam. "Not just your dad. Her leaving did something to you too."

He nods. "I guess so. I shut people out like he does. That's why I left him, because he never loved me or anyone else, not since Mom. I don't want to follow his example."

"You won't." I think about Rhonda saying they had a conversation and my stomach ties in knots. Is that why he shut her out? Is he realizing now how big a mistake that was?

"I moved to Port Gibson for a reason, Ruby. You asked before."

He looks at me expectantly, but I can't handle hearing about Rhonda, not today. I tell myself it's because I don't want to be to blame for his separation from her, but I'm not even sure I buy that.

I change the subject, instead. "What I don't get, what makes zero sense, is why the Marked knew my name. I'm sure Aunt Anne wouldn't send them looking for me, and she didn't go to join them anyway. She and my Uncle are probably around here somewhere, right? Plus they said 'he' when referring to the guy who told their boss about me, right?"

I look up at Sam, expecting his face to reflect my baffled astonishment.

It doesn't.

He didn't seem surprised when they knew my name earlier today, either. I narrow my eyes and pull away. "Why weren't you surprised?"

He doesn't answer.

"Tell me, Sam." I push away from him completely. I might be afraid of things, good and bad, but I'm standing alone now, and I want answers. "What do you know? What aren't you telling me?"

"It's complicated," he says.

"What is? Why are you lying to me?"

"I haven't lied." He leaps to his feet in a dizzying blur. "I've never, ever lied to you. I wouldn't, I swear. I never lie, especially not to you."

"Keeping things from me *is* a lie." I bite down hard on my lip. Lately, every time someone keeps something from me, it comes back around to smack me in the face. Wesley, my aunt, my dad. I brace myself. What new horror is about to jump from behind a wall and slam me to the ground now?

"Look, it's just that, the night of the attack . . ."

"The night my aunt got Marked, you mean? The night you didn't tell me about it until after she left? That night?"

"I didn't even see you until after they left, but yes, that night." He growls and runs a hand through his hair, pulling the rubber band out. His hair falls, wet and stringy all around his face. His sculpted features are even more achingly beautiful in the rain, and his eyes shine like twin flames, more gold than green in the moonlight.

"They were looking for you that night, all the Marked kids. That's why your uncle made me promise to keep you safe. He knew they'd come back for you." He looks away, clenches his fists, and looks at me again. I can barely make out his next words. "I did lie, I guess. I told you I didn't see anyone you knew, but I saw him that night, briefly."

"Who? My uncle? Tell me he's not Marked, too. I can't handle anyone else—"

"No, not your uncle. Him. Your freaking boyfriend, Wesley. The Marked's precious new *boss,* or maybe his best friend, I don't know."

"Wesley?" I ask, incredulous. "He can't be the boss. He's been Marked for like a week!"

"I know it seems unlikely, but it's true nonetheless. He led the attack. Your aunt got Marked because he sent people after her specifically. He was desperate to find you, and he was raving."

"How do you know all that?"

"Because I almost shot the little jerk, okay? I saw him just after some skinny little spaz Marked your aunt. He came alone, after the initial attack, and we captured him. I have no idea how he escaped. He had a lot to atone for, but someone freed him while we were out dealing with fallout from the attack."

"Why would he return? You said he asked for me?"

"He came to reason with your aunt, who wasn't handling being Marked very well. He kept saying that all they needed was you."

"It makes no sense."

"He said some ludicrous crap, Ruby. That they couldn't survive without you."

"That, I mean, look . . ."

"He gave me this for you." Sam holds out a scrap of paper.

I spread it out in the rain, but I can barely read the soggy words.

Ruby—

We need to talk. Our kiss changed everything. You could feel it too, I'm sure of it. You didn't meet me like you said and I need you now, desperately. Turn yourself in to the Marked and I'll guarantee your safety. I'm important with them. Trust me, and I won't let you down, not again.

Truly,

Wesley

I read it twice to be sure I didn't misunderstand anything.

"You've had this for days, Sam. Why not show me earlier?"

Sam stands like carved rock, rain dripping over his perfect features, but not touching him, not moving him.

"Tell me!"

"Why? So you can run back to him? To that spoiled brat who almost *Marked* you?" Sam clenches his fists.

"No, you idiot. Because I could've talked to the Marked and found out what they wanted. We'd know why they're searching for me, why they're attacking the Unmarked to find me. Who knows how many other people have been Marked, all because I didn't know they wanted me!"

"You can't talk to them or turn yourself over to them! Your uncle saw that and everyone else on the Council agreed. It's not like they're going to be reasonable, or rational! They think you're some Promised One! It's ridiculous, Ruby. He's convinced them all that you're the panacea, that you'll save them all, just so they'll bring you to him."

"It's not their decision to make, and it's not yours either. I'm not a little girl anymore. I could've talked to Wesley, at least. He wouldn't hurt me, Sam. I know he wouldn't."

Sam grabs my arms and pulls me against him. "I know what he wants. Why don't you?"

I shake my head and water drips into my eyes. I blink it out.

"He wants you. He gets Marked, and what does he do?"

I stare at him blankly.

"He knowingly goes to the Last Supper and tries Marking you. When that doesn't work, he rallies his new troops and comes after you. He thinks you're his, and he's used to getting whatever he wants. He wants you so badly that he doesn't care what happens to you or anyone else as long as he gets you back."

"That's ridiculous." I try to pull away, but he won't release my arms. "Sam, it's absurd."

"Did you read his note?"

"That's not what it says."

"Fine," Sam says. "I know, because it's what I'd want. It's what I'd want to do if I were him. That's why I hate that little jerk. He wants what I want, and I get it. You don't want to hear this, but you're going to. I moved here because I wanted you to notice me. You never did when we were younger, but it didn't stop me from trying. The difference between us is that he's willing to hurt you, and that I can't forgive."

His words turn the world inside out. Sure, we've been flirting lately, and I think we almost kissed, but Sam *moved back* for me? My jaw drops.

"How could you not know?" he asks. "When I moved to Port Gibson, I came over every day for weeks."

"I never saw you."

"You were always gone with him. You spent all your free time on projects with Wesley. I even signed up for a few, but you didn't notice I was there. You only had eyes for him."

Sam's emerald eyes bore into me, glints of gold burning me up. I was freezing a minute before, but heat floods my body. I want to reach for him, but I can't. We stand like that, staring at each other, for a long moment. Then two.

I shake my head. "You never talked to me, and you never came over when I was even home. I had no idea how you felt. You barely spoke to me, and when you came back, you were different. A man who had won every award the Unmarked offered, girls swooning at you from every angle. I didn't know what to say to you."

"You know me now." Sam pulls me against him, and this time his head lowers to mine without interruption of any kind. He crushes my mouth with his. I'm dry wood drenched in gasoline and he's the spark. The flames reach the stars, impervious to the rain and the cold. I lean into him, pressing against him while his hand moves from my back up to my hair. His fingers cup the base of my scalp. He lifts me off the ground with his other arm, and I want to fly like this all night.

He breaks the contact between us too soon and collapses

cross-legged in a large puddle. I sway, standing alone. In that moment, I miss something I hadn't even known existed. My heart slams against my chest. My fingers long to wrap around his neck.

He reaches up with one hand and takes mine. He tugs until I let him pull me down next to him. I try to kiss him again, but he shakes his head.

"Why not?" I ask, feeling a little broken. I want to forget everything again.

"Ruby," he rasps.

I shiver.

"What?" I tug his head back down toward my face.

"No." He wipes water from my lips and caresses my cheek. "We need to talk. We have too much to discuss, and too much to do."

"I don't want to talk."

"Job will be back any minute," Sam says. "I don't even know how you feel."

I let the rain wash over me and think about my feelings. I like Sam. He's smart, capable, caring. He's almost hotter than my eyes can handle. But he's a little too authoritarian. He always thinks he knows what's best for me, and sometimes tries to make decisions without talking to me first. He keeps things from me.

"I don't know how I feel," I say. "Frankly, I'm tired of people treating me like a child, and maybe a little sick of feeling anything at all. I've felt too much lately."

"I've put all my cards on the table. You have this boyfriend, the leader of the Marked, and he's got a whole army following us. Rhonda says you guys are getting married, and I don't know what to think."

Rhonda. Who likes Sam, and sacrificed her life for me.

I shove another foot away from him and wind up in a mud puddle. "Why does everyone call him my boyfriend?

He's my friend. I had a crush on him for a while and we kissed, disastrously, one time. That's it. I like you Sam, in case you hadn't noticed, but I don't always like the decisions you make."

He frowns. "What does that mean?"

"You're smart. You're funny. You're prettier than anyone deserves to be. You—"

Sam coughs and his eyes bulge. "I'm pretty?"

"Fine, you're hot. Is that better? You're hotter than anyone should be, and I feel safe with you. I like all of that. What I don't like is how you make decisions without me *that concern me.* So, yeah, I don't know how I feel right now."

"But you think I'm hot?" Sam grins.

I roll my eyes.

"It's a start," Sam says. "I've liked you for ten years, and you finally know. And you think *you're* a coward."

"Are you saying you've liked me since we were kids?"

"Well, not in the same way." He grins. "But yeah. Do you remember when we first met?"

"No." I try to remember, but it feels like I've always known Sam. We didn't meet on a certain day, nothing so tangible as that. He was just there at the beginning, and he'll be there at the end.

"My dad's best friends with your uncle." His hand reaches across the distance between us and holds his palm out to me. Sam would never hurt me. I know that.

I take his hand.

"My dad knew your dad, too. They worked together at some point. My dad took me out to Nebraska when your dad died. That's the first time I remember seeing you, and you were the most beautiful thing I'd ever seen. But sad, like you thought the sun was gone forever. I've wanted to bring it back ever since."

I don't remember much about those first weeks. "I'm sorry," I say, "I—"

"It's okay." He brushes my hair back from my eyes. The rain has slacked off, so it's no longer pelting us. Of course, maybe that's because Sam slid closer, and his body's shielding me. "I don't expect you to remember, but I recall the very moment I knew I liked you more than anyone else I'd met. You'd just found a tiny, wounded bird."

The bird I remember. "I'll never forget that evil cat."

"You were such a little thing," he says, "always. That cat was enormous. It caught a sparrow and was playing with it."

I shudder. I'd grabbed a stick and hit the big, shrieking, hissing cat, swinging the stick at it until it ran away. I'd taken the bird to my aunt, desperate to save it. I hadn't saved my dad, but I could save that bird. I had to save it.

And I did. Well, my aunt did anyway.

"You fought that cat off and sat by that bird for days. Weeks, maybe. You fed it worms and bugs you dug around in the dirt to find."

Then it comes to me, and I remember Sam too.

"You were there," I say. "You brought me oatmeal."

"I told you to eat, and you protested. You told me you were fine."

"You threatened me. If I didn't eat my breakfast, you'd bring me worms next. You'd force feed me like a baby bird if you had to."

"I said that, yes." He chuckles. "You were so stubborn. And too thin, even then."

He squeezes my hand. "That's when I knew I needed you. I've never doubted. It's also how I know you aren't a coward. You've always been courageous."

"For shooing off a cat?" I arch one eyebrow. "I wasn't that small."

"Ha," Sam says. "It wasn't that part that impressed me. It

was that you took a chance on that bird, knowing it might die. You stared death in the face and said 'Screw you. You can't take anyone else.'" Sam squeezes me. "I wish you saw what I see. Nothing would stop you then."

I look up at Sam, at his gorgeous eyes, his chiseled jaw, and beyond it to the strength inside. If he'd shown me how he felt back then, I might never have noticed Wesley existed. "Why didn't you ever talk to me?"

Sam looks sheepish. "I wanted to, but I didn't have much to say. You were always playing the piano. Dancing. Painting. Reading. Studying. I didn't know how to talk to you. I didn't have anything to offer. I'm not a science prodigy. I'm not creative or genius smart."

Neither am I, but I don't want to fight about it. "So you ignored me instead?" I ask.

"No." He shrugs. "I hung out with Job. We had nothing in common either, but that doesn't matter much to guys."

"I always wondered why you two were so close."

"Being Job's best friend meant I had a reason to be near you."

As if on cue, Job's head appears across the street. I really hope he found us someplace dry, because I'm sick of being wet, and I don't need the rain anymore. I'm done with crying for a long time.

CHAPTER 20

We have plenty of time to move further apart while Job walks up the road to where we are, but neither of us moves. I lean against Sam's chest, my hand caught in his. Job's eyes widen, but he only says, "I found a place."

When I stand up to follow him, the wind cuts through me like an iced arrow. I start shivering and can't seem to stop. A cold front came in while we escaped in the rain, and even with my jacket on, I've forgotten the meaning of warm. Job leads us across the small bridge and past several roads before turning down a street. He motions for us to follow him into a sagging yellow house. Two shutters have fallen off, and another hangs at an angle. Bird nests line the porch over-hang, and the steps sway when I climb them.

I hesitate in the doorway, eying Job nervously.

"It's clear," he says. "A lot of these homes were vacation homes, so no one died inside."

Sadly, this house is in the best shape of any on the small street. Too many storms hit the coast for buildings to fare well without regular upkeep and repairs. The humid, salty air destroys what the storms don't. We follow Job through the doorway and around a corner to the kitchen. It isn't much warmer inside.

"I found some food that isn't rancid or spoiled. I figure we should conserve as much of the food in our packs for the trip home as we can."

He points. Several open cans sit on the table in front of mismatched seats.

"Where'd you put the bad ones?" I ask.

He points to a pile in the corner of bulging and warped cans, all unopened. "What about the ones that surprised you?"

He points to a window that's still open a crack. Better outside than in. We all learned a few things in the years after the Marking. One was how to spot cans that have gone bad. The bulging cans are obvious, but sometimes they look okay, and foam, or bubble or outright smell foul once opened. Extremes of heat and cold are the biggest cause of canned good spoilage, but time's a worthy enemy, too. Usually by now, in relatively temperate climates, one in five cans has survived.

I take the smallest chair, not much more than a stool. It doesn't look like it could bear Sam's weight or even Job's. I squash a spider egg sack and sit down. The boys find seats on either side of me. Sam takes the wooden kitchen chair, displacing a lizard in the process, and Job sinks down on an ottoman, moved into the kitchen by way of the family room I assume. I peer into my can. Pork and beans. Gross.

I must have curled my lip because Sam holds his can out to me. "Trade? I'll eat anything."

I glance at his can. Chunks of chicken swimming in meat juice. Even worse. I shake my head. "No, thanks."

"I've got vegetable barley soup if you'd prefer that." Job's eyes still look sad, but only kindness is directed at me.

"Thanks."

Job trades our cans with a small smile. "There's more," Job says, "but I grabbed the best ones first. I only had to toss three out the window, but the rain's strong enough no one will notice."

I eat the soup and then scope out the remaining cans. Tomato sauce. Black beans. Green beans. Peaches. More canned chicken. Job did pick the best first. I crack the peaches, but tiny bubbles rise up through the juice. Bacteria. I'm not brave enough, or enticed enough by the options, to keep trying.

Sam pulls jerky from his bag and shares it around. Job, undaunted, tries the remaining cans and finds two more good ones. "We have another can of chicken and a can of clam chowder. Any takers?"

I shake my head.

"I'll take them both." Sam slurps the chicken juice first, pours clam chowder over the remaining chicken and wolfs it all down.

Some of my disgust must show on my face.

"What? It takes a lot of fuel to maintain all this." He flexes his pecs.

I've never seen Sam flex before. I guess I've never seen him flirt before, either. It's weird, but good weird. I grin. "I appreciate your sacrifice."

Job looks from Sam to me, and back again, understanding dawning. "What's going on?"

Sam shrugs. "I like your sister. I have for a while, actually. She's trying to decide whether she likes me back."

If I expected a big reaction from Job, I'd have been disappointed. His eyes widen again, but after a moment, he simply scratches his head. "Maybe I missed something. What happened to Wesley?"

Sam growls.

Job turns his hands palms out. "Okay, sure. She could do

worse."

"We're good?" Sam asks.

"As long as you treat her well."

"Great." Sam pulls out more jerky and tosses some to Job, not unlike tossing a treat to a dog for good behavior. I wonder if he'd have whapped Job on the nose if he'd freaked out. The image makes me snort-laugh.

Sam raises one eyebrow at me. "Let's talk about tomorrow."

"Not much to talk about. At first light, we cross the bridge and tell them we want to join," Job says.

"You and me," Sam says. "Ruby stays."

When I shoot up off my chair, it sways precariously. "No way. You were just saying the reason Rh—" I stop, suddenly unable to say her name. "You were telling me that I needed to go, that you needed me to be there to find the cure."

"Maybe we do," Sam says, "but we can go scope out the situation first, and make sure it's safe. It's a recon mission, and we don't need you for that."

"You'll tell me to come in how, exactly? Smoke signal?"

"That's what I wanted to talk about."

"No," I say. "Absolutely not. Only I can get into that safe."

Job looks confused. I fill him in.

"That's why Rhonda stayed behind," Job says. "I wondered, but it makes sense. Rhonda's always been a pragmatist."

I look down at the table.

The boys hash out a plan. We'll scope things out, search for a boat, and take it around the northeast side of the island, looking for the Palisade Palms. If we're caught, we pledge our service to WPN.

"I'm going to look for some buckets to catch rainwater," Sam says. "Our canteens are almost empty. I've got treatment tablets, but I'd rather treat rainwater than puddle water."

Job says, "I searched for a boat today without luck, but tomorrow we can look a little further from the bridge. It'll all go much easier if there is a boat close by." Job leaves with Sam. I'm cold, so I stay put.

I think about our plan. It's not so great. We don't know if my uncle has reached WPN yet. We don't know what WPN knows about me, or about the cure. I'd like to think they know nothing, but somehow the Marked are out looking for me. It could be that Wesley's desperate to find me like Sam thinks, but that feels wrong somehow. I've known Wesley for years. He's never been controlling or manipulative. If I'd gotten that note sooner, I'd have gone to see him. I'm still a little pissed Sam kept it from me.

But also, I get a little flutter in my belly when I think about him being jealous. Basically, I don't know what I think about any of that.

Whatever I feel for Sam, I want to keep him safe, and I love Job like a brother. Fear grips my belly and familiar ice floods my veins. Fear controls my life and I'm sick of it. If I'd simply called the police years ago, I could've saved my dad, and probably the whole world. If I'd read his journals sooner, instead of wallowing in guilt, I'd have insisted we do something to retrieve the cure. If I'd refuted Rhonda earlier today, I'd be facing the people who want me, including Wesley, instead of leaving my sister in my place. Each time, fear controlled my actions.

Never again.

In a moment of perfect clarity, I recognize that Sam and Job got me here, and they're undeniably stronger, faster and more dangerous than me. But that might be exactly what we don't need. WPN's dangerous. Its population is armed to the teeth, and evil enough to plan the massacre of a bunch of kids who are already dying.

I might have a better chance of getting the cure without Sam and Job along.

The biggest problem is that I'm not sure how to get to the Palisade Palms precisely. I mean, I know where it is geographically, at least as well as any five year old could on an island the size of Galveston. I'm confident I'll recognize the building if it hasn't collapsed or been destroyed by a storm, but I have no idea where it is in relation to WPN's power structure.

I do have an idea about how to get in, but my plan won't work for Job and Sam. I have something no one else has—a skill set that has nothing to do with my blood or my family. It's all me. I have experience in Sanitation, a job no one wants, a work choice that disappointed my family so thoroughly.

What's the one job that goes everywhere? Janitorial. Everything gets cleaned. I spent the last eight months in Sanitation back home, so I know everything there is to know about disinfecting, boiling, cleaning, sanitizing, polishing and removing stains and filth.

Surely WPN could use another person willing to do manual labor. Once they confirm I'm not Marked they'll let me in. And I'll get to the Palisade Palms, one way or another. The boys will never agree to send me in alone, but I've worked out the rudiments of a plan by the time they return. They find me rummaging in the pantry.

"Any luck finding a boat?" I ask.

Job shakes his head. "We weren't even really looking. We did find buckets to collect rain."

"Still hungry?" Sam asks. "I found more food."

"Not really," I say, emerging triumphant. "I wanted something special, and I found it." I pull out a plastic container, and shake the lumpy, bumpy contents. "Sugar lasts forever!"

Job rolls his eyes. "You and your tea."

"It's been a bad day. Mint tea helps me sleep, and it'll help you too. We all need good rest before tomorrow." I lean over and pull out my dried herbs, hoping I brought mint. I did, thank heavens.

"You have a plan to heat that, sunshine?" Sam asks. "Because otherwise, no offense, it's going to be gross no matter how much sugar you add."

"Says the guy who ate cold chicken chunks swimming in congealed clam chowder."

Job chuckles. "I kind of like you guys together."

Sam's grin splits his face from ear to ear.

"I have a can of Sterno and a little rack for it. Hang on." Job pulls out a tiny can from his bag and holds it out to Sam. He pulls it back when Sam reaches for it. "I'll even let you use it if you promise to refrain from calling my sister pet names around me from now on."

"I've called her sunshine for years in my head." Sam keeps grinning and then, fast as lighting, snatches the fuel out of Job's hand. "How's this for a counteroffer. I keep using 'sunshine,' and you realize it doesn't bother you after all."

"Fine, but no putting your tongue in her mouth." Job pretends to gag.

Sam lifts his eyebrows. "I think bargaining with her brother about what I can do and say sets a bad precedent. Ruby?"

I roll my eyes. "You two are absurd." They both stare at me as I rinse three of the empty cans out and fill them with water from one of Sam's canteens. Sam lights the little heater and I set one can on the rack over it, and dump the water and tea leaves in.

Sam watches a moment longer before turning toward the doorway. "I'm going to look for a decent place to sleep. Dry bedding, maybe some dry clothes."

Job says, "I'll come. No way are you making some little love nest and sticking me in another room."

I'm relieved they're leaving, but I don't want them to know that. "Well hurry. This won't take too long and I don't want the fire to burn out and the tea to get cold."

I fill two of the other cans a third of the way with water and drop a sleeping pill into each can. The pills are a little gooey from my wet pocket, but mostly intact. With any luck, they'll dissolve fast. I add a second to Sam's for good measure. He's pretty big. One knocks me out, but I probably weigh less than half what he does. I stir as vigorously as I can without spilling the water. I agonize while the tea leaves steep. I stir in the sugar and heat each can for a bit to dissolve it. When it's ready, I pour some of the water off into each of the other cans, and then reach into mine to pull out the soggy leaves before dividing the infused water. I finish seconds before I hear boot steps on the stairs.

"No way," Job says.

"Look, it makes sense. Ask her yourself. The only safe room is the family room, and she's gonna want to sleep next to me because it's cold, and she'll be warmer than if she's sleeping alone." Sam winks.

I hope he isn't kidding. That night in the truck was the best sleep I've gotten lately.

"I do want to sleep by him." Even if it makes it harder to sneak away. The thought of a few minutes, or even an hour with him before I walk like a sacrificial lamb to the WPN compound sounds heavenly.

"Fine," Job sighs heavily. "But don't forget I'm four feet away. Ridiculous, both of you."

I hand Job a can.

"Drink up, and calm down," I say. "We need to get some sleep."

Job fumes. "She's still sixteen, Sam. Don't forget that."

Wait, what day is it? I mentally count.

"Actually," I say, "I'm seventeen tomorrow."

"Fan-freaking-tastic," Job mutters.

"Oh, relax," Sam says.

I hand him one of the other cans. Sam sits down on his chair next to me.

"My intentions are completely honorable." He leans over and whispers, "Happy Birthday, Ruby, a few hours early."

Job sips his mint tea and pulls a face. "This tastes strange."

No, no, no. They need to drink it. If I can't get the sleeping pills in them, I'll never sneak out without waking them up.

"Too delicate for your girly constitution?" Sam smiles mockingly, but when he takes a swallow, he gags a little. "It's got a real kick to it." He turns to me. "How's yours? Are we sure the sugar didn't spoil? It's kind of bitter."

"Sugar doesn't spoil." I sip mine, which tastes fine. That means it's definitely the sleeping pills. I need another scape-goat. I make a face, too, and drink a little more anyway. "Maybe I didn't rinse the cans well enough, but I was trying to conserve water. Mine tastes a little like chicken."

Job drinks more. "At least it's warm. I think you're right though, I can taste the chowder, which does not mix well with mint."

Sam shrugs. "It's not awful, just a little bitter."

Thank goodness. They drink slowly, but they both finish.

"Bedtime?" Sam asks, and my heart spins in a circle.

"Sure."

"I think there may be some clothes you can change into upstairs," Sam says. "In the bedroom at the top left. If you hear a sound, it's a family of squirrels. Don't worry though, they're in the wall by the window. I think the dresser and closet are fine."

I grab my flashlight, a water bottle, and my toiletry bag.

I'm delighted to find a veritable treasure trove upstairs, untouched by squirrels. A very girly girl lived here Before, and I droop a little, thinking that she must've died. I yank off my wet clothes, pulling and shimmying where they cling to me, trying not to let any of it rub on my abused palms or sliced finger. My skin pebbles in the cold air as I struggle with the holster. I consider calling Sam up to help me remove it, but I think of Job's never-ending whining and reconsider. I dry off with a musty smelling towel and slide into dry underwear that actually fits.

Clean underwear feels divine after walking in soggy panties for an entire day. I even find a pink lacy bra. Thankfully my benefactress and I wear about the same size. She doesn't seem happy to be our size though, because it's a padded, push-up bra. It lifts my very modest chest up more than I would have thought possible. I tug a shirt on over everything else and turn to look at myself in a cracked full-length mirror that hangs askew on the wall. With the help of my flashlight, I understand why she picked a push-up bra. Her scoop cut shirt looks awful, but I think of one positive side benefit.

No one in the world will suggest I take the suppressant if I'm wearing this.

I look nothing like myself. It's like Rhonda's staring back at me in the mirror, which I thought I'd like, but today it depresses me. I rummage around for another shirt, but they're all the same, absurdly low cut. While I appreciate the dry underwear, my clothing cannot dry fast enough.

I zip a windbreaker up over the shirt, and try on some jeans. Despite her taste in tops, her jeans are amazing. I towel off my hair with a hand towel from the bathroom in the hall. I put on some floral scented deodorant that only smells a little off, brush my teeth with the last of the water in my canteen, and reapply the mascara Rhonda gave me. I find some gel in the same bathroom and run some through my hair. It stings on my cuts a bit, but it still smells like peaches and cream, so I figure it's worth it. I'm a new person. I take a handful of the toiletries down with me to stuff them in my bag.

By the time I clomp into the family room, a fire roars in the fireplace. "Aren't we worried about smoke this close to WPN?"

"Not in this rain," Job says. "We need something to help dry out these clothes and keep us from freezing in here. We won't add any logs to it, so enjoy it while it lasts."

The boys pull both sofas and some chairs over near the fire, and then drape their wet clothes over the kitchen chairs to dry. I cross the room and put my clothes over the chairs too, finding open spaces where I can. I put my underwear on the far side where it's less obvious. I notice the boys' underwear on the ottoman and turn back quickly, curious what they're wearing underneath the blankets wrapped around them.

"Hey, you guys aren't naked, are you?"

"Wouldn't you like to know?" Sam raises one eyebrow.

"Eww." Job glares at Sam and drops his blanket. Sam follows suit. Apparently, there was a male occupant of the home as well. My benefactress was the perfect size for me, but Sam and Job didn't fare as well. The man of the house was quite small. The pants Sam and Job wear hit them at the knee, and the ankle respectively.

I can't help laughing. "You two look ridiculous."

Sam crosses the room in a flash and picks me up, tossing me up in the air and catching me. "Ridiculous, huh? Why are you wearing a coat in front of a blazing fire?"

He reaches down and tugs it up and over my head in one smooth motion.

"Wow," Job says. "Everyone's clothes are too small."

Sam stares at me, and *not* at my face.

"Eyes up, compadre," Job says. "And let's put that jacket back on."

Sam's gaze flies up to my face, and he blushes. My big, brawny Sam blushes.

"Yeah, good call," Sam mumbles. "Sorry."

I pull the windbreaker back over my head and Sam leans over and says, "You better not wear that to WPN tomorrow."

"Wouldn't dream of it." I lean against him, tucking my head under his chin. I'm still mad at him for not telling me about Wesley, but this feels divine.

"You may be tiny, but we fit together perfectly," Sam says.

I sigh by way of response.

Job groans. "Ugh, this is weird. I'm going to turn this way." He lies down on his sofa and turns in toward the cushions. "But," he calls over his shoulder, "that doesn't mean I can't hear you. Don't forget that I can't un-hear things. Don't. Maul. My. Ears."

Sam winks at me and leans back on the sofa, pulling me down against him and stretching out. It's a full-length sofa, but it wasn't made for someone like Sam. He turns sideways and bends his knees to avoid falling off and brings me even closer, his front to my back. Deja vu. Not long ago, we slept like this in a truck. My world had recently changed drastically, and now it's changed yet again. Mostly for the worse, but in this one thing, better too.

He whispers in my ear, and shivers shoot through me head to toe. "We have all the time in the world. For now, sleep. I'm here, and you're safe. I'll always take care of you."

Just for a moment. I'll let him hold me for a moment until he falls asleep. When his breathing evens out, I'll slip away. It's a good plan. Except that I'm so tired, I fall asleep too.

Thankfully, I wake with a start sometime in the middle of the night. Sam's smooth breathing and steady heartbeat make it hard to pull away. Job's soft snores a few feet over reassure me that he's asleep, too. Now's the time.

I shift, moving Sam's arm so I can escape.

Sam stirs behind me and whispers, "You okay, sunshine?"

I shiver. This still feels unreal, and I have the strongest desire to curl back up and go to sleep next to him. "Yes, I'm fine. Sleep." He nuzzles the back of my neck and shifts. I wait in agony for his breathing to even out again. Minutes drag, but after what feels like an hour, he finally sleeps again. This time when I move his arm, he doesn't wake.

I quietly gather my damp clothing and stuff it in my bag. I found some paper and a pen while riffling through the upstairs room. I scribble a note, messy because pressing down on the paper hurts my scraped palms. I leave it on the kitchen table.

Boys-

Don't be upset. I realized something last night. I can go where you can't. I have experience in Sanitation, and cleaning crews go everywhere. You wanted to leave me, but I'm the only one who really needs to be at risk. I'll get the cure and meet you back here.

Stay here. Be safe. Wait for me.

In case you want to ignore me, don't. I'm doing this to keep you safe, so please honor my wishes. I know you won't want to listen so I'm telling WPN that I'm running from two guys I saw shoot some men in League City. I'm giving them your descriptions. If you follow me, they'll shoot you on sight.

Stay put. For once, it's my task to complete.

Ruby

I'd never actually tell WPN anything of the sort, but it would defeat the whole purpose of my leaving them if they follow. They have to believe they can't come after me. They'll hate sitting around, but it's what's best for everyone. WPN would never suspect a little girl of trying to steal information. Heck, maybe I'll get in and realize they're as desperate for a cure as everyone else. Maybe this King Solomon's reasonable after all. Maybe I can tell him what's going on and he'll walk me over to the lab himself.

I can't count on that, though. I always assume the worst and hope to be surprised. I rarely am.

I sneak out the front door, walk down the street and move quietly toward the bridge from the mainland to the island. The moon overhead lights my way. I expect guards on the bridge, but for the first mile or so, it's completely empty, devoid of sound, activity, and life.

What a birthday. I'm running away from everything I love into the unknown, but at least I'm not sitting at home, alone and scared. I notice the first lamppost has a sign on it. The light from the post allows me to read the words. "Warning," is printed in large block letters. "Intruders will be shot without exception." I look up ahead to a brightly lit guard-house fifty yards or so in front of me.

I ignore the sign. It's probably meant to scare away Marked kids or other threats. Surely the guard won't perceive a lone girl approaching on foot as a major concern. About ten feet further, an identical sign is posted. Fifteen feet further along there's a third. The hairs on the back of my neck stand up and my stomach sours. I can't help anyone if I die alone on a bridge. I'm only twenty yards from the little guard hut. Surely he'll see I'm unmarked, alone, and unarmed. Before I take another step, I hear a loud crack and a bullet hits the road a few paces away from my right shoe.

I turn and run back the other direction. I run until my lungs hurt, until my legs cramp, and then I keep going until I run off the end of the bridge and right into a brick wall.

Whump.

A warm, familiar, breathing, brick wall.

Sam.

He's as gorgeous as ever, but boy does he look pissed.

CHAPTER 21

His hands clamp onto my upper arms like vises. "What do you think you're doing?"

"Obviously I'm headed back to find you."

"Now that you've been shot at, you mean?"

I wince. "They have all these signs up on the other end of the bridge. I'm not sure we could've enrolled if we wanted to. They shoot at anyone who gets close."

Sam frowns, drops his arms from mine and takes a step back. "You dosed me."

"I was trying to be noble."

"You're an idiot."

"Maybe so, but you're standing here when you shouldn't be. Why didn't it work?" I narrow my eyes at him, which he can see thanks to the backlight from WPN's creepy shooter tower. "I doubled your dose."

Sam shrugs. "Job's snoozing away."

"You aren't."

"I have an unusually fast metabolism."

He should be passed out for hours yet. "Don't think I'm dropping this, but maybe we better chat about this later."

229

Now that Sam's stepped back and my heart rate has slowed, I realize he's armed to the teeth. "You headed for war? Geez Sam, where'd you get all this?" I gesture at the clips covering his chest. He looks like Rambo, a character from one of my uncle's favorite old movies.

"Maybe war," Sam says. "I was coming to save you."

I frown. "I left you to keep you safe, not so you'd storm after me."

"You're an idiot," Sam mutters.

"You've said that, thanks."

"You left me behind to come on your own. You think your problem is that you aren't brave and rushing off alone will make you a hero. What you don't get is that you've never been a coward. Your problem all along has been trust, not fear."

"What are you talking about?"

"Years ago, you didn't call the police because you didn't believe they could protect you if your dad couldn't. You didn't tell your aunt about any of it because you didn't trust her to love you if she knew. Then your stupid aunt and uncle lied to you about your dad and mom, and now you think you were right. You think you can't trust people."

"Wow, I didn't realize you're a psychologist."

Sam shrugs. "It's simple really, and you were right, for the record. You can't trust people."

"I was right to ditch you?"

He shakes his head and pulls me close, shoving cold and sharp clips up against my jacket. "I'm not *people*. People suck. I'm Sam, and I'll never let you down. You can trust me. Your problem all along has been that you trust the *wrong people*." When he leans down to kiss me, I don't stop him.

His lips on mine erases the last residue of fear. My heart swells, and I lose track of time. By the time he finally pulls away, I'm glad the sleeping pills didn't work.

"What do we do now? Spend all day tomorrow looking for a boat? We can't just walk in. They'll shoot us."

"I think you're right, about walking in, and about leaving Job. Rhonda was an asset, but Job's nowhere near Rhonda in accuracy and reliability. He's never been in any operations, either. I don't know if it's occurred to you, but if WPN hasn't heard about you yet, they may soon. The Marked have lost their minds. The sooner we go in, the greater our chance of actually reaching that safe."

"When do we go?"

Sam sighs. "Probably now, if you're up for it. If they send scouts because you snuck onto the bridge, we don't want to be standing around, and Job's safest where he is, asleep and quiet."

I feel a pang of guilt for forcing his hand.

Sam touches my face. "You did what you did. Don't regret it. I roll with momentum. My strengths lie in doing anyway, not as much in planning and strategy."

Sam crouches down and pulls out the maps I brought from my uncle's office. I'm glad he grabbed them when we left the truck. He points at the island. "You said your old apartment was where?"

I kneel down next to him and point to the right side of the island. "It was on the beach. When we crossed the bridge, we turned left. We drove a long way down that main road. I don't remember much else, other than the name. The Palisade Palms."

Sam squints at the map, moving his flashlight quickly. "These maps are old, and it's here. Look."

I peer down at where he points. "Palisade Palms, close to the Galvestonian." Far east side of the island, like I said. "If they have guards all up and down the bridge, how will we get there? By boat?"

Sam doesn't respond quickly. He's still studying the map.

"We should have gone around the island to Eighty-seven and taken a boat down. I should've looked at these maps sooner instead of heading for the bridge. . . well, there's nothing we can do now. The Marked holding Rhonda are smack in between here and there."

"Maybe we should head back to the house before the sun comes up," I say.

He curses. "We need to find a boat; something small, without a motor. Then we'll have to hope we can make it from here to the island without being noticed. It doesn't help that these maps are from Before. We have no idea what WPN has done since."

Sam starts to fold up the map, but I reach over and snatch it away. I spread it back down and extend my hand for the flashlight. "Before we go hunting for a boat and try to float in the dark, against waves and currents and who knows what, maybe we see what that is." I point at a skinny line that runs parallel to the main bridge line.

Sam peers down at the map. "Don't you think the people who shot at you might notice us walking down that bridge? It's not far from the forty-five."

I shrug. "I didn't see it when I was walking. In fact, the closer I got to that lit up guardhouse, the less I could see around me. It's called light and dark adaptation and it'll keep the guards from noticing us on that side road, too. Or at least, I think it will."

"When this map was made, this Highway Seventy-five was already out of use. I have no idea if it's safe." He taps his lip. "We can't risk a flashlight if we do this. I have great night vision, so maybe it's worth a try. We can always backtrack and look for a boat to use tomorrow night."

Sam folds the map and puts it away. I worry that ditching him hurt our chances at being something. I put my hand on his. "I'm sorry I left without you."

He looks me dead in the eye. "You know about light adaptation, but this is what I do. I've been trained for it. When we get to the island, if we make it tonight, you're going to do exactly what I say. No more gallivanting off."

"Did you just say 'gallivanting'?"

Sam grins. "I did."

I grab his jacket collar and pull him toward me. He presses his lips to mine, and I talk against them. "No more gallivanting." The sensation of his lips smiling against mine sends my heart racing.

I reluctantly pull away, and Sam and I begin the walk down toward the retired bridge on the map. We backtrack for what feels like at least half a mile before turning down an overgrown road that must've been old highway seventy-five. Sam doesn't move like a normal person. He's quieter, more sure of himself, and agile in a way I can't dissect. I've never felt particularly clumsy, but my feet stumble, my knees bob and I scrabble over tree roots, bumps, rocks, and shale like everyone else I know.

Sam doesn't stumble in the dark, he never slides on scree, and he doesn't trip over weeds or roots, not a single time. Two sleeping pills, and he still woke up and followed me out here. He never misses a shot, and I saw him in hand-to-hand combat at the Unmarked Games. No one should move that fast. Something's different about him. I just don't know precisely what or why.

Finally we reach the base of the bridge. A railroad track runs alongside a narrow metal road. The whole thing sits much lower than the Forty-five bridge, as though it had been built much earlier with less materials and more rudimentary technology. If it were summer, there'd probably be a lot of overgrowth, but for now, everything's brown and dead.

"I think this might work," Sam says. "Give me your hand."

I reach for him in the dark. He turns toward the front of

the bridge and pulls me along with him. Once we climb up onto the bridge platform, he places my hand on his lower back. "This'll be annoying, but I don't want you any further away from me than we are now. If we communicate at all from here out, it'll be by whisper. Unless you hear me, don't say a word. Keep close and do what I do."

It's slow going for the first few hundred yards, but most of the dead vines and plant life disappear once we get fifty yards or so away from land. The metal road's pitted and rusty, and in the moonlight it looks like the surface of an alien planet. At least it's intact. We keep to the middle where there are less holes and gaps.

A mile or so from the mainland, my foot punches through a hole and my entire body collapses toward the ground. The second my hand leaves Sam's back he spins and grabs both my forearms, lifting me before I've even sunk all the way. We're almost parallel to the guard station that shot at me, which sets my stomach churning, but our road has no light. We can see them, but I remind myself that they can't see us. I wish I'd paid a little more attention to the details when I learned this principle.

We pass the first guard house without incident, and then another. I figure we're near the middle of the bridge when the road ends in front of us. If I squint, I can barely make it out. There's a road . . . and then there isn't.

We're screwed.

We're going to have to turn around and pick our way back. Trying again tomorrow's our only option.

Sam puts one hand over my mouth, and the other behind my head. He tilts my head to the side, toward a tower with a bridge reaching much higher, higher even than the Forty-five. The guard tower to our right casts a large pool of light on the main bridge parallel to our location.

"How certain are you that they can't see well around the guard towers?" he whispers faintly in my ear.

I close my eyes to try and recall what I learned. I whisper back. "His eyes are using cones since he's surrounded by a pool of light. He needs rods to see in low light, and they'll be non-existent because they overlit their guard towers. It's a security oversight."

Sam nods. He motions toward the tower at the edge of the road. It rises far above where we are, at least three flights of stairs above us. Sam shifts from the road portion, to the railroad tracks, and climbs over a concrete barricade, never releasing my hand. I let him help me over and stand at the base of what looks like a very unsound method of crossing. It's almost like a giant ladder was tossed over the top of this old bridge, where a section broke and collapsed.

"Was this on the map?" I ask, careful to keep my voice down.

Sam shakes his head in the moonlight. "I don't think so, but it was probably set up so when boats needed to pass through the channel, this section could lift up. This bridge sits much lower than the big one."

"But what about the road? Why does it disappear?"

Sam shrugs. "Maybe by the time they had boats big enough to cause a problem, no cars used this anymore, so they only spliced the road for the railroad track."

It makes sense, but I don't like it. I follow Sam up three slippery flights of stairs to the top of the bridge splice. The wind's stronger here, and my hair whips my face where it has escaped my braid. The sea spray is warmer than the air near Port Gibson, but still cold enough to sting. The railroad tracks narrow, with large gaps between the iron beams we have to walk along. To make it even scarier, the entire thing's slick with saltwater.

I know I need to move, but I can't quite do it. My hands

shake, my heart pounds, and it's hard to breathe. Sam whispers in my ear. "You've got this, and I've got you."

I slide one foot along the beam and my heart races. I force my eyes upward, focused on the beam in front of me, and Sam's back. Not the drop. Not the drop. Besides, if I do fall, I can swim. I'll be fine. That's what I tell myself, anyway. I've barely taken twenty steps when my boot slips on a slick part, and I stumble forward, sure I'm about to nosedive into the gulf below. Sam's hand wrenches my wrist, but he keeps me upright until I regain my footing.

My heart leaps to my throat the second and third time I slip too, but I know Sam's there, and I trust him. He never once missteps or even slides. I have no idea how he keeps his balance, let alone mine and his when I almost fall.

I breathe a huge sigh of relief when we reach the other end. I practically slide down three flights of iron stairs to the barricade, my legs wobbly and my knees weak now that the adrenaline rush has ended. I practically leap across the concrete barrier to reach the corroded iron road again. That unstable metal road looks like the floor of my own room by comparison to that horrific metal beam in the sky. We creep past another guard station before we reach the end of the bridge. I glance over at where the Forty-five meets the island to the right of us. Sam continues to walk along quietly as we pass a huge guard tower, but I pause.

He yanks me along, no apology, no backward glance. Probably because the sun will be up soon, and when that happens we'll be in trouble. We walk along the bridge, hovering above land for a few hundred feet before the metal beneath us finally gives way to concrete. By the time my boots strike land, my neck and thigh muscles are cramping and my stomach aches with hunger. My fingers and toes throb with cold.

Sam pulls me against him and squeezes my shoulder. "You did great. Can you make it a little further?"

I nod, and we jog toward a few dozen metal railroad cars stopped on the tracks just past the water. As the sun's first rays light the sky, Sam lifts me into an old rusty railroad car and slides the door closed behind us. We startle a fox and I insist on moving down to the next car. Sam kills a few bugs before laying down in silence and pulling my head onto his chest. We chew on the last of Sam's jerky before collapsing into a pile to sleep.

Sam shakes me awake in the middle of a great dream.

I start to say, "What's going on—" but Sam puts a hand over my mouth. He helps me stand, and I follow him out of the train car. My eyes fly wide at the sight of three men slumped on the ground outside. I glance at Sam, but he shakes his head and keeps walking. I stare long enough to confirm their chests still rise and fall.

The sun sits low on the horizon, which means we slept for a while. I try not to think about how Sam handled those men, or what might've happened. If he wanted to tell me, he would have. We jog along the railroad line, but it isn't too long before I lag behind.

"I don't see anyone around," I say. "Can we take it easy? We aren't being chased, right?"

Sam slows slightly and speaks softly. "I was going easy. I forget how small you are sometimes."

"What's the rush?"

"This train track runs until Thirty-Seventh Street before cutting to the north, unless my map's outdated. We need to turn and head south on Thirty-seventh to make it down south. It only gets us about halfway there. Those three men were looking for whoever left footprints off Highway Seventy-Five. When they wake up, they'll go for backup, and be after us again."

"Why didn't you kill them?" I can't help asking.

"I wouldn't have felt guilty shooting them if that's your question. I probably should have." He stares at me for a moment, looking for judgment. He won't find it this time. "If we get caught, it'll be way worse for us if we've killed their people. If we keep moving, get in and get out, hopefully it won't matter. People I knock out tend to stay that way for a good while."

"Why are we following the train track?"

"It's clearly not in use." He points at several busted tie plates. No train could traverse that. "Also, there aren't any houses on the map for the length of the tracks, probably because of noise when it ran. Unless WPN's changed that, it makes this an easy way to create no footprints, and avoid people."

"How far does it run?"

Sam grunts. "Looks like about eight miles."

Eight miles, and that's only half way. Ugh. I'm really starting to hate my size, or maybe it's that I'm out of shape. I don't ask any other questions, and I try to jog as fast as I can, but I'm depressed. My feet hurt, I'm dirty and stinky, and I'm tired of traveling. The Palisade Palms looked much closer on the map. The sun sets as we reach the end of the track at Thirty-Seventh Street. The signs have been replaced, the white lettering bright and easy to read.

We continue walking briskly along Church Street, past a park, a few houses, an abandoned brewery. The roads have been maintained here, and vegetation doesn't engulf every-thing. Unlike the surrounding area, none of these buildings appear abandoned.

We make good time and don't attract much attention, until we reach Twenty-Fifth Street. Sam stops and eyes the road sign like it's a viper about to strike. People come and go through storefront doors on both sides of the street now. Street lights click on while we walk past.

"This is where it gets tricky," he whispers. "I'm guessing we'll be surrounded by people from here on out."

"Please don't kill anyone," I say.

Sam nods but he doesn't make any promises. Although he doesn't have a gun in his hand, I can see the signs of weapons on him, bristling here and there like the spines of an angry porcupine. The outline of his holsters, the tip of a knife on his belt. At least his Rambo clip carrier is tucked beneath his jacket.

He reaches over to casually take my hand, and I realize he's passing me a small black firearm. I glance at the safety, which is on, and slide it into the waistband of my pants. Without my holster, I don't have many choices. By the time I've stowed my new weapon, the outlines of weapons on Sam are gone. It's an astonishing and impressive transformation, and I wonder how he hid them all so well.

Sam takes my hand and whistles as we turn to walk down the street. Just a guy and a girl strolling along. We amble casually until Nineteenth Street, where the business district ends.

"We're going to stand out worse soon," Sam whispers. "Try to smile."

I glance at his mouth. If that's his attempt at a smile, he needs practice. People will think his foot's stuck in a mousetrap. "Maybe drop the smile."

"Why?"

"It looks a little creepy."

He shoots me a hurt look but drops the rictus of pain in favor of his normal scanning gaze. "Only eighteen blocks between us and Beach Drive. We might pull this off."

On the first block, a girl walks a yellow dog.

On the second block, an elderly couple pushes a small

child in a stroller. The little boy stuffs his face with popcorn, and points at Sam.

On the third block, an old woman planting flowers turns and stares at us. She drops her spade.

On the fourth block, a small dog barks and barks. The man who comes to retrieve it smiles at me, but scowls at Sam.

On the fifth block, faces press against windows in at least four homes. No one leaves the house, and no one waves.

By the sixth block, Sam grips my hand tightly and our brisk walk graduates to a jog.

On the seventh block, men in black gear pour out of an alley and drop to a knee. I duck behind a tree, but Sam pulls me along. "Keep moving. Targets in motion are almost impossible to hit."

On the eighth block, Sam fires four times. Three men drop and another limps.

On the ninth block, a huge black van turns the corner behind us, peeling out in a mad rush toward us. Sam fires one shot and it spins into a palm tree, metal crunching, men shouting.

On the tenth block, Sam shoots a fire hydrant and the spray slams into the men closest to us. He shoots three more men, and they all collapse.

On the eleventh block, Sam changes clips. He does it so fast I don't even see the old one. He shoves me under a car while he clears the men behind us, and then we run another fifty yards.

On the twelfth block, Sam slings me on his back and runs. I stupidly assumed he was kidding before. We move twice as fast this way. Sam holds a gun in each hand. A guy pops up from the left side, and Sam clips his shoulder so he drops his gun. Sam fires a second shot a millisecond later and a man on the second floor of a beach house screams.

I've never seen anyone fire dozens of shots and not miss a single one. In the dark, while moving, and carrying someone. Not even the movies from Before depict anything quite so unbelievable. Except, I witness it with my own eyes.

Three clips later, we're only a few blocks away, but behind one of the men Sam shoots, a little girl crouches near a tree. She's sucking on her thumb and holding a yellow blanket. Sam might be able to do this forever, and we might even reach the Palisade Palms, but how many will die? If I allow him to carve a path there, who are we?

I'm not willing to risk lives like my dad. Sam's good enough not to shoot children, but is shooting her dad, or her brother or her grandpa any better?

I slide off Sam's back and hold up my hands. I shout the words. "We surrender."

Sam's eyes bulge. "We do not surrender." He has a gun in each hand, and he glances right to left. "I can take you all down, one by one. Back off, or I'll do it."

I reach out and put my hand on his chiseled arm, running my fingers over the veins popping out of his forearm. "At what cost, Sam? Civilians are everywhere." I shake my head.

He lowers his arms slowly, like it pains him.

Three men in black gear rush toward us. Sam drops his guns to the ground, and the men grab them. They shove Sam up against a nearby car and handcuff his hands behind his back. They barely even notice I'm there.

My gun's still tucked into my waistband, and my hands aren't cuffed when they march us back along Church Street, the same way we came. Along the way, the people Sam shot are being treated. Arm wounds bound. Leg wounds cleaned and splinted. Not a single body bag.

"Were you aiming to incapacitate?" I whisper.

Sam doesn't look me in the eye, but he says, "You asked me not to kill."

"No one could be sure of where they hit anyone else in the dark, not firing that fast. You shot and shot without looking."

"I'm always sure."

I think back to our lessons, to the awards he's won. I can hardly believe it.

"Did you kill anyone?"

"Not if they have competent medical care."

The men shove us both against the wall and pat us down. They find my gun, and eight other firearms, four knives and two throwing stars on Sam. Throwing stars? Really? Sam still won't meet my eye when they shove us into a small empty storage room in an office building to wait. I wish I knew what we were waiting for.

"Are you ever going to look at me again?" I ask. "I'm sorry I surrendered, okay? I didn't know what else to do. I saw that little kid with the blanket, and I couldn't. What if she got hurt? Or another little kid?"

"What about all the Marked kids who are dying?" Sam asks. "Rhonda? Or Wesley? What about all of them? They'll all die now."

I sigh. "Unless we get a chance to explain."

"That's why we're here. Someone in charge will question us."

"Oh, good. Maybe they'll let us—"

Sam grabs my arm and pulls me close. He whispers, "Let me do the talking. I know I failed you out there, but I have a lot more experience with this than you do. I also have a fallback."

"Wait, how did you fail me?"

Sam looks away.

"Are you being so weird because you think this is your fault? That you lost somehow?" I laugh, even though I know it isn't funny. Nothing's funny right now, but for some reason I can't help it. "Sam, no one on earth could've gotten us closer than you just did. You might've made it all the way if I'd let you, unless you ran out of bullets. I have no idea how you did what you just did."

"It wasn't enough."

I try to hug him then. I can't because, handcuffs, so I sort of lean against him and squish my face against his. I hope he knows what I'm trying to do.

A small grin surfaces on Sam's lips and I take it as a win. Sam obviously had a terrible childhood if he thinks what he just did wasn't enough. "That was the single most amazing thing I've ever seen in my entire life."

He doesn't have time to respond before the door swings open. The man who walks in holds a gun trained, not on Sam, but on me. Five more men follow the first man inside. They all hold guns aimed at my head.

A young man with blonde hair and sparkling, light blue eyes enters the room last. His face is young, not much older than me. Maybe the same age as Sam.

"Who are you?" he asks Sam. "And why are you here?"

"I won't talk to you," Sam says. "I'll only talk to Solomon."

"*King* Solomon's quite busy, and you don't get to make demands." The tall man's wearing a grey uniform, with some kind of star on the lapel. "If you make any more, I'll shoot your friend."

Sam doesn't flinch. "That's not how this works. I'll give you a piece of information, and then you'll scurry off to get your boss."

The man scowls. "What piece of information are you going to give me that will save her, now that you've pissed me off?"

"My name," Sam says.

"Why should I care about your name?"

Sam cocks one eyebrow. "Because I'm Samuel Roth. You'll

believe me because you'll actually get information on what just happened before you interrogate me again. I shot seventy-nine people out there while on the move, and not a single one died. No one you know could do that. The five men you have holding guns on my *friend* wouldn't be enough to stop me from killing you, if you did something stupid like shooting her."

The tall young man blanches, and leaves the room for a few minutes. When he returns, he's much more deferential. "Mr. Roth, we've notified King Solomon. He'll be here shortly."

A very thin man in a black suit enters with a tray. It holds a pitcher of water and two glasses. He sets it on the floor and the men all file out quietly after him.

"What was that about?" I ask.

"My dad leads the Unmarked," Sam says. "Solomon knows that, and he's probably heard some of the things I can do. In case he didn't believe the person he's holding really was Samuel Roth, now he has reasonable evidence. I'm pretty sure Dad's been communicating with Solomon, at least a little bit, for years."

"You're kidding, right?"

Sam clenches his jaw. "I wish. I saw a letter from a David Solomon to my dad last Christmas. He wouldn't give me any information and seemed angry that I mentioned it at all."

"That's creepy."

"It is," Sam says, "but if it keeps us alive, it'll be the first favor my dad's ever done for me."

CHAPTER 22

The good looking young man in the gray uniform returns twenty minutes later to lead Sam into the next room. Sam doesn't object, but it annoys me to be left behind. Why don't I get to meet this King?

David Solomon, what a pretentious name.

He can't be named after one famous Biblical king? He needs to be named for two? Pretentious, bloodthirsty, and nefarious. He wiped out the US government, after possibly releasing Tercera to begin with. And he's planning to wipe out the kids who managed to survive his decimation of the world. Sam's in the room with him while I'm stuck twiddling my thumbs.

I'd especially like to meet him, because if he did release Tercera, odds are good he knew my dad. Maybe he knows Jack, or perhaps he's actually the partner. There's no way he was born with the name David Solomon, and then happened to become some bizarre religious icon.

I may not be face-to-face with him myself, but maybe I can hear what they're saying anyway. I run to the wall and press my ear against it. The words I make out now and again are too muffled to comprehend. I shift around and find a spot that's a little better, but I still can't understand most of what's said. I look around the storage closet and see the tray with the water. I pick up one of the glasses and press it to the wall. This should help, if my understanding of acoustic coupling isn't completely wrong.

I hold my ear to the glass and grin. I may not be able to shoot eighty people, but science is awesome in its own way.

Sam says, "I already told you. The girl lives or there's no deal."

A light baritone voice I assume belongs to King Solomon responds. "I have eighty injured people, Sam. Eighty! It's not about me. Surely you understand that. I have to give them something. Eighty people are going home with gunshot wounds. They have arms, legs, and shoulders that don't work right anymore because of you. You haven't even told me why."

Sam says, "The girl is the only reason it stopped when it did. Believe me, you can't punish her and not me. The reason for our presence isn't mine to tell, but I'm here for her. She lived here Before, and needs something of her father's. I can't tell you more than that. If you'll let me retrieve it with her, I promise you my father will pay a handsome fee for my safe return."

"It must be valuable for you to risk your life and hers, not to mention the lives of all those people." King Solomon lowers his voice and I can barely make out what he says next. "Especially since you could've had your dad send me a message about it instead. That means it's either valuable, or it's something you don't want me to know about."

Sam says, "If you think I'd ask my dad to do me a favor, you don't know him very well."

"Meet me halfway Sam. Tell me what you came to

retrieve. I'm going to see it anyway if I let you go. Where's the harm?"

"I already told you. You don't listen very well. It's not my decision to make."

"You still maintain you're the muscle, and she calls all the shots?" King Solomon laughs. "Your dad likes to brag you know. I've seen your aptitude tests, and you're more than a sharpshooter. More than a gifted warrior. Your mind works differently than most people, but it's faster, and quicker, just like everything else."

Sam doesn't speak.

King Solomon changes tactics. "Does your father know you're here?"

I don't hear anything, so I assume Sam shakes his head.

"How do you know he'll pay me anything to rescue you from an unsanctioned mission?"

Sam says, "I'm all he has."

"But the girl," King Solomon says. "He won't pay for her?"

"She's not important to anyone but me." I have to admit, that stings a little, probably because it's true. "Allow us to grab her dad's belongings and I promise you, my dad will compensate you for your men's injuries."

"I'm afraid we're at an impasse. I obviously can't make any deal without knowing what I'm giving up, and no matter who owned it Before, all of Galveston belongs to me now."

Sam growls. Two chairs scrape the floor as both men stand.

"Only my girlfriend can decide whether to tell you about her dad."

I inhale sharply, but doubt anyone can hear me. I wish I'd been there to see his face the first time he called me his girlfriend. My heart leaps against my ribs, and I realize that for all my indecision, I've already decided about Sam. I want him as much if not more than he likes me.

"Fine. Let's ask her, then." Footsteps sound in the other room. My eyes widen. They're coming for me.

I scramble away from the wall, but don't have time to put the glass down before the door opens. The same five men with guns enter the room and circle me, firearms trained at my head again. It's getting old. There's barely any room left in the storage closet with us, but somehow Sam fits, and after him, another man does, too.

The other man isn't as tall as Sam, but he's tall by anyone else's standards. He isn't old, and he isn't young. He isn't fat, but neither is he thin. He doesn't have blonde hair, but it's lighter than most people with brown. He has freckles on his nose, but nowhere else on his face. His large, straight teeth, and angry blue eyes stare straight at me.

He's a fairly memorable looking man, but I wish I could forget him the moment I see him. Unfortunately, he's not someone I'll ever forget.

"What's your name, girl?" he asks me.

I recognize the voice as the man from the other room, the man I assumed was King Solomon. I can't believe I didn't recognize the voice earlier. I should have.

Sam must sense my confusion, because he says, "Ruby, this is David Solomon, the king of World Peace Now."

I want to do something. I want to yell at him, or better yet, pull a gun and point it at his head. I've imagined this meeting over and over, dreamed of it even, but never under these circumstances.

With five men pointing guns at me, instead of doing what I want, I mutter, "Nice to meet you." I train my eyes on the floor so he won't see the hatred burning in them.

"I'm pleased to meet you Ruby. Sam's been telling me all about you, and how you came to retrieve your dad's old belongings. I thought you might be able to fill me in a little more. What's worth risking both your lives, and shooting close to a hundred of my best people?"

My mouth's drier than sand in the desert, and my vocal cords knot up painfully. My hands ball into fists tight enough that my nails dig into the soft part of my palms.

"Well, won't you share? A successful compromise requires both parties to give a little."

When I finally look up at King Solomon, my chest fills with a rage I've never before felt. Sam's expecting me to beg him to let me look for my dad's journal. Or perhaps he thinks I'll tell him how I thought my dad might've been on the cusp of a cure to Tercera.

I don't beg, and I won't. Not if I stand here for a hundred years.

Five men ready to shoot an unarmed girl. Seems like overkill, which doesn't surprise me, not with him. I should be polite. I should be deferential, but I can't. Not now, not looking into the eyes of this person, the one person I hate more than anyone else in all the world.

Instead, I do the most measured thing I possibly can. My hands shake, my blood boils, and I say, "Go to Hell."

Sam's eyes fly wide and King Solomon's mouth falls open. The men with guns shift and mutter, and Sam tenses.

"Excuse me?" King Solomon's surely unused to people speaking to him this way.

I clear my throat. "You didn't understand me?" I look him right in the eyes this time. "I'll enunciate. I told you to Go To Hell."

King Solomon turns to Sam. "Your girlfriend has lost her mind."

"I have not," I say. "You may not recognize me, but I can't say the same. Ten years ago, I hid in a closet. Ten years ago, I did nothing when you broke into my home with threats and a gun. I watched you murder my father more than a decade ago, but I'm not a little girl this time. My name is Ruby Behl. Does that name mean anything to you? I may not be able to shoot you now that you've disarmed us, but at least I can tell you to go to where you belong, with the demons and the fire and the never-ending penance." I want to spit in his face, but . . . guns.

I don't know what kind of reaction I'm expecting, but it isn't a smile.

I flail like a fish when King Solomon pulls me tight for an embrace. I shove him off and clock him on the head with the glass I'm still holding in my hand. He slumps forward, and then stumbles back.

The stockiest of the five men grabs me by the back of my neck and shoves a gun against my temple. The rest happens so quickly, I can't follow it, but one minute there's a gun pressed to my head, and the next, Sam has disarmed the guards, knocked three of them out cold and is holding a gun on King Solomon, who's pressed against the back wall.

I'm not sure my brain can process much more when the door to the storage closet flies open and a woman walks inside. She's short with curly blonde hair and dark blue eyes. She has fine features, a small, pert nose, and a tiny frame. She wears a fitted blue pantsuit and a simple strand of pearls around her neck. Tiny crow's feet crimp the corners of her eyes.

Wrinkles aside, she looks exactly like me.

"David, the perimeter guards turned up another intruder just off the bridge to the island. He's young, too. He won't tell us his name." She glances around the room and her hand flies to her mouth. "What's going on?"

"Don't worry," King Solomon says. "It's all a misunderstanding." He smiles at the woman brightly. "Ruby's alive!"

CHAPTER 23

Sam still holds a gun to King Solomon's head.

"It's not a misunderstanding," I say to Sam. "I hate him." I look at the gun in Sam's hand. I hear bootsteps thundering toward us in the hall. This might be my only chance.

"Give that to me." I hold out my hand to Sam.

"Are you sure?" he asks me. "I can do it."

I shake my head. "It has to be me." He hesitates for a split second before handing it over. It's a large gun and it's heavy in my hand. I press it to King Solomon's head. "You deserve this. You shot my dad."

"I probably deserve it," he agrees. "But I didn't shoot your father."

My voice comes out high and squeaky. "You deny shooting Donovan Behl?"

Several more guards have reached us, and they're yelling at me to put the gun down. With nine people already crammed into the small space, there isn't any way for them to reach King Solomon, at least not without shooting us and stepping over our corpses. They're thinking about doing exactly that, but they're hesitating. Why?

I can't quite suppress a smile when I realize why. "They're worried if they shoot me, I'll press this trigger as a reflex."

The man standing nearest the door snarls. "We will shoot you little girl. Put the gun down now."

"Stop," King Solomon yells. "No one shoots her, not even if she shoots me. Leave us alone."

No one turns to leave or even lowers a gun.

Solomon's face flushes and his nostrils flare. "GO!"

"Your Highness, she—"

King Solomon turns his head slightly, and his eyes spear the gray-haired guard. "Leave."

The guard grunts, but he turns and leaves. The other guards grab the unconscious ones and within thirty seconds, they're all gone. Only the woman remains, a bewildered look on her face.

King Solomon glances back toward me. "I shot the man you knew as Donovan Behl, Ruby, but he wasn't your father."

The gun shakes in my hand. "That makes no sense."

"Ruby, Donovan Behl wasn't even his real name. His name was Donald Carillon and I know he wasn't your father because. . . I'm your real father."

The small woman standing in the doorway sobs.

King Solomon frowns at her. "She was there, Joey. She saw me shoot Donovan that day. She was hiding in a closet."

I lower the gun. I don't know what else to do. The woman looks exactly like me. It was the first thing I thought when she walked in.

I barely hear the words she whispers, "Do you have a birthmark?" Her eyes shine through unshed tears.

King Solomon smiles. "You had a small red mark behind your left ear when you were born. It looked exactly like a ruby. That's why we named you as we did. Well, that and Proverbs 31:10."

None of this makes sense. I know my dad, of course I do. This man killed him.

I shake my head and lift the gun again. "I watched you fight with him, and then shoot him. You killed my dad."

"Actually, my gunshot wasn't what killed him. Didn't you know about the fire? When I left, I called 911. They were en route and Don would've been fine. But by the time they got there, someone had lit his body on fire. They put out the fire, but Donald Carillon didn't survive."

"Carillon?" I shake my head. "I've never even heard of a Donald Carillon."

The small woman takes a gulping breath. "He took the name Donovan Behl when he stole you from me. His real name was Donald Carillon. Carillon means bell tower in French."

"No." It can't be true. My father is Donovan Behl. He tucked me in every night, read to me, and fed me. I know he loved me. His name was Donovan Behl. This man killed him. "You're lying."

"Check her ear," King Solomon says to Sam. "You'll see the birthmark."

Sam glances at him and then turns back to me. "Do you want me to check?"

I don't want him to do anything. I want to shoot this man, go and get the cure and go home. I shake my head. "No."

The woman who looks like me stares with undisguised longing in her face. "You look and talk just like Anne Carillon, his twin sister. Tell me, is she alive?"

My heart stops and I'm the one taking gulping breaths. It can't be true. It can't. She can't be my mother. I close my eyes and think back on the photo, the one photo I have.

It's her. The woman in front of me is the same woman holding Donovan Behl's hand in that photo. My aunt and uncle lied to me about my dad, about his death, and his creation of Tercera. And about my mom being dead. Could they have lied about this, too? Was Donovan Behl a kidnapping monster?

"Wait."

Sam holsters one gun.

"Check," I say.

Sam takes one step toward me and gently moves my braid out of the way. He shifts my ear and his exhale, a tiny breath I normally wouldn't even notice, guts me.

There must be a birthmark, like they said there would be.

"Your name's Joey?" I ask the woman. I look at her, her eyes, her hair, and her small frame. I'm so much smaller than Rhonda and Job, smaller than my aunt and my uncle, smaller than my tall, broad shouldered father. So much smaller than everyone else in my family. But not smaller than her.

"I'm Josephine Solomon. Before I became Josephine Solomon, I was married to Donald Carillon."

King Solomon grunts.

She touches his shoulder. "I was married to Donald when I met your father. I fell in love with David, and divorced Donald. When he found out I was pregnant, he claimed the child was his. He didn't believe that you were David's. He went crazy over it, but no one guessed he might abandon his job and flee his entire life to kidnap a child who wasn't even his. It took me completely by surprise when he showed up at the hospital. We searched for you everywhere."

I lower my hand, and King Solomon stands up and brushes off his pants.

Sam gently takes the gun out of my hand and whispers in my ear, "Maybe it's better if I hold on to this."

I want to curl up in his lap and pretend none of this happened. Except I can't do that. "You didn't search everywhere, obviously."

King Solomon says, "We tried milk cartons, news

programs, every police station in the area. When you were five years old, almost six, we got a call. Donald's business partner, a man named Jack, told me where you were." King Solomon glances at Sam, and then back at me. When neither of us speaks, he continues. "He figured out who Donovan Behl really was, and felt we should know the location of our daughter. Donald threatened to release a deadly virus he'd created in the process of developing some kind of super vaccination, unless Jack kept your location secret."

Drums pound inside my head, and I can't think straight. King Solomon knows my dad's partner was named Jack. He knows Dad made Tercera. I bite my lip hard. I need to think this through. Aunt Anne always refers to Dad as Don, never Donovan. My dad and my aunt both have straight, dark brown hair. I knew my hair color came from my mom, and Rhonda and Job got their light hair from their dad, but now I don't know what I know.

Except that my Dad would never have released Tercera to keep me from my mother. Not in a million years. I read his journals. Jack wanted to sell it, not Dad. "You're saying the man who raised me was a kidnapper, a liar, and he released the virus that wiped out the world? Because I've always heard the leader of WPN did that." I cross my arms.

"Why would we release a virus?" Josephine asks. "We rushed down here to find you, but we were too late. Your father shot Donald to protect you from him. An injured man couldn't possibly continue to hide a child, but then we couldn't find you. And it turned out Donald had already released the virus."

They know a lot of facts. I study each of Josephine's features, and while I do she gazes at me tenderly. I should be delighted, but I'm not. I want to shred something, or smash a glass, or scream. She must be my mother, so why don't I want to hug her or shout for joy? Maybe because I'm grown, and it's the first time I'm seeing her. Or perhaps it's because her story doesn't line up, not quite.

If Dad was such a monster, how could he also be a devoted and loving dad? Because he was. Not to mention, how did my dad release Tercera if he died weeks before the first documented cases? If they knew he created the virus, why didn't they tell the authorities, and let them dig around for the cure? Something cold snakes up my spine. David Solomon wiped out the United States government, and I saw him shoot my dad. What if he *has* the cure, and kept it for himself? I need answers, but I also need to tread carefully.

"What about Aunt Anne?" I finally ask. "Are you saying she's a Carillon, and she knew my dad kidnapped me?"

Josephine sighs and frowns. "Anne loved Donald, probably a little too much. It's common with twins. She supported everything he did, even bad decisions."

"You knew her. You think she'd keep a child who wasn't really her brother's blood?"

"Donald believed you were his child," King Solomon says. "He and your mother tried to have children for years with no success. Your mother conceived you within a month of beginning her relationship with me. You are my daughter."

"You two have lots of other kids too?" I ask. "Do I have brothers? Or maybe a sister?" In the middle of this nightmare, this one thought fills my heart with hope.

"No," Josephine says. "We haven't had any others."

"Then maybe you're the one who's infertile," I say. "Maybe Donovan *is* my dad. You don't know."

King Solomon slaps me across the face and I stumble back a step.

Sam punches King Solomon in the nose, and grabs his arm. He twists it around his back until King Solomon cries out. Guards knock at the door a moment later. "Your Highness? Are you all right?"

"I'm fine," he calls out tersely. "You aren't needed." King Solomon struggles against Sam.

Sam lowers his face to King Solomon's level. "This is my only warning. If you raise a hand against Ruby again, I'll kill you. I don't care whether you're her dad or not, and I don't care what your people will do to me. You do not hurt her. I shouldn't have to tell you that, if you're her Dad, but here we are. Do you understand?"

King Solomon's eyes flash and the muscles in his neck tense, but he nods. Sam releases him.

King Solomon brushes his shirt off and shrugs his shoulders a few times. "This has been a lot to take in, for all of us. We've known for years and years about you, but seeing you in person. And thanks to Donovan," he practically spits the name, "you're just hearing all of this. You probably need some time to sort through it. I shouldn't have overreacted, but it's new to me, being a father. We'll give you as much time and space as you need."

Blood drips from King Solomon's nose down to his mouth, and onto his shirt. He wipes his face with his sleeve and winces. It's enough for now.

"We're so happy you're alive." Josephine's eyes well with tears again, and she takes a step toward me, arms extended.

I shy away. She may be my mom, but I don't know her. I don't want her touching me now, seventeen years too late. And she's married to this man who orders everyone around and slaps me.

"I'm glad you're happy." I don't know what else to say.

Josephine drops her arms and steps back. "We want to make you happy, too."

I think about my dad, bleeding on the floor, and I'm not happy. I want to hurt her, like her husband hurt us. She left him, and she left me. She's been alive all this time, and she never found me. "What if reclaiming my dad's things,

Donovan Behl's belongings, and leaving with my boyfriend is what will make me happy? Sam's more than capable of keeping me safe. I have a life and a home and a family already, and you aren't part of it."

As much as I'd like to watch my mom's face, I keep my eyes trained on King Solomon instead. If he has the cure already, he'll know what I'm here to retrieve.

His face doesn't show a thing. "Your quick departure would break your mother's heart, but we wouldn't stop you if you truly wanted to leave us. Speaking of, why don't we take you somewhere you can rest."

Rest. I haven't truly rested since. . . I don't know when. Even in the house on the outcropping, before we left Job and — Josephine mentioned they found someone when she came in the room. "Did you find my brother, Job? He's tall, thin, and has blond hair like mine."

Josephine raises one eyebrow. "Brother?"

I huff. "Yes, brother. Cousin by blood perhaps, but raised as a brother to me."

Josephine flinches. "The boy we found is tall and thin with dark blond hair. It's straight and much darker than yours, but yes. I imagine it's him."

I grit my teeth. Even if Job and I don't share blood, and I'm not convinced we don't, he's more my brother than she is my mother. She doesn't need to point out that Job doesn't look as much like me as she does. I have eyes.

"We'll all share one room," Sam says.

"While I acknowledge she's only just returned to my life, I'm certainly not allowing my daughter to share a room with her boyfriend." King Solomon glares at Sam.

Sam counters. "She's only safe with me."

"There isn't a soul at World Peace Now who would harm my daughter."

"Stop saying that!" I stomp my foot. "I am not your

daughter. Sam and Job and I will all share a room. Nothing will happen with my *brother* in the same room. Even if it *did*, seeing as how you're not meeting me until now—my seventeenth birthday—I don't think it's your place to dictate where I sleep, even if we do share DNA."

King Solomon's nostrils flare. His hands clench and unclench. I don't know whether my words pissed him off, or the fact that I'm dictating to him. I gather it doesn't happen often.

Josephine steps near him and touches his arm. She speaks softly. "It's her birthday. She hasn't seen us in seventeen years. Give it time."

"It's fine for now." King Solomon opens the door, and I notice the same young, blonde haired guard from before hovers outside. "Adam, take them to the palace and release the other prisoner into Ruby's care. They'll share the Blue Room. It has several beds." He forces a smile. "It was designed for visiting families."

"It'll be perfect for my family. Thanks."

As I leave, I notice a tear trails down Josephine's cheek. My anger with her dissipates and my heart constricts. I try to imagine how I'd feel if I were her. She found her long lost daughter, and instead of expressing joy, her daughter called her a liar and yelled. No matter what else is true, it seems likely she's my mother. I close the space between us and pull her against me. Hugging someone else as small as me feels odd, but it's also reassuring somehow. She smells like peppermint, and I breathe in deeply.

She holds on a moment too long, and I have to shake her a little to escape. Even that diminishes my anger. I've never had someone want to hug me so badly that I have to pull away. Isn't that what a mom's supposed to do?

This time, when I duck into the doorway, Josephine's smile brightens the room.

I stumble along behind Sam and Adam in a daze, still processing what happened. My dad went on the run with me, I have a birthmark, and my dad created Tercera. On the other hand, I don't believe he would've released it, and I doubt my dad would steal a child unless he was sure that child was his. He never yelled, he took good care of me, and I know he loved me. Besides, he had his own lab. The answer to my paternity was one genetic test away. Surely he would've checked. My aunt and uncle may have lied to me, but they're some of the best people I know. I really believe the lies they told were to spare me confusion and sadness.

None of what I've learned changes that I watched David Solomon shoot my dad. He doesn't even deny it.

Adam stops in front of a dark van. I glance at Sam, who still has at least two guns. The one he took from a guard, and the one he took from me. Sam checks the van before gesturing for me to enter. Adam doesn't move to stop any of that. The van's clean, shiny, and new. WPN's either manufacturing new vehicles or maintaining the ones they have extremely well.

The van rolls down the road smoothly. No potholes, large cracks, bumps or other interruptions hinder us. We pass house after house en route to the palace, which is apparently on the other side of the island. They're all freshly painted. No trash clutters the streets, and the bushes and grass are all neatly trimmed. I don't notice a single garden, which makes me wonder how all these people are being fed while living on an island.

The van pulls up in front of an enormous white plantation home with eight white pillars, four on either side of the front doors. A stairway almost thirty feet wide leads up from a circular drive. The stairs climb and climb up to massive double front doors that hang open, presumably in anticipation of our arrival. I'm guessing they don't have a major fly problem this time of year. Two guards stand on either side of the doorway.

Adam climbs out of the van first and comes around to open the door. Sam leaps out and holds out a hand to help me. I don't take it, because I'm not a princess. I'm perfectly capable of climbing out on my own.

"Please follow me up the stairs, your Majesty," Adam says.

"No, no, no." I frown. "Don't call me that, please."

"I apologize for my poor behavior earlier. I didn't realize who you were." Without his haughty attitude from earlier, he looks no more than twenty.

"I held a gun on your king. I'm still the same person. Don't call me majesty or highness or princess, okay?"

Sam snorts.

Adam's eyebrows draw together and his eyes widen alarmingly. "Your Highness, we must—"

"I'm not anyone's highness," I say, stopping him. "If I'm not your king's daughter, then I'm not a princess, and you shouldn't call me that. And if I am, then you have to listen to me when I tell you not to call me that, right?"

Adam nods stiffly. "We must show respect."

"Great, because Ruby is a respectable name, and that's good enough. Just plain old Ruby."

Adam sighs. "This way your, er, Ruby."

He walks up the stairs toward the doors and Sam shrugs at me and follows him up. Two guards in front of us bow. I grit my teeth. News travels fast within WPN. I wonder how they conveyed the information so quickly.

The floors of the palace are marble, and the entry way boasts even more columns. A chandelier glints and sparkles over our heads. Adam walks us up to a woman with a fluffy navy dress and a gray apron. "Ruby, this is Alice. She manages the palace and its staff. She'll show you to the Blue Room."

Adam bows, turns on his heel and marches out. Alice beams at me. Her almost white hair has been twisted into a tight bun, but her face looks much younger. She's thin and tall and her eyes light up when she speaks. "It's such an honor to have you here, your Highness."

Sam snickers.

I force a smile. "I'd really prefer if everyone would call me Ruby. I'm not majestic, nor am I high. In fact, I'm so short that being called 'Highness' feels like an insult."

Alice's face falls. "Yes, milady. I'll call you Ruby, milady."

Sam turns away to hide his smile. Milady is almost as bad as your majesty. What's wrong with these people? We follow Alice down a vast hallway with dozens of doors, up a grand staircase, and down another, smaller hall. We finally reach the Blue Room.

I walk through the doorway and look around. A large, upholstered, floral-print sofa sits next to two big, blue, accent chairs. I walk through a side door and find a bathroom that's bigger than my kitchen back home. Notably, there's no bed.

"Uh," I say, "King Solomon told me there were beds in here? As in plural?"

Alice says, "Oh yes, there are, milady. This is the sitting room."

It should be called the Blue Rooms. She leads us through a door in the back into another room with blue wallpaper, a blue crystal light fixture, and blue carpet. Navy blue curtains hang on a four-poster bed, which fills the center of the room. Smaller twin beds with blue checked bedspreads flank the large one on either side. Job's sitting on one of the twin beds when we walk into the room.

"Ruby!" He jumps to his feet and runs over to give me a hug. When he pulls away, he's frowning. "You left me."

"To be fair, I left Sam too," I say.

Sam clears his throat. "She came back for me because I'm so awesome."

I roll my eyes. "Someone shot at me. I ran from that smack into Sam."

Alice clears her throat. "Is there anything I can fetch for you, milady? Some refreshment perhaps?"

Job's eyebrows climb his forehead. "Milady?" He looks from Alice to me, and back to Alice. "Who are you talking to?"

"I'm addressing her Majesty, Ruby Solomon."

Job coughs and coughs, and then starts choking. I have to get her out of here before Job chokes to death.

"We're good for now. Thanks, Alice."

Alice bows to me and leaves, closing the door behind her.

"What the hell is going on?" Job asks. "First they act like they're going to kill me. I'm tied up in a chair with a bright light in my face, and I swear the only thing missing were bamboo shoots under my fingernails. For no reason, a minute later, they bring me to this opulent mansion and plop me down in this room without a guard, or a care in the world. Now that woman's calling you Ruby *Solomon*, and curtsying?"

"You missed some stuff." Sam pulls the curtains to the side and sinks down onto the four-poster bed. "Turns out, King Solomon thinks Ruby's his kid."

Job laugh-snorts. "I'm sorry, he thinks what?"

I try to explain. I'm skeptical of the whole story, but Job takes it a little further.

"No way in hell is any of that true."

I sigh. "The woman sure looks like my mom, from the one photo I have."

Sam grunts. "She also looks a *lot* like Ruby."

Job paces. "Well, that's certainly conclusive."

"I'm not an idiot, Job. I know it's not proof, but she

seemed to be as upset as I am, and there's a lot to corroborate her story."

Job's eyes flash. "My parents would not have been fine with Uncle Don kidnapping you, and they wouldn't have lied about it. Not to you, or me, or the police."

"Right," I say, "because Aunt Anne would never, ever lie to me. She'd never conceal, for instance, that my dad *engineered Tercera*. Or that he developed a cure before his murder."

"Maybe they didn't tell you that because you were so young, but do you really think they'd lie about who you are? Do you think you aren't even my cousin?" Job's anger falls away and he slumps down on the bed like a puppet with his strings cut. "Do you think we're not even related?"

"I'm not saying that."

"What are you saying?" he asks.

"I don't know what I'm saying." I collapse on the bed next to Job and drop my face in my hands. "I don't know up from down, but I know I love you as much as a brother. Maybe more."

Job pulls me against him. "Are you happy? A little excited that maybe you aren't an orphan?"

I don't know what to say, because I am. If it's true, it means I have a family. Not a borrowed one, but a real family that loves me. I know my dad loved me, but he's been gone a long time. I wish I knew whether this King Solomon was the villain I believe him to be. Slapping me in the face doesn't give me much confidence, even if I was questioning my mom's honor at the time.

"How can we figure out whether they're telling the truth?" Job asks.

Sam's voice rises up from where he's lying on the four poster bed. "What do they stand to gain from lying?"

I can't think of a single thing.

"Maybe," Job says, "they know Uncle Don created Tercera,

and they need you to find the cure. If they can get you on their side, they'll finally get it."

I lean back against the headboard so it's easier to talk. "It's not zero sum. A cure would help everyone. But even if that's true, why lie about me being their kid? That's a bizarrely twisted way to go about it. They already had me in a storage room. They could've won me over way easier. Plus they didn't have time to confer. Solomon announced 'Ruby's alive' and they both started explaining. It couldn't have been fabricated on the spot."

Sam sits up. "I agree. If it's a lie, it's one they both believe. It also explains why WPN's headquartered in Galveston. If Solomon knew your dad, or you know, Donovan, or Donald. Man, if they're telling the truth, this is strange. But if Solomon knew Donovan invented Tercera, he might have stayed here to look for anything he could parse together from the research." His eyebrows draw together. "It might be how they figured out the accelerant WPN used to wipe out the government."

By all counts, King Solomon's a sociopathic villain. He can't be my father, can he?

"Or," Job says, in a voice so quiet it's barely more than a whisper, "maybe they stuck around here to look for you."

This morning I was an orphan. Now I have too many parents to go around. I have no idea what kind of people they are, and I'm beginning to think the same about the man who raised me the first six years of my life.

A knock on the door to the sitting room startles me. I walk out to answer it with Sam on my heels. Josephine stands on the other side. I guess my time to process my feelings has run out.

CHAPTER 24

"Hello Ruby." Josephine changed out of her power pantsuit and ditched her pearls. Now she's wearing a light blue cotton dress with navy birds on it. "I thought you might be hungry."

My stomach growls and I smile. "Yeah, I guess I am." Except she didn't bring any food with her. "Uh, where would the food be?"

"Your father and I thought maybe you'd want to eat a late supper with us?"

I flinch. "Please don't call that man my father. My dad was smart, funny, kind, and he loved me all the way to Jupiter. He told me every single night after he brushed my teeth, read me *Green Eggs and Ham*, and tucked me in. If you want me to spend any time here, you have to stop referring to David Solomon as my father. I watched him shoot Donovan Behl. He may be my biological parent, but he will never, ever be my dad."

"I'm truly sorry you saw that." King Solomon appears from around a curve in the hall. He also changed clothes and is wearing light pants and a collared shirt. Obviously they dressed down to make me more comfortable. I'm not sure whether it's manipulative or sweet.

Josephine wrings her hands and I feel guilty for being so abrupt. Still, they deserve to know how I feel. At least this time no one slapped me. In fact, he didn't even frown.

"If you're telling the truth," I say, "then it's a terrible thing that happened to you. Maybe that means my dad was kind of crazy, I don't know. But to me, he's still Dad."

"You don't believe us?" Josephine whispers.

"I don't know what to believe," I say honestly. "Did you even try to find me when my dad supposedly stole me?"

"We were so shocked when it happened. We tried normal channels first," Josephine says. "We hired a lawyer, requested a DNA test, and demanded custody legally. Donald didn't show up to the injunction hearing, or any other hearing after."

"So you gave up?"

"Of course not," Josephine says. "But perhaps we can discuss this while we eat in your . . . in David's office. Documents might help, and we have quite a few."

I glance back at Sam and Job, who are standing two steps behind me.

"Maybe we could spend just a few moments alone," Josephine says. "The office isn't very large."

Sam makes a sound that closely resembles a growl. "She's not going anywhere without me."

I bristle at his proprietary arrogance, but ultimately, I agree with him. "Not without Sam and Job."

"This is the cousin?" Josephine asks.

Brother. I want to correct her, but figure she's probably heard it enough already. "He came to help. He's a scientist for the Unmarked."

King Solomon opens his mouth as if to argue, but Josephine puts her hand on his arm. He shakes it off, but doesn't say anything to contradict me. He scowls at Job, spins on his heel and stalks down the hall. Josephine waves for me to follow. I take a step or two and glance back. Sam and Job aren't far behind.

When we reach King Solomon's office, several women in gray uniforms follow us inside and set up trays in front of the chairs. King Solomon sprawls behind a monstrously large desk in a large wingback chair that closely resembles a throne. Sam takes a seat in the back of the room near the door where he can see all the exits. He pats the seat next to him and I take it. Job sits on my other side.

Josephine unlocks a filing cabinet behind the desk and rummages around inside. She opens and closes several drawers before pulling out a green folder. Her eyes well with tears. She wipes them away and sets the folder on the desk.

I stand up to look, trying to ignore the man sitting in the chair in front of me. His staring makes me uncomfortable. The paper in the folder reads: The City of New York, Vital Records Certificate, Certification of Live Birth. Below that, it lists my date of birth, and my full name, Ruby Ruth Thomas.

"Thomas? Why's my last name Thomas?"

Solomon sighs. "Why are you showing her that? What does it prove?"

"I'll explain." Josephine points at the bottom of the certificate.

It reads: "Mother's Maiden Name: Josephine Matilda Stefan" and just below that, "Father's Name: David Thomas."

I quirk one eyebrow at Solomon. "How many dads do I have? I'm counting three at this point."

King Solomon grunts. "My given name was David Thomas, but when I decided to become a pastor, David Solomon was more fitting. I changed my name officially, legally. Not because I was on the run." He points at the certificate. "That's me."

I laugh. I can't help it. "You're telling me my dad's real name is Donald Carillon. He changed it to Donovan Behl to steal me from you. But your name isn't your name, either. You changed yours from David Thomas to David Solomon so people would associate you with a famous religious figure. So, who am I really? Ruby Carillon Behl Thomas Solomon? This is nuts. That paper doesn't prove anything. That could be anyone."

King Solomon's face turns red. He obviously doesn't see the humor in this. He opens up the bottom right drawer of his desk and shuffles some things before he produces a small rectangular piece of plastic. He slams it down on the desk. King Solomon's face smiles up at me, but the name on the small plastic card reads David Thomas.

"I may have changed my name, but that's the only thing I have in common with Donald Carillon. You are my daughter, not his. Ruby Ruth Solomon."

"Be that as it may," I say, "I—"

Boots on wooden flooring make a lot of noise. A lot of boots make more noise, enough to hear from pretty far down the hall. Several guards rush into the office, interrupting us. Adam salutes King Solomon. "Your Majesty, a significant number of armed Marked children are amassing near the bridge."

King Solomon's eyes fly wide, and he turns toward me. "Do you know anything about this?"

I'm not sure what to say. Rhonda almost certainly told the Marked about the Cleansing WPN has planned, but I doubt I should tell him that. Besides, I have no idea why they're here. Maybe they're here to look for me. I am their "Promised," whatever that means.

I shake my head.

Josephine sighs. "Perhaps they've found out."

"Then we move up the time table. Adam, fetch General Kovar. We need to revise and expedite our strategy." King Solomon turns back to me, his previous anger gone. "We may have to postpone our meal, but don't worry darling. You'll be perfectly safe. That's a promise."

Don't worry, Ruby. Your name-changing, face-slapping, possible biological donor plans to keep you safe by annihilating thousands of ill children, among them my sort-of-ex-boyfriend, my maybe-cousin, and my accessory-to-a-kidnapping aunt. Perfect.

King Solomon whispers to one of the guards in the hallway. I can't let him kill them out there if I can stop it. Even if I find a cure, it won't matter if everyone I want to save is dead.

I throw my cards on the metaphorical table. "Don't do it. We heard about the Cleansing, and it's a mistake. The suppressant's failing, but we're here because we think Dad may have developed a cure."

King Solomon spins around so fast that I stumble back. "Excuse me?"

"We came to Galveston to find the cure. Some of Donovan's journals mention it."

"Where are these journals?" Josephine asks.

"My aunt and uncle kept them," I say, "but I read them a week ago, and I might know where to find it. If it exists, you don't need to kill the Marked. They won't be a threat anymore."

King Solomon narrows his eyes. "They're a threat right now, to my daughter and my people."

I appeal to his pride. "Imagine if the great King Solomon healed the infected masses instead of killing them."

"Ruby, we scoured the island for years and found nothing," Josephine says.

"Dad had a hidden safe," I say. "I remember where it was."

"God works in mysterious ways. I've wondered for years why this happened to us." King Solomon pulls Josephine under his arm. "Maybe our daughter's suffering has been like Joseph's sojourn to Egypt. Her path set in place to save these children."

Sam's eyes widen. This guy's cuckoo.

"And the cure would be located?" King Solomon asks.

"Back at our condo," I say. "Is the Palisade Palms still standing?"

Josephine nods. "It survived all three hurricanes since the Marking, a small miracle itself."

"God's hand's always working among us," King Solomon murmurs.

I can't tell whether he's posturing or whether he believes this crap, but it annoys me either way. "God's plan began with letting almost everyone on earth die?"

"When humanity becomes too wicked, God has no choice but to purify the population." King Solomon's eyes bore into mine. "He did it once with a flood. Is it so far-fetched to imagine He might use a virus?"

"So everyone who died was wicked?" I ask.

"Death isn't a punishment in and of itself," King Solomon says. "Many who died ascended to heaven, a blessing above anything we can possibly imagine. I do not presume to tell God who should live and die, or pass judgment on His methods."

I force myself to remain calm. "You don't?" Sam squeezes my hand, but I can't stop. "Accelerating the virus and killing the entire US government wasn't your doing?"

"No one took the threat seriously," King Solomon says. "Without a cure, which no one had turned up in an entire year, our only hope was to isolate those of us who were uninfected. I did what I had to do to preserve the uninfected."

"*You* did it then? Not God?" I ask.

"At his direction," he says. "God has a reason for what he does, then and now."

"That doesn't make any sense," I say. "Some of the best people I know died. If God was punishing them, then I want nothing to do with God."

King Solomon's nostrils flare and he slams his hand against the doorframe. "Death is not the end. You're a perfect little heathen, aren't you?"

Josephine steps in front of him. "We have time. For now, we can take her to the Palms to look into this cure. Before we take steps we can't untake. She showed up just before the Marked began this assault."

"I find that timing curious." King Solomon scowls.

Josephine tilts her head. "You said yourself, perhaps *this* is God's plan. He may want us to spare them."

King Solomon nods. "Very well. Give me time to make some arrangements. We'll head to the Palms directly."

"All of us."

He stomps out of the office with Josephine at his side, leaving the three of us in his office unattended.

"Are we finally headed for the Palms?" Job asks.

I pick up the birth certificate. "David Thomas may be my father." I slam it down on the desk. "But he isn't my dad. I don't know if Donovan Behl went crazy or not, but he loved me, cared for me, and tried to do right by me."

Job nods. "I agree."

"But I'm worried."

"About what?" Sam asks.

"If my mom's right, then Donald Carillon's blood doesn't flow in my veins."

"You're still my sister," Job says. "No matter what."

"I agree." I wrap my arm around Job for a side hug. "But my blood won't open that safe."

Sam swears.

"A place only my blood can reach," I say. "That's what his journal said. I remember, because I wondered at the time whether that meant it had to be *his* blood."

"Are you saying we can't get the cure after all?" Sam asks.

I shake my head. "I think we can. Or, more specifically, I think Job can."

"Me? Why me?" Job looks around the room. "Do you think my mom's secretly my aunt?" He smirks in a way only someone entirely sure of their lineage would smirk. The way I would have smirked yesterday.

"No, idiot." I pick up the birth certificate. "I may not have Donovan's blood, but you do. You're his twin sister's son. Scientifically speaking, your blood is basically what I thought mine was."

"What do you want to do, then?" Job asks. "Tell them I need to open it?"

I shake my head again. "That's the thing. I don't want that guy to know. He took my dad from me. Whether my dad really died from a fire or not, without that gunshot, he'd still be alive. Now it's my turn to pay him back. I want him to suffer."

"What do you have in mind?" Sam asks.

"I need to find something to hold some of Job's blood," I say. "Help me look."

I start opening drawers in the desk. Sam walks to the doorway and assumes a guard position. With his hearing, he's the best one to tell us if anyone's coming. Job's looking in the skinny drawer at the top and isn't paying me any attention. In the bottom drawer on the left, I find something strange.

A tranquillizer gun.

Two pouches full of darts rest next to the gun. One's labeled T. The other is labeled A. I have no idea why, but I grab them and stuff them into the waistband of my pants over my lower back and pull my shirt and jacket out and down to cover them up. It might be helpful to have a tranq gun, depending on how things go.

"This might work." Job holds a fountain pen.

"How's that going to work?" I ask.

"Like this." He unscrews the whole thing and pulls out a small vial from inside the pen. "This one's empty." He stabs his thumb with the nib of the pen and squeezes his blood into the empty vial then screws it all back together and hands it to me. "Make sure you hold it up or it'll pour out the end of the pen."

I'm stowing the vial in a torn spot in the liner of my jacket that I can reach through my pocket when Sam waves at me. I shove the drawers shut and walk around to my seat. Job's already sitting.

"Everything's ready," King Solomon says. "But if it yields nothing Ruby, please let me handle things with the Marked as I see fit. I've been protecting my people from unfathomable threats for over a decade. Believe me when I say, I don't take fatal action lightly, and I've pondered and prayed about the Cleansing through long hours of study." He turns on his heel and stalks down the hall.

Josephine waits for me to reach her and falls in step next to me. She walks as close as she can without tripping over my feet. Whenever I glance her way, she smiles.

A van idles at the bottom of the grand staircase. It's gray, but otherwise looks a lot like the van we rode over in. The roads are smooth most of the way, but the closer we get to the far north side of the island, the bumpier the roads grow. No one speaks.

"This is a Hail Mary," Solomon says to Adam in a low voice as we arrive, "but sometimes those work. If it doesn't, we have Plan B already in place."

Adam nods, but frowns as though he regrets it. It makes me like him a little. "We do."

"Good." Adam exits the car first, but King Solomon follows closely behind.

I look out the window as four other guards exit a car stopped just behind us. When I step out, the view of the Palisade Palms slaps me in the face. If any place from my childhood felt like home, this was it. Almost every one of my favorite memories took place inside this building, and the man standing next to me ruined them all that day.

Since then, this building has starred in every nightmare I've endured. The two curvilinear towers shoot up into the sky a few steps from the beach, the same way I've dreamed about them a hundred times.

We park to the left and walk past the basketball court. Two small boys are bouncing a ball on it. Their eyes widen when they see the five guards with us, and the ball bounces sideways and rolls away.

"We lived in the east tower."

Josephine's mouth turns up in what looks like sympathy. "I know, sweetie. People still live here, but we've kept your old apartment intact and uninhabited to preserve the evidence."

I can't believe it. I've been preparing myself for it looking entirely different, but it's going to look exactly the same. We ride the elevators in silence. I don't realize my hand's shaking until Sam reaches over and takes it in his. When he interlaces our fingers, my heart swells. I may be alone in this, but I'm not abandoned. Sam's behind me, and Job too.

The elevator dings and we step into the lobby on the twenty-seventh floor. I gasp. Everything looks exactly as it did. The carpet's worn, but it's the same light gray. The same beach landscape hangs on the wall, and the wire mesh trashcan sits next to the elevator, with an ashtray built into the top.

The doorknob on my bright blue front door twists easily, the door swings open smoothly. I want to stop and take it all in, but there's no time with an army at the bridge. So many sick kids might die if I delay. I tighten my grip on Sam's hand and he follows me through our old entryway and toward my dad's lab.

The marble floors are dusty, but otherwise exactly as I remember them. I pause in the family room. There's no blood on the floor in front of the fireplace where my dad lay after being shot, but there are burned tiles and blackened places. I shudder. Someone tried to clean it up, but there was a fire. My mom didn't lie about that. Thinking about my dad burning alive, at the hand of yet someone else makes me want to collapse into a heap and sob uncontrollably. The army of Marked kids who Solomon might shoot is the only thing that keeps me moving.

My mind reels when I pass the coat closet where I hid. My feet turn toward my room, but I'm not a little girl, not anymore. I force my feet to walk toward the heavy wooden door to Dad's home lab. I only went inside a handful of times, because dad's lab wasn't safe. Entering without permission was against the rules.

I breathe in through my nose and out through my mouth twice. I tune out the sound of shifting feet, impatient sighs, muttering and whispers. I lean forward and turn the knob.

It should disturb me to see my dad's place without my dad in it, but it bothers me less than the rest of our old home. He died in the family room. I hid in the closet. I lived in my room. I made food in the kitchen with him, and we ate together in the dining room. I have memories most everywhere, but only a few here. The beakers, test tubes, and machines that whirred and buzzed gather dust now, trans-forming them into something foreign. Something I don't recognize at all.

A vast mahogany bookcase spans the far-left wall. A built-in desk sits just to the right of it. I close my eyes and think of the time my dad and I were eating ice-cream cones. He suggested we make play-doh. I was so excited that I practically ran to the lab ahead of him. We made the dough in flasks over a controlled fire, but in the end, it was so thick and hard to stir that I collapsed on the floor, whining. Dad took over.

I was sitting on the floor playing with purple and green play-doh when I heard a whump. I looked up just in time to watch another book fall off the bookcase and land on my foot. I began bawling, loudly.

"Don't cry, dumpling," Dad said. "I'll show you a secret."

I shake off the memory and gulp some air to keep from crying. I cross the room to the built-in desk and the Eiffel tower clock still resting on the top of it.

"This is it," I say. "This little decoration is the key."

"The key to what?" King Solomon's brow furrows. "That clock contains the cure?"

"I hope it'll reveal the cure. The tip of the tower has a small reservoir." I reach into my pocket and slide my hand into the hole in the liner. I slide the fountain pen out and unscrew it. At the same time, I blow into the tip of the Eiffel Tower clock to distract everyone else. Dust flies up into my eyes. I wipe them off and blow on it again, and again. The third time, no dust flies out. "If my blood matches my dad's, this safe will open."

Sam keeps King Solomon and Josephine near the back wall with a looming stance, giving me the space I need. Adam and four other guards array themselves on either side of

King Solomon, glaring at Sam and Job. I press my finger to the top of the reservoir, but I don't press down hard enough to break my skin. Instead, I squeeze on the pen until blood squirts through the nib. I turn my face toward the bookcase full of battered, scientific treatises and journals expectantly.

Nothing happens. My heart pounds in my ears.

I came all this way. I've lost so many people—Wesley, Aunt Anne, Rhonda.

All for nothing.

Then it happens. Books fall from the bookcase several shelves up as the safe door swings open. I catch two of them, but the third falls to the ground right next to my foot. Heart in my throat, I crouch down to look inside the open safe.

A hardback leather journal, larger than the ones I read back in Port Gibson, rests in the safe. A small wooden box sits on top of it. My heart constricts—Mom's ring box. I forgot about that in my fervor for the cure. I open the box.

The enormous diamond heart, surrounded by canary yellow diamonds, sparkles up at me, undimmed by time or dust.

"My ring," Josephine says.

I turn to look at her as if for the first time. She really is my mom. I smile at her and she beams back. I'm not sure whether the journal holds the cure, but I feel like it was almost worth the trip, just for this moment of connection.

Then I think about Rhonda, Wesley, and Aunt Anne and I feel guilty for ever thinking it.

I'm completely shocked when King Solomon grabs me by the back of the neck and shakes me like a terrier shaking a snake. Before I can guess his reason, what with my brains being scrambled like eggs, he's grabbed my mother by the shoulder.

"A slut and her whelp."

He shoves us both toward the door and we sprawl to the

ground. The ring skitters toward the wall and I lunge for it, forgetting entirely about the journal that slid under the desk. I hear Sam struggling with the guards and hope he's okay.

"You told me you hadn't been with him," King Solomon says. "You swore there was no possibility that Ruby was anyone's daughter but mine. You're a lying whore."

Solomon kicks my mom in the ribs. She doesn't make a sound. She should've cried out. Why doesn't she? I tuck the ring in my pocket and watch my mom. Solomon kicks her again, and this time she curls into it, still not making a peep.

This isn't the first time he's beaten her.

I stand up. "Leave her alone, you filthy pig."

He turns toward me. "Or what? Your boyfriend can't help you."

One glance shows me he's right. Adam and his men press guns to Job and Sam's temples.

King Solomon's been in absolute power in Galveston for so long, I don't think he even considers that I might not curl up into a ball and accept whatever he orders. Like his guards. His people. My mom. He's missed every part of my life, so he doesn't know one major thing.

I am nothing like my mother.

I pull the tranq gun out of my waistband and pull out a pouch, the one labeled T. "I don't need my boyfriend." I put a dart in the gun.

"No!" Solomon leaps backward, slamming into the bookcase in his efforts to back away.

"If your guards take those guns off of Sam and turn them on me for one second, Sam will kill you all." I smile. "But what's the big deal? It's just a tranquilizer. It'll wear off and you'll be fine."

"That's not a tranq," he rasps. "It's Tercera."

I look down at the dart with horror. T for Tercera. He

keeps a gun with Tercera darts in his desk to infect people at will?

"You wouldn't dare to question God, huh?" I ask. "Because you play God already. Is that it? You infect anyone you don't like, anyone who questions you?" He shakes his head, but I ignore it. "You beat my mom. You shot my dad. You murder whoever you want, and you plan to murder all the Marked? You're irredeemably evil."

Then I realize that if T means Tercera . . . what does A mean? Antidote? Or Accelerant?

"Do you already have the cure? Or do you infect people and then accelerate the disease?" He either uses Tercera to execute people, or he's been sitting on a cure all this time without sharing it. I don't know which explanation is worse.

"What, no answer?" I lift the gun. "Then let's find out."

My mom cries out, but it's too late. I shoot the dart, and my aim's true. It hits Solomon squarely in the chest. His eyes fly wide and his hands claw at the edge where it protrudes. My mom lunges for me, but someone stops her. I glance sideways. Sam used the distraction to disarm the guards, all of them. Job leaps across the room and stops my mom from touching the newly infected King Solomon.

I pull out the other pouch.

I load a dart marked A into the gun, and aim it at King Solomon. "Which is it, *Daddy*? Will this cure you? Or accelerate your death, like you accelerated thousands?"

Before he can answer, I fire the second dart. King Solomon raises one arm to block and the dart hits his forearm.

I smile darkly. "Now tell me again about how the people who die fulfill God's will."

King Solomon begins to froth at the mouth. I'm guessing that's not the effect of an antidote. I turn and walk out of the room.

By the time I reach the elevator, Job appears, forcibly hauling my mom with him. She struggles against him, pulls at his shirt and cries pitifully, but he gently tugs her toward the doors all the same. Sam's only a step behind him, the leather journal safely under one arm.

Bless him. Sam does everything right.

CHAPTER 25

By the time the elevator reaches the bottom floor of the building, my mom's sobbing wordlessly on Job's shoulder. At least it's mostly quiet.

Sam slides into the driver's seat, so I take shotgun. He wastes no time putting the van in gear and driving down Beach Drive toward Seawall. I hold my dad's journal in my hands. For a moment, I can't bring myself to open it, but after we hit Seawall, I crack the cover.

I discover pages and pages of unintelligible notes and equations. Great. It might contain the cure, but how will I know? Panic grips me. We can't leave the island without it. If we make it out of here, there's no coming back. Impatient and scared, I flip to the end.

There it is, the last entry, just like before.

I've done it. Ever since I developed that disgusting virus in my attempt to create a universal vaccination, and my partner decided he wants to sell it knowing it had a long lead time, I've been desperate to formulate a solution. Recently, I tested my designer virus against it. The Triptych virus transmits by touch, and it replicates fast, faster than any other virus I've seen. My new virus doesn't replicate as fast and it doesn't transmit by touch, not yet anyway. It requires a blood transfer, but my new virus eats the old one up.

I know because Jack and I got in a fight and a vial broke. I caught Triptych myself. I thought I might not catch it when the vial broke because that strain needed to bind to blood to operate properly, but because I'd cut my finger, the sample I had bound to mine. I could've infected the whole world. The strange mark I coded into it appeared on my forehead within half an hour of exposure, just like I intended. Ruby was watching TV in the other room. She came in when I cried out, in spite of my warning.

I've never been so afraid.

I dosed myself with my attack virus. I almost dosed Ruby too, but it hasn't been properly tested. I don't know what side effects it may have. After my blood tested clean again, I dosed a frantic Ruby with the antibodies I developed first. I made them to protect her from Triptych, but they'll boost her immune system across the board. It should be enough to keep her safe forever. I gave her triple the load I calculated she would need to be safe. She had a pretty bad reaction last night after I dosed her, but she's fine, now. I know my actions were paranoid, but I can't help it. Since her mother left me, she's all I have.

Jack called me a few minutes ago, irate. He's calling my bluff. The funds from selling Triptych will fund our ongoing research he says, including fine-tuning the cure. He knows I'll work night and day if he does release it. Jack knows nothing about my success with the antibodies I gave Ruby. He only knows I've been formulating a cure, not the form it takes. I told him I'll never agree to sell, no matter what, but it may not matter. He stole a sample of Triptych before I installed my new safe. I told him if he sells it, I'll report him, even if it means they come after Ruby and me.

It might have been a lie. I don't think I can risk her. I don't care whether Ruby's my biological daughter, so I never checked. I took her to punish her mother at first, but I kept her to protect her from *the monster that stole Josephine from me. That awful action, the worst thing I've ever done, has filled my life with light. She's the best thing I've ever taken part in. She's everything to me. Her blood now carries something that's more mine than any DNA. She holds something I made to protect her. And I've hidden the key to Jack's mess in the one place I value above all others. In the body of my daughter.*

I drop the journal and it slides to the floor of the van.

I've been the cure all along. That's why Wesley's kiss didn't Mark me. It wasn't lip-gloss—of course it wasn't. I should never have believed that.

I could've saved Wesley, Rhonda and my aunt. I gasp when a horrible thought hits me. If my dad hadn't been murdered, or if I hadn't been stolen, or if my Aunt and Uncle hadn't run and left his research, or if any of those things hadn't happened, they could've used my blood to keep the world from dying. My cowardice killed my dad, and my dad's death doomed everyone in the world, even more than I already thought.

My breathing accelerates, and I close my eyes and focus on slowing it. I can't hyperventilate until after we've escaped the island.

I focus on the good news. David Solomon has no idea what this journal says. If we get off this rock quickly, he never needs to know.

Sam reaches over and takes my hand with his big, strong one. Sam's my rock, and he's with me. Job's safe, and hopefully Rhonda and Wesley will be soon. And after seventeen years without her, I found my mom. We freed her from the monster—who might actually be my biological father.

As much as I wish we'd known what Dad hid in my blood all along, for the first time in a decade, today's a better day than the one that came before it. I have Sam, my mom, my dad's journal, and we're leaving Solomon to die in the same way he's doomed so many others to suffer.

I'm still scared, but I know how to move past that fear and do what needs to be done. For now, maybe that's enough.

***

Make sure to check out the next novel in the series, *Suppressed,* available now!
Suppressed: Sins of Our Ancestors Book Two

The third book, *Redeemed,* is available now, too!
Redeemed: Sins of our Ancestors Book Three

If you'd like a FREE full length novel, sign up for my newsletter at www.BridgetEBakerwrites.com! I'll send you a free copy of my novel, Already Gone, a twisty, complicated YA romantic suspense.

Finally, if you enjoyed reading MARKED, please leave me a review on Amazon (and GoodReads or Book Bub!) It makes a tremendous difference when you do.

THE END

ACKNOWLEDGMENTS

My family: My mother has been my number one fan for thirty-seven years. She helps me in every way possible. My big kids, Eli and Dora, have read draft after draft with enthusiasm. My sister Emma has been there to pick me up whenever I need it.

My friends: Erin Shepard waves her pom poms whenever I'm drafting. Rachel Fordham checks in religiously and keeps me going. Nacoree Elsdon reads quick and gives excellent feedback. Last but never least, Shauna Holyoak is the best writing friend a girl could ever ask for!

My developmental editor, Peter Sentfleben, is AMAZING! His feedback is clear, clean and always spot on. He's been supportive every step of the way, and without his help, my blurb would have read: Pretty please read my book. (I wish I was kidding.)

Big thanks to Linsey Stuckey for handling my cover photo shoot, and Ashlyn Holleman for being my model! (And to Marie for sharing her daughter.)

Thanks to The Writing Gals for making a wonderful home and sharing their enthusiasm, knowledge and talent. It inspired me to take the plunge, without which, MARKED would never have been read by anyone other than my family.

Finally, a Texas sized thank you to Whitney for being the best husband, father, and book writing supporter of all time. No one compares to you. Really.

Bridget loves her husband and all five of her kids (most days). She has a springy dog, backyard chickens, two goofy horses, and two demanding cats. Every day is a battle between playing with kids, riding her horse Splash, and writing. If her publication speed has slowed down, you can blame the kids and the horse.

She makes cookies all the time, and thinks they should have their own food group. In a possibly misguided attempt at balancing the scales between overconsumption and exertion, she kickboxes every day. So if you don't like her kids, her cookies, or her books, maybe don't tell her in person.

9 781949 655018